The Origin of Dracula

Irving Belateche

Laurel Canyon Press
Los Angeles

Laurel Canyon Press, March 2015
Copyright © 2015 by Irving Belateche

This book is a work of fiction. Any references to historical events, real
people, or real locales are used fictitiously. Other names, characters,
places, and incidents are products of the author's imagination, and any
resemblance to actual events or locales or persons, living or dead, is
entirely coincidental.

Library of Congress Control Number: 2015902638

ISBN: 978-0-9840265-6-2

Edited by David Gatewood
www.lonetrout.com

Cover design by Ivano Lago
www.newebart.it

Formatting by Polgarus Studio
www.polgarusstudio.com

Author Website
www.irvingbelateche.com

Printed in the United States of America

Laurel Canyon Press
Los Angeles, California
www.LaurelCanyonPress.com

Also by Irving Belateche

Einstein's Secret
Science Fiction Thriller

H$_2$O
Science Fiction Thriller

The Disappeared
(A short story)
Supernatural Thriller

Under An Orange Sun, Some Days Are Blue
Autobiographical Novel

Chapter One

Some of us have done something in our past that haunts us forever. Something we'd rather bury and forget.

But we can't.

It's always with us.

At first—and I mean right after we commit this transgression—it's always on our minds. But eventually—and by eventually I mean a long, long time afterward—we can go an entire day without thinking about it. Then, if we're lucky, after enough time has passed, we may even be able to go an entire week without thinking about it.

For some of us, this haunting transgression was minor. But because it involved another person, someone on the receiving end of our offense, someone we badly deceived or cheated or hurt, it's seared into our souls and can't be forgotten. We feel tremendous guilt about it, and it fills us with shame and self-hatred.

But for others, the offense was more than a minor transgression. It was something truly horrible. Unforgivable. The guilt and the shame are so strong that we can't ever hope to bury it and forget about it.

Instead we learn to live with it.

I was in this second category. And the only silver lining was that, even though I couldn't forget my transgression, the haunting memory was fading. It was becoming less real and more like a vivid nightmare from which I had long ago awoken. It was becoming less fact and more fiction.

But just as fact can transform itself into fiction, fiction can also transform itself back into fact. Fiction can suddenly come back to life with a vengeance. And the most frightening part of this—the part that brought me to the edge of madness—was the discovery that the boundary between the world of fact and the world of fiction is porous.

There is another world, as real as the world we know, hidden in fiction—in stories and in novels. And my transgression was linked to this world—as real as any other world.

More particularly, it was linked to one specific novel.

But I wouldn't learn this until my transgression came back to life and dragged me into that world and into that story.

*

As I sat behind the reference desk at the Cherrydale Public Library, waiting for my shift to end, I wasn't thinking about my terrible sin. Time had worked its magic. Twenty years had passed, and those years had done a good job of cleansing my mind of the truth. My transgression was still a nightmare that I couldn't shake, but it no longer had the impact of reality.

I was scanning a list of books on my computer, books the library was considering purchasing, and I noticed that non-fiction books dominated the list. The buyers for the Arlington County library system, to which the Cherrydale branch belonged, had finally acquiesced to a growing trend: the popularity of non-fiction books at the expense of fiction. The debate about whether to follow this trend had been raging in library systems across the country. And now, after holding out for many years, it appeared that the Arlington County libraries had decided to hop on the bandwagon.

I applauded this decision because of my own relationship with fiction. I'd once been an avid reader of fiction, but then I gave up on it, concluding that novels—from the classics to mass-market bestsellers—offered nothing of value. Proponents of a liberal arts education claimed you could learn important truths about life in great works of fiction.

I believed that was a con job.

Reading fiction was a waste of time. Fiction was make-believe, and make-believe was of no help when it came to dealing with reality. Don't think that I thought this actually mattered to anyone. I understood that practically no one cared about this philosophical debate. A vast majority of people who read fiction did so for entertainment value and not to learn life lessons, even if, as some argued, those lessons were there.

My strong distaste for fiction—*hate* is the better word—stemmed from once believing in it so deeply. The truth was that fiction had once saved my life, which was the primary reason I'd become a librarian. But when Lucy died, fiction wasn't there to help me. It betrayed me.

My love affair with fiction began my sophomore year of high school, right after the first death that shattered my life. My father died of a sudden heart attack—a devastating blow for my mother and me. We'd been a tight-knit family, so my father's abrupt death left a big hole in our lives. Our dinner table turned from a warm place where my dad and mom recounted their workday dramas to a dead place dominated by painful stretches of silence and a somber void. The couch in our living room turned from a place of fellowship, where on Sundays my dad and I cheered on the Washington Redskins, ridiculing their ineptness and applauding their triumphs, to a place that evoked all-consuming grief, an unbearable sadness.

After my dad died, I couldn't bear to enter the living room on Sundays.

Both my mom and I withdrew from our friends and from each other. I still went to school, as if everything were normal, but I socialized a lot less, preferring to spend my free periods, including lunch, studying rather than hanging out with friends. My mom still went to work, also as if everything were normal, but she no longer brought home stories of office successes, mishaps, and scandals.

But even as I was withdrawing from the outside world, I was entering a new world. The world of fiction. Up to that point in my life, I hadn't been much of a reader. I'd been a good student and had read what was required in school, as well as a few of the popular books my friends were reading, but that was it.

After my dad died, my reading habits changed drastically. I read one book after another without any breaks in between. The obsession started innocently enough, when I finished up the entire year's required reading for my English class in a couple of weeks and then moved on to the suggested reading list.

My mom also joined me in this obsession. Maybe it was her way of staying close to me, or maybe it was her way of seeking refuge from the emptiness that permeated our house. We pored through Melville, Dickens, Twain, Hemingway, Fitzgerald, and Steinbeck, then moved on to more modern authors, like J.D. Salinger, Harper Lee, Arthur Miller, and Kurt Vonnegut.

While my mom read many genres, I became enamored of supernatural novels. My days and nights were spent in the supernatural worlds of Edgar Allen Poe, M.R. James, Bram Stoker, Shirley Jackson, H.P. Lovecraft, Richard Matheson, Peter Straub, and Stephen King.

By the end of my senior year of high school, my mom and I had reintegrated ourselves back into life in the outside world. I was hanging out with friends again, and she was filling me in on her workplace dramas again. We were no longer withdrawn from each other, and life had gone from sad to good again.

I attributed this recovery to "novel therapy." Our broken hearts had been healed by fiction. Though my mom and I had withdrawn into an inner world, it wasn't a world of hopelessness and despair. It was a world every bit as vibrant as the outside world—engrossing enough that it kept us from focusing on our shattered lives.

Fiction had saved me, and that salvation had lasted until nine months ago, when suddenly my life had once more been shattered. Lucy, my wife, had been murdered—and I had found myself turning again to novel therapy for help.

But this time it had failed me.

And this failure made me reassess what had happened all those years ago. Instead of dealing with my father's death, I realized I had run from it. Novel therapy had given me shelter from the storm, when what I should've done was face the storm. If I had, then when death struck again, I would have had a chance of rising from the ashes. If I'd dealt with reality back then, I would've been able to deal with it now.

But as it stood, Lucy's murder had crushed me, and it had left Nate, my young son, with a shell of man as his father.

*

I clicked over from the list of non-fiction books to my email, to see if the last RSVP to Nate's birthday party had come in. It had, and it was another "yes." Considering the party was on Sunday, only two days away, this was late notice. Not that it really mattered; one more guest wasn't going to make a difference. Nate had wanted me to invite all of his friends, and I had. With or without this last RSVP, we were going to have a full house.

Spoiling Nate for his seventh birthday was the right thing to do. This would be his first birthday without Lucy, so I was okay with whatever he wanted. It was also a way for me to make up for being sullen, withdrawn, and inattentive over the last nine months.

But the truth was that the party wasn't going to change anything. Nate was looking forward to it, but I'd just been pretending. I was dreading it. I'd planned a magnificent day—a magic show, a variety of party games, cake from a high-end bakery, and gelato—but regardless of how much fun it'd be for Nate, for me the party would only accentuate Lucy's absence. I'd be mourning her death the entire time, no matter how hard I'd try not to.

The practical matter of the party's expense wasn't going to make it any easier to enjoy either. I was spending way more than I could afford. But that could be said of all my purchases over the last six months. With only one income, my finances were in bad shape. Lucy and I hadn't bought life insurance, so when she died, what little financial stability we had died with her.

That was my fault. As soon as Nate was born, she'd wanted to buy life insurance—for both of us. But my foolish view was that we were too young to worry about it. It took me a full six years to finally consider it, and just as we'd started looking into policies, tragedy struck.

And then it was too late.

I clicked out of my email, checked the time, and logged out of my computer. Before Lucy's death, I'd always had a burst of energy at the end of my shift, a second wind that came from looking forward to my evening with Lucy and Nate. Nate was a great kid, bursting with insightful questions that kept me on my toes, and Lucy was a great companion, my best friend, curious about my day at the library, and quick with an intriguing tale about her own day at work.

But after her death, that second wind disappeared. I became a nocturnal creature, staying up most of the night, then catching a couple hours of sleep right before taking Nate to school. So by the time my shift was over, I was exhausted. Prior to this new routine, I'd always been asleep by eleven, awake by six, and alert all day. Now I felt like I was living in a netherworld, and this made it hard to connect with Nate. He lived outside this netherworld.

What I didn't know, and could never have imagined, was that this change in my routine was a gateway into another world, a frightening world beyond the horror of losing my wife. My exhaustion and unnatural hours were the way into this other world. My tenuous grip on reality—accompanied by an unrelenting dull ache in my gut—was required for what was to follow.

I looked up from my computer to see Barbara Price, one of the senior reference librarians, marching toward me, ready for her shift. Barbara was gruff with the library patrons, rude and impatient when answering their questions. I felt sorry for the patrons who had to deal with her.

"All yours," I said as she walked through the wooden gate and entered the reference area.

"Hopefully I'll make it through my shift without getting too many stupid questions," she said, smiling conspiratorially as if I shared her sentiments. "Friday is always stupid question day."

I stood up, relinquishing my seat. "At least you've only got four hours." The library closed at seven on Fridays.

"That's four hours too long." She sat down and logged on to the computer. "Did you look over the Virginia display?"

I glanced to the far end of the library, which featured the display—her display. Books on Virginia's history, all non-fiction, except for one slim volume written during Virginia's colonial period. "I did—it looks great."

"I thought so, too. Do you want to add anything to it?"

"Nah. It doesn't need anything more." Even if it did, I knew better than to make a recommendation. She'd solicited suggestions from the other librarians, then scoffed at their suggestions behind their backs.

"Have a good weekend," I said, and headed toward the front foyer.

"You too."

That wasn't going to happen. There were no longer any good weekends, any more than there were good weekdays. The reference desk was the only anchor in my life. Every minute away from it was spent floating aimlessly in a choppy sea with no port of call. Still, this weekend, for Nate's sake, I planned to force myself to at least *act* like I was standing on solid ground. I'd channel the little energy I had into that. I loved Nate more than anything in the world, and I desperately wanted to build a new life for him. But right now, pretending to have a good weekend was the best I could do.

Even though my mind and spirit were adrift, I was there physically for Nate. I was always one of the parents who arrived first to pick him up from the afterschool program. But that stemmed from my guilt. Before Lucy's death, Nate wasn't in the afterschool program; I'd arranged my shifts so that I could pick him up right after school. Lucy and I hadn't wanted Nate to be one of those kids who had no choice but to spend his entire day away from home. But now, because I needed to work as many hours as possible, Nate had become one of those kids.

I hurried to my car, an older Camry, climbed in, and headed to McKinley Elementary School. Friday afternoon traffic was heavy. The Northern Virginia suburbs had long ceased being just a bedroom community for Washington, D.C. Major businesses were located in every county, and when you threw in the federal government offices and the major shopping districts, it all added up to a thriving metropolitan area with way too many cars on the road, especially during rush hour.

I navigated through the typhoon of traffic with one hope in mind: that this evening would be the one that ushered in significant change, that this evening would be the one where I'd finally sail out of the netherworld and into port—a port of normalcy. The new normal, the one without Lucy.

I'd driven home many times over the last few months with

that single hope in mind, only to be disappointed.

But this evening would turn out to be the one that delivered. Not on the hope, but on the change. Significant change. Change that was about as far as you could get from a new normal. I was about to sail out of choppy seas and into a maelstrom of chaos.

Chapter Two

When I walked into the classroom, Nate looked up from the book he was reading, *Encyclopedia Brown Saves the Day*, and flashed me a huge grin. He hurried to the back of the room, grabbed his backpack and a small, model house made from popsicle sticks, then raced over to me.

"Two more days, Dad," he said, his blue eyes sparkling with anticipation.

"Yep—and I heard from Will's mom. Will's coming, too."

"That means everyone's gonna be there."

On the way home, Nathan was a chatterbox. This had both an upside and a downside. The upside was something I'd convinced myself to believe as opposed to something I knew for sure: when Nate rambled up a storm, it meant he wasn't noticing I wasn't there for him. The downside was something I *did* know for sure: Nate's monologues didn't require many responses, so they made it easy for me to not be there for him.

"Dad?" he said. "Will he?"

Will he what? I thought. I knew his question had something to do with the birthday party, but my attention had drifted too much to know any more than that. I glanced at him. He was leaning forward in the back seat, restrained by his seatbelt, eagerly awaiting my answer.

"I'm sorry, honey," I said. "I was thinking about tonight's dinner. Will he what?"

"Will the magician show me some tricks?"

"Of course. I already talked to him about it."

"What kinds of tricks?"

"A card trick, a disappearing coin trick, and a couple of tricks that are going to be surprises."

"Four tricks?"

"Yeah. And maybe more, if there's time."

"Good. I'm going to do them for my afterschool class. Ms. Johnson said I could do them next week."

"That sounds like a good plan." I checked the rearview mirror. Nate was beaming with pride.

"Can I pick up the cake with you?" he said.

"Sure."

He had insisted on being involved in all facets of planning the party. Lucy had usually planned his birthday parties, so this might've been his way of staying close to her. But it had also crossed my mind that he thought I wasn't up to planning the party, or worse: he could tell I wasn't totally there for him and wasn't capable of planning *anything*.

He didn't talk much about Lucy anymore. We had talked about her death a lot during the first couple of months. Mostly about how random it had been. She'd been murdered in a carjacking and it was hard for him to understand why the thief had picked her out. The irony was that his instincts would turn out to be better than the police's, but who would've guessed that then?

Over the next seven months, there had been a healthy geometric decline in these conversations about Lucy's death. There were a lot of studies about how young kids dealt with the death of a parent. Many concluded that a good number of kids had a hard time accepting that a dead parent was gone forever. These kids believed their dead parents would come back and walk right through their front doors as if death weren't permanent.

But Nate seemed to grasp that his mom wasn't coming back. In those first couple of months, many of his questions were in one way or another attempts to confirm that her death was irreversible. He wasn't expecting her grand return. Instead, he was getting used to the idea of no return. And as it stood now, he'd done a hell of lot better at accepting the tragic loss of his mom than I had.

I turned onto Fillmore Street, pulled up to our house—a small, white craftsman that Lucy had always described as warm and cozy—and parked. Nate grabbed his backpack and popsicle-stick house and scrambled out of the back seat. As we walked toward the front door, he turned the popsicle-stick house over in his hand, examining it.

"I like the afterschool class, Dad," he said.

Warmth bloomed in my chest, and my thoughts suddenly lost their bitter edge. Nate was happy with the afterschool program. He didn't see it as a bad turn in his life, which made it a good turn in my life.

I leaned down and kissed him on his forehead. "Good for you, sweetheart. I'm glad you like it."

"Yeah. The extra stuff we do is good. You don't have to change your work to pick me up. "

That warm sensation bloomed again. He wanted me to know that it was okay that he had to stay late. He was a good kid, doing his part to make our new life work. Of course, there was another interpretation. He didn't want to hang out with his shell of a dad.

I unlocked the door and we walked into the house. "Do you have any homework for the weekend?"

"No—I mean yes, but I did it already."

"Great."

He plopped his backpack down on the couch. "Can I watch TV?"

"Sure—until dinner is ready."

He headed toward the den, toting his popsicle-stick house. I grabbed his backpack and headed into the kitchen. I'd taken over Lucy's job of going through his backpack to check and see if he'd been assigned homework or if the school had sent home any notices. He was pretty good about telling me if he'd been given homework, but it was a different story when it came to those notices. If I didn't dig them out, sometimes they'd remained buried in the bottom of his backpack for weeks.

At the kitchen table, I unzipped the backpack and pulled out his workbooks. While flipping through them, my thoughts drifted to the long night ahead, the part that came after cooking dinner and washing the dishes and getting Nate ready for bed, all of which was the "normal" part of the night. What came after all of that was my transformation into a nocturnal creature. Reading one newspaper after another on my iPad. Sitting zombie-like in the den watching movies. Camping on the edge of my bed, going through photos of Lucy. Wandering from room to room, tidying up an already tidy house. Standing in the back yard, staring up at the stars in the dark night sky, wondering why Lucy had been taken from me.

I closed Nate's math workbook, pulled out his vocabulary workbook, and noticed a white, letter-sized envelope peeking out from under another workbook. My first thought was that it was a notice from school, another one that without my intervention would've sunk to the bottom of the backpack and stayed buried there for a while.

As I pulled it out, it dawned on me that the school rarely sent notices home in an envelope. Usually they arrived in the form of a brightly colored flyer. Turning the envelope over revealed that there were no markings on either side. If it was a notice from school, surely it would've said, "To the parents of Nathan Grant." Maybe it was a note from the afterschool program or an invitation for a play date. But this was wishful thinking on my part—I'd already concluded that it was neither of those.

From the second I spotted the envelope, a queasy, sickly feeling started to grow in the pit of my stomach. Holding the envelope in my hand made the queasiness worse. The envelope's texture felt unnatural. It was smooth, as it should be, but it also felt cold and clammy, almost wet, even though it was completely dry.

If I hadn't opened the envelope—if I had just thrown it away—would my life have remained undisturbed by the horrors that followed? I'd never know. Because I *did* open it, and I pulled out the folded sheet of paper inside.

I unfolded the paper—it was a letter, clean and neat, printed on a laser printer. The letter started with my name, *John*, with no salutation before it. No formal *Dear* or informal *Hi*. Then came the first paragraph, made up of one simple and powerful line:

The past isn't dead. It isn't even past.

I recognized the quote immediately—William Faulkner—and the words hit me like a punch to the gut. I couldn't breathe. I knew exactly what these words referred to, and I didn't want to keep reading.

But I did.

The body washed away and disappeared. The river took it downstream and out of your life.

Until today. Now it's washed up onto your doorstep.

My heart was thumping heavily, pumping fear throughout my body. My awful transgression had come back to haunt me. The past wasn't dead.

The time for revenge has come, the letter continued. *I will kill your precious son on his seventh birthday.*

I fought to breathe and tried to will my heart to stop its

manic thumping. The queasiness in my stomach had turned into painful nausea.

If you have any doubt about the veracity of my threat, I suggest you check in with your partners in crime. You'll find a connection that will serve as proof of the devastating damage I can wreak.

There was almost no doubt in my mind that this threat was real. The past had been waiting patiently, more patiently than was humanly possible, to spring forth and attack. This wasn't revenge as much as it was justice. Over the protests of my thumping heart and overwhelming fear, I forced myself to read the rest of the letter and tried to convince myself that it was a hoax.

This is a game, and in a game each player has a chance to win. You will have one chance to save your son. If you can find me and tell me my name, tell me my true identity, I will spare your son.

A tiny ray of hope.

The letter wasn't signed, but it did end with a name:

Dantès.

I immediately understood that since this wasn't his real name, it was part of the game, just as the Faulkner quote had been. The person who'd written this letter had chosen Dantès as his pen name for one reason. Anyone who'd finished the required reading in his or her high school English class would know the reason: Edmond Dantès was the main character in the most famous tale of revenge, *The Conte of Monte Cristo.*

The game had already started, whether I wanted it to or

not. I put the letter down and slowly inhaled, then exhaled, forcing myself to breathe more calmly. Again, I tried to will my heart to stop its violent thumping, but it wouldn't. My painful nausea grew more acute.

My physical reaction to the letter, along with the questions spinning wildly in my head, made it hard to think straight. I continued to breathe in and out slowly, hoping this would help me regain at least enough composure to gather my thoughts. It was urgent to prioritize what needed to be done. Then, from my scattered, rambling thoughts, one imperative emerged:

I have to stop Dantès before he kills Nate.

That was all. Nothing else mattered.

But how?

By heading over to the closest police precinct. Right now. Playing Dantès's game was the wrong move. Trying to discover his real name, his identity, was the wrong move.

But going to the police meant telling them what had happened twenty years ago. *So what?* If it would save Nate, I'd do it.

I focused on my surroundings, searching for a foothold on reality. But there was a creepy, ghostly veneer over everything—the kitchen walls, the stove, the cabinets. They didn't look real; they appeared to be projections from some place beyond this world. This veneer was familiar. It was how the world had looked right after Lucy's death. Everything outside of me had appeared ethereal and eerily phony. The only reality had been that I'd lost the love of my life.

This time, the only reality was the threat to my son's life. But unlike after Lucy's death, now there *was* something I could do about it. Death hadn't come yet, and I had a chance to combat it before it did. To hell with the veneer. I'd ignore it. This wasn't like last time. Death hadn't won this round yet.

I needed to get to the nearest police precinct, present the letter, and confess to the secret I'd been keeping for twenty years. But I'd have to bring Nate with me.

A second later, I found myself walking into the living room, letter in hand, debating what to tell him. That debate was interrupted when a frightening image came to me: Dantès placing the letter in Nate's backpack at school. My skin was damp with sweat, and the few clear thoughts I'd managed to string together started to unravel.

In the hallway to the den, I stopped and once again started breathing in and out slowly, hoping to abate my rush of panic. Dantès hadn't harmed Nate. Not yet. And that led me to another rational thought: it was possible that a parent or a kid or a teacher at Nate's school might've seen Dantès slipping the letter into Nate's backpack. If so, the police would have a witness to question.

Before stepping into the den, I glanced down at the letter, and for the first time saw it as the police would: a piece of paper that didn't come with proof that the threat was valid. The police would have to investigate before proceeding, and that would take time. Time I didn't have. I had less than two days to save Nate: Friday, which was almost over, and

Saturday.

And the clock was already ticking.

Getting the proof that the threat was real meant taking one trip before talking to the police. The trip Dantès had suggested in his letter. The trip he knew I'd have to take, as if he was one step ahead of me. *Check in with your partners in crime. You'll find a connection that will serve as proof of the devastating damage I can wreak.*

That meant visiting either Lee or Quincy or both—the only two people in the world I never wanted to see again. And what if Dantès's proof was another unfathomable horror? What if he'd already extracted revenge by murdering one of their kids? But who knew if they even *had* kids? The fact was, I knew nothing about them.

After that fateful night at Cold Falls, the site of our transgression, we'd sworn never to see each other again. It was our way of forgetting. In retrospect, we'd have drifted apart anyway, but it wouldn't have been as abrupt. Our decision to go our separate ways and not so much as even talk to each other had lasted to this day. It was one of the reasons why that night had become less real to me over the years, and more like a nightmare I couldn't totally shake.

I stepped into the den, went over to my desk, and fired up my laptop. Tracking down Lee and Quincy seemed like an easy task, since every time I'd tried to find out what had become of a childhood friend, the Internet had lassoed them in fairly quickly.

Nate was glued to an animated Nickelodeon show and

wasn't paying attention to me at all. A few months ago, I'd started working in the den as a way of remaining physically close to him, so by now my presence had become part of the background for him.

He let out a deep belly laugh, full of delight. For me, those laughs were always a quick snapshot of what happiness sounded like, and I longed to be part of it. They were a reminder that our life could get back to some kind of normalcy.

But now Dantès had changed that.

It didn't take me long to find out that Lee and Quincy had one thing in common. They didn't have Facebook pages, Twitter accounts, LinkedIn profiles, or any other kind of Internet presence that Google could immediately find.

If I'd had the patience and focus to dig a little deeper, Google would've returned a hit on Quincy. A hit that would've verified that Dantès was playing a vicious game. But my focus was too scattered, so as soon as it became obvious that tracking down my partners in crime using Google searches was going to be tough, I pulled out my credit card and paid $14.99 to one of those despicable websites that sells personal information.

One minute later, I had both Lee's and Quincy's phone numbers and addresses.

Quincy lived in North Carolina, and Lee was local. Very local. Like me, he lived in Arlington. Both of us had settled down close to where we'd grown up. Still, based on the kind of kid Lee had been, I figured that talking to Quincy was the far wiser choice. But that reasoning lasted no longer than a second. Under the circumstances, it was critical to talk face to face, and there was no time to drive down to North Carolina. So Lee was my only option. Hopefully he'd changed over the years.

"Nate, we're going out to dinner," I said, keeping my voice calm. I'd pick something up for him on the way to Lee's place.

"Great! Can I watch the rest of this before we go?"

I glanced at the clock on my computer screen. His show would be over in less than ten minutes, but every minute was critical. "If you want to go out, we have to go now."

"Please."

I stood up. "I don't mind making dinner instead."

"No—I want to go out!"

After Lucy's death, I'd spoiled him by taking him out to dinner three or four times a week. That had stopped when the reality of our financial situation had come home to roost. But by that time, eating out had become one of his favorite activities. He had a list of preferred places: Paglia's Pizza, Subway, Granny's, Chipotle, and Le Petit Café.

"Then let's go." I grabbed the letter. "How about Subway?"

"Really?" He was now beaming. "Can I get chips?"

"Sure."

He grabbed the remote and clicked off the TV.

In the foyer, I grabbed jackets for both of us. As I slid the letter into my jacket pocket, I glanced back at the living room. Everything was still coated with that ghostly veneer.

Chapter Three

We picked up Subway sandwiches—an activity now ridiculously mundane compared to the real business at hand—and ten minutes later we were driving through one of the older neighborhoods in Arlington. Here, "bash and build" hadn't totally taken over yet, so among the splashy new McMansions were a good mix of small houses, including Lee's—a modest, red brick rambler.

I parked out front, then stared at his front door. Though he lived just a few miles away from me, it felt like I'd traveled halfway across the world. Or twenty years back in time.

I turned to Nate. "I'll be right back. I'm going to talk to an old friend for a minute or two." My plan was to stay on Lee's doorstep so I could keep an eye on Nate. "You can eat in the car."

"Really?"

"Yeah—just this one time."

"Why?"

"It's an early birthday present."

Nate's eyes widened as he unwrapped his sandwich. I never let him eat in the car, so this was another treat.

I climbed out, feeling for the letter in my pocket, and for the first time I realized my stupid mistake: the letter could have Dantès's fingerprints on it, and I'd been handling it willy-nilly. Well, too late now, but I'd be more careful from here on in.

I hurried up Lee's walkway, braced myself at the door, and pressed the doorbell. As three chimes rang inside, a new scenario hit me. What if Lee was behind the letter? What if he was Dantès? After all, only he, Quincy, and I knew about our secret, and if one of them was behind the letter, it had to be Lee. But why would he threaten Nate? Money was the only answer that came to mind. But if this was a shakedown, wouldn't he have asked for money?

The front door swung open, revealing an unshaven man with pasty, lifeless skin, uncombed, wild hair, and bags under dead eyes. He was wearing a dirty white terry-cloth bathrobe, cinched around his waist. Though his disheveled appearance took me by surprise, there wasn't any doubt that the man standing in front of me was Lee. The wiry teen was now as thick as a linebacker.

"Long time, no see," I said, not sure how else to start.

"Get the hell out." He started to swing the door closed.

My hand automatically whipped out and stopped the door. "Please, I need to talk to you for a minute. It's important."

"Whatever you're selling, I don't want it." He pushed on the door, but I held firm.

"Just give me a few seconds."

"Don't you remember the deal?" His tone was harsh. "We never see or talk to each other again. We didn't say except for a few seconds."

"Lee—I wouldn't have come if I didn't have to. Just hear me out."

"Nope." Again, he tried to push the door shut, but this time I pushed back hard—my desperation taking over—and the door opened far enough for me to catch a glimpse of the living room. Dirty dishes covered the coffee table. Crumpled shirts and pants covered the couch. And vases, stuffed with wilting flowers, covered the end tables and mantelpiece. It didn't take a genius to see that Lee was in bad shape.

"What's going on?" I blurted out. "Are you okay?"

"What's going on? Karma's a bitch—that's what going on." His dead eyes flashed with anger. "It took a hell of a long time to catch up, but it finally did."

Had Dantès murdered his son or daughter? I glanced back at my car. Nate was munching on his sandwich.

"Is that your son?" Lee asked.

"Yeah—Lee, please tell me what's going on?"

His body slumped and his anger dissipated. "My wife was—killed."

"… Wow… I'm sorry…" I was overwhelmed with sympathy for him—the same crushing blow had felled me.

Then the coincidence of it all hit me. Our wives had both been killed.

"Now will you leave me alone?" he said. His body sagged even more, like a balloon that had just been deflated.

For the second time in less than an hour, my mind was reeling. It wasn't karma that had killed his wife. It was Dantès. *This* was the proof of the damage he could wreak. My legs turned wobbly and my mouth went dry as another horrible possibility washed over me:

Had Dantès killed Lucy, too?

"My wife was killed, too," I said, and let that hang there, letting him make the connection.

"What?" He stared at me for a full ten seconds without another word. Something was stirring in his dead eyes. Then: "You're saying this was revenge for what we did—after twenty years."

"Dantès."

"What the hell is 'Dantès'?"

"The king of revenge—from *The Count of Monte Cristo*."

"Are you fucking crazy? You came over here to talk your brainy bullshit?"

I pulled the letter out, no longer worried about fingerprints. If Dantès was getting away with murder, he was also doing a damn fine job of cleaning up after himself. "Read this."

"Why?"

I looked past him into his living room, at the signs that his life had been shattered. "I'm not saying it's going to help, but things might make more sense."

Lee hesitated for beat, then shook his head, as in *What difference is this going make?*, and took the letter. He unfolded it and started to read.

Was it possible that Dantès had murdered two people to make his point? Or had he murdered Lee's wife just so I'd make the connection to Lucy? Either scenario proved that Dantès was cunning and ruthless. Nate had been handed a death sentence.

As Lee read the letter, the movie featuring Lucy's death started playing in my head. I'd stopped it from playing three months ago and was proud of that. For a long while, it had been the only show in town. The film combined the facts from the police report with gruesome elements conjured up by my imagination, which in turn was fed by the many horror and supernatural books I'd read.

As the film unspooled, I watched it with fresh eyes. The anomalies in her murder were suddenly clues, indications that the killing hadn't been random, just as Nate's instincts had told him. Lucy had been targeted.

She had worked late that night. Other young attorneys at Brown & Butler often worked late, but she would stay much later than most. While the others tended to work late almost every day, staying until nine or ten, she'd put in her extra hours all at once, working until one or two in the morning a couple of nights a week. That was to make up for the other days when she left on time so she could spend her evenings with Nate.

That night she'd been the last to leave, which was usually the case on her late nights. She'd taken the elevator downstairs, walked past the security guard, then down the back corridor and out into the parking lot. I'd often wished that the guard had offered to escort her to her car.

Detective Wyler, the detective assigned to the case, had told me the killer was waiting for Lucy in the shadows, probably right up against the building. He'd wanted the keys to her Accord, which I later learned was the most stolen car in the U.S. That fact alone made the case open and shut. The killer's motive was crystal clear, so everything else fell into place, regardless of the inconsistencies.

But now those inconsistencies made sense. They made *more* than sense. Those inconsistencies revealed what *really* happened that night.

From the evidence, it was clear that Lucy hadn't struggled. And Detective Wyler said she'd made the right decision not to fight back. But the thief had decided to shoot her anyway. Wyler chalked this up to bad luck. Most car thieves don't kill their victims.

But that hadn't been the only inconsistency. This thief hadn't even waited for Lucy to get to her car. He'd shot her in the head when she was still yards from the car. Detective Wyler said most car thieves waited until the victim unlocked the car and opened the door—but not this thief. The theory was that he was either impatient or an amateur, or both. That's how Wyler explained this inconsistency away.

But now the way the tragedy had unfolded made sense. It hadn't been a random and amateurish attempt to steal an Accord. It had been a targeted execution.

Lee looked up from the letter. "Do you want to come in?"

"Sure."

*

I ushered Nate through the living room, toward Lee's kitchen. He eyed the mess but didn't say anything, probably because he was more interested in digging into his bag of chips, which he hadn't opened yet. Chips were an even more special treat than eating in the car. I never bought them for the house.

Lee's kitchen turned out to be a disaster area, too. The counters were littered with dirty frozen-dinner trays and Styrofoam takeout containers featuring dried-up, half-eaten meals. Dishes were piled high in the sink.

I led Nate over to the kitchen table, which was miraculously litter-free. The only thing on it was a small TV. Maybe this spot was Lee's sanctuary. "Nate, can you wait for me in here? Or is it too gross?"

Nate sat at the table, placed what was left of his sandwich down—he'd wrapped the remaining third back up—and asked, "Is it okay if I don't finish the sandwich, Dad?"

What he was really asking was whether it was okay to start on the chips before finishing his sandwich. He knew I liked him to first finish his proper food before starting in on his junk food.

"Okay," I said. "And you're fine in here?"

He ripped open the bag of chips. "Yeah."

"I'll be in the living room. Come get me if you need anything, okay, sweetheart?"

"How long you gonna be?"

"Ten minutes or so."

He glanced at the kitchen counters. "I want to go soon."

"We will. I promise."

He pulled a chip from the bag, popped it in his mouth, crunched it, then took a longer look at the kitchen counters. His brow furrowed, betraying his anxiousness.

"Don't worry. Everything is fine," I said, wishing I could sound more convincing. "I'll be right back."

I entered the living room and found that Lee had cleared off the couch. The crumpled shirts and pants were now in a giant heap on one easy chair. Lee was seated on the other.

"Did you go to the police?" Lee said.

"No." I took a seat on the couch.

"But you're going to."

"Of course. What choice do I have?"

Lee's eyes shifted from me to the dead flowers on the mantelpiece.

I waited for him to say something more, and when he didn't, I spoke up. "How long has it been?"

"Two months." His eyes watered, but his face was stoic.

I wanted to say something helpful, or comforting, or uplifting, but I didn't have anything that fit the bill. When Lucy died, nothing anyone said to me helped. Still, I tried to think of something to say to fill the silence. But it was Lee who spoke first.

"You're thinking that this motherfucker—Dantès—killed my wife," he said. "And yours."

"… Yeah. But I don't know that for sure."

Lee looked down at the letter. "I'm going to hunt him

down and kill him."

My pulse quickened, and I sat up straighter. I was shocked, but not as much as you might think. This was the Lee I remembered from childhood.

"That's not why I came here, Lee," I said calmly, but my calmness rang false. "We have to—"

"Don't tell me what we have to do. I loved Grace, and that bastard murdered her. I want him dead."

Even though Lee had married and settled down to what looked like an ordinary middle-class suburban existence, he hadn't changed. He was reactionary, impatient, and unreasonable. And most of all, he was angry—his natural state.

Of course, it was possible he *had* changed, and that his anger wasn't the kind of anger I remembered. Maybe this was raw grief channeled into a sudden anger—an anger that gave him a way out of his troubles. Rather than sitting in his house, paralyzed, unable to bring his dead wife back to life— the same insurmountable problem I had—he'd just been granted the opportunity to fight back. To mete out revenge on the person who'd driven him to such despair.

"We have to go to the police," I said.

"I told you what I'm doing."

"But they can track Dantès down."

"Bullshit. You're not thinking straight."

"Me?"

"Yeah. Do you want me to play it out for you?"

I didn't respond immediately, so he pressed on.

"You show them the letter, and then what?"

"Then we have to tell them what happened at Cold Falls," I answered, knowing that wasn't what he wanted to hear.

"And when they check that out, what are they going to find?" He took a beat to let that sink in. "They're not going to find a damn thing. Zippo."

I shifted uncomfortably. We'd been lucky. As far as I knew—and I'd researched it a few times over the intervening years—there had never been any reports about what had gone down that night. That meant the police wouldn't have any evidence from that night—nothing they could use to track Dantès down. Our good luck—that our heinous deed had never been recorded, except in our own lives—had suddenly soured into bad luck.

"They can investigate the present crimes, the murders of our wives," I said. That was right—I *was* thinking straight. "They might find clues to who Dantès is right there."

"What happened to your wife?"

"She was killed when her car was stolen."

"And the police already investigated, right?"

I was silent. I had a good idea where he was going with this.

"Let me guess," he said. "They don't have diddly squat."

"They have a theory, but now I can show them it's wrong. The letter changes everything."

"Come on, John. Give me a break. The letter doesn't say this guy murdered your wife. It doesn't say anything about her. And it damn well doesn't say he murdered Grace. *We* know it's him, but the police don't. Sure, they'll investigate the letter, but do you really think they'll come up with anything? I'll tell you this: Grace's case is definitely closed. An accident. A hit-and-run driver. What about your wife's case? It's closed, right?"

My eyes shifted away from his, which gave him his answer.

He pressed on. "You really think you can convince them to reopen her case? To investigate? To look for new evidence?" He leaned forward in his chair. "And even if you could—and you can't—how much time do you have? When is your son's birthday?"

I knew my answer would make his case, but I volunteered it anyway. "In two days."

"So you're telling me that you're going to convince the police to reopen the case and that they're going to solve it— all in *two days*?"

No, I thought. And I was sure of that. No matter how you sliced it, it would take months, *if* they were willing to reopen her case, which was a pretty big if. The only thing they'd investigate was the threat to Nate, assuming they believed the letter wasn't a hoax. "What makes you think *you* can find the killer in two days?" I said.

"I didn't say I could. What I said was that I'm going to hunt him down and kill him."

I looked over at the chaos of clothes on the easy chair, then at the dirty dishes strewn across the coffee table.

Lee saw that and said, "Don't worry. Now I have a reason

to get my shit together." He stood up, and my stomach churned as I suddenly had an inkling of his plan.

"You're going to wait until he goes for Nate," I said.

"What?" His eyes went wide—he was genuinely surprised. "Hell no. I'm going after him now."

I believed him, but I also knew he'd be there on Sunday to take a shot at the bastard if he couldn't track him down before then. And if he didn't get him on Sunday, I had no doubt he'd spend the rest of his life tracking him down, if that's what it took.

"Lee, I can't do this your way," I said. Even if Lee and I could actually find this man—and that was another big if, since I certainly didn't have those kinds of skills and I doubted Lee did either—I couldn't kill him in cold blood. It was morally wrong. I didn't have the psychological makeup to commit murder. I wasn't a vigilante, and there was no way I could put myself in that frame of mind. Vigilante justice was only meted out in books and movies. It was fiction, not fact. The only way to catch Dantès was to go to the police.

"I didn't ask for your help," Lee said.

"I'm going to the police."

"Did you hear anything I said?"

"Of course I did."

"Okay, go to the damn police, but leave me the hell out of it."

"How can I do that?"

"That's your fucking problem." He motioned toward the kitchen. "And like I said, you're not thinking straight. What

about your son? You go to the police and they don't do shit
for who knows how long, how are you gonna protect him?"

"Send him into hiding." From the moment I'd gotten the
letter, I'd known I had to find a place where Nate would be
safe—but as soon as I said it out loud, the absurdity of the
idea became obvious, and Lee pounced.

"Send him into hiding? Like you're some kind of covert
ops expert?" Lee's lips were curled in a smirk, another of his
traits: a cocky arrogance.

I ignored it. "While the police track down Dantès, I was
going to send Nate to his grandmother's in Illinois."

"It's not going to work," he said.

"Why?"

"Isn't it goddamn obvious?"

It was if I wanted to admit it to myself. And since I didn't,
he did it for me.

"You're not going to get away from this guy—you're not
gonna be able to 'hide' your son from him. Who knows how
long he's been tracking you? At least long enough to
coordinate killing our wives and maybe a hell of a lot longer.
He knows what he's doing, and you don't. There's an old
phrase for what's going on, John: you can run, but you can't
hide."

His smirk disappeared and his lips tightened as if he was
thinking about the implication of that himself. He ran his
hand through his messy hair and sat back down. In a softer
tone, he said, "Do you remember that night?"

"Of course I do."

"Do you *really* remember it? Everything?"

I couldn't be sure, but I thought he was referring to some of the strange surreal elements from that night. We had never talked about those. There'd been no reason to. Instead we had talked about covering up our transgression and going our separate ways. But now I wanted to remember *every* detail from that night. I needed to. One of those details might yield up a clue to Dantès's identity.

Chapter Four

Lee, Quincy, and I had talked our parents into letting us camp out by ourselves for one night in Cold Falls, a Virginia state park. This was a big deal because we were eighth-graders and we'd never gone on an overnight trip that wasn't supervised by an adult.

We had picked Cold Falls because the state park held a special fascination for kids in Northern Virginia. The land had once been prime Native American land, and word was that it hadn't changed since those days. Kids, including Lee, Quincy, and me, believed that this land was mysterious and magical. That somehow the Native Americans reached out from the past and glorified it still.

Lee's parents didn't care one way or another whether he spent the night there. They didn't give a crap about him, and even back then I knew they were awful parents. They were rednecks, but that wasn't what made them awful parents. Back then, the Virginia suburbs weren't totally gentrified, so there were plenty of redneck parents, and just like any other parents, the majority of them were good parents doing the best they could for their kids. What made Lee's parents awful was the same thing that made any parents awful: how they treated their kid.

They preferred doing anything else—especially heavy drinking—to taking care of Lee. So Lee ended up a rough-and-tumble kid, and he was well on his way to becoming a delinquent by the time I met him in middle school. His parents were always leaving him with his uncle while they headed off to get drunk or high with their friends. Lee would spend Mondays, Tuesdays, and Wednesdays with his parents, and then they'd drop him off at his Uncle Harry's for the rest of the week and the weekend. So whether he was at Uncle Harry's or at Cold Falls for this particular weekend didn't matter to them.

Quincy's parents were more like mine. They paid attention to what their son was doing. But Quincy was a forceful kid, and he convinced his parents to let him go with a straightforward argument: *It's not like I'm going camping far from civilization. It's not even far from home.* Cold Falls was twenty-five miles from D.C., mostly a place for picnics and day hikes. And though the park was called Cold Falls, there weren't any falls, so that wasn't a danger.

Though Quincy convinced his parents with that argument, it didn't quite work when I used the same argument on *my* parents. They wouldn't agree to let me go. So as that weekend approached, I resorted to temper tantrums, which was unusual for me because I was an easygoing kid. I yelled at my parents, over and over again, *You don't think I'm brave enough! You don't think I can handle it! You don't think I can take care of myself for one night!*

After a couple of days of that, my dad started to see it my way: this camping trip was an important test of my independence. Letting me go would prove that he had faith and confidence in me. Keeping me home meant he thought I was a baby and a loser. So basically, I was able to guilt him into taking my side.

Then he tried to convince my mom that the trip would be good for me. After all, wasn't Cold Falls the perfect place for such an important life lesson? The Boy Scouts, Girl Scouts, and other youth groups often camped there for that exact reason. In addition to the trails and picnic areas, Cold Falls had two small campgrounds near the Potomac River. Those campgrounds offered a good introduction to the wilderness without the risk of being stranded in the middle of nowhere should something go wrong. Hospitals, police, et cetera, were all close by.

By Friday, my dad had talked my mom into it.

To this day, I wish he hadn't.

We spent Saturday morning getting ready. I packed a change of clothes, a flashlight, and a radio. My dad went out and bought me a sleeping bag while my mom made sandwiches. In the early afternoon, my dad drove me out to Cold Falls.

When we pulled into the parking lot, Lee was already there, with a backpack, sleeping bag, and grocery bag by his side. He said he'd ended up taking local buses to the park and that he'd shopped for his own food. Even though his dad had promised to swing by Uncle Harry's and pick him up, he'd never showed, and Uncle Harry didn't have a car.

Quincy and his dad arrived a few minutes later, and Lee and I were happy to see that Quincy had remembered to bring a tent. Then the five of us checked out a glass-enclosed map next to the ranger station—a large wooden cabin. After that, we started hiking the Gray Owl Trail. It would take us to the Clear River campground.

The day was gorgeous—blue sky and warm sunshine—so there were quite a few other people on the trail: a mixture of families, couples, and serious hikers. After we'd hiked about an hour, the trail narrowed and the forest thickened, adding shadows and mystery to the woods around us. It felt like our adventure had started.

We arrived at the Clear River campground a few minutes later and took measure of it. It consisted of seven campsites where the undergrowth had been cleared and the dirt packed down. Each site was separated by twenty yards of trees and brush. Nowadays, you won't find many campgrounds like this, where the campsites are so isolated from each other. We thought this was fantastic—exactly as we'd imagined it.

None of the sites were occupied, so Lee, Quincy, and I proceeded to carefully examine each one as if we were making a critical decision. Quincy's dad and my dad begrudgingly went along, but it was clear that they thought all the sites were the same: large, irregularly shaped patches of dirt, each equipped with a metal barbecue set into concrete.

We managed to find differences though. Some sites were

more shaded. Some were a bit smaller. Some featured rocks laid out in a circle, where previous campers had built fires. But the biggest difference, at least to us, was the proximity to the Potomac River.

Lee liked the site closest to the river, which was also the site farthest from the trail. Quincy and I agreed with his choice. And it was the campsite most surrounded by the wilderness.

"Are you sure you want that be that far from the trail?" my dad said, concern on his face.

"This is good," I said, embarrassed that he was worried about us.

My dad glanced at Quincy's dad, looking for support, but didn't get any. "Well, if anything goes wrong," Quincy's dad mused, "I don't suppose being a little closer to the trail is going to help. You'll still have to hike back to the ranger station."

My dad stood up tall, an indication that he didn't like that response. Quincy's dad must have understood my dad's body language because he followed up with: "You all know how to get back to the ranger station, right?"

"Yeah, we're not stupid," Quincy said, also embarrassed by his dad's concern. He grabbed the tent. "Help me set this up, Dad."

While Quincy and his dad were setting up the tent, Lee, my dad, and I hiked through the woods to the Potomac, about fifty yards away. There was no trail here, and we ended up at the top of a steep embankment, where huge gray boulders sloped almost vertically down to the river below.

"You guys need to be careful out here," my dad said. "Stick to the campsite once it gets dark. And use your flashlights." He looked down at the Potomac. "And don't climb down these rocks. If you want to get a closer look at the river, hike down that way." He motioned downriver to where the edge of the forest stood even with the bank.

But Lee was staring down the cliff in front of us as if he was already planning to ignore my dad's warning. After all, climbing down these boulders was the very kind of adventure that had drawn us here.

My dad headed back to the campsite and I followed. Lee spent another few seconds staring down from the precipice, then pulled himself away.

Back at the campsite, my dad reminded us that if we got hurt or ran into any problems, we should immediately go to the ranger station. A ranger was on duty twenty-four hours a day. My feeling back then, which stuck with me to this day, was that regardless of his reminder, my dad knew in his heart that if something terrible happened to us, we were in trouble.

As it turned out, he was right on the money.

We said our goodbyes, and our solo camping trip officially began. The first thing we decided to do was hike the rest of the Gray Owl Trail. The round trip would take about three hours, which gave us plenty of time to get back before nightfall. We took our canteens—bottled water was not yet de rigueur—and shipped out.

It wasn't long before we were disappointed. The hike was

fairly crowded, so it wasn't much of a wilderness adventure. The large number of hikers stripped the forest of any mystery or danger. Lee was so pissed that he marched straight off the trail and into the woods.

We followed him, leaving the day hikers behind, and entered a more intimidating forest, where trees came at us from every angle, where bushes stood unyielding in our path, and where ground creepers grabbed at our sneakers. As the challenge of this hike grew more difficult, our mood improved.

But that didn't last long. We were about to get a taste of the horror that awaited us in the night to come. After about twenty minutes of roughing it off-trail, and enjoying every minute of it, Lee stopped in his tracks and put his finger to his lips, shushing us. We stopped talking, and he pointed to a bush thick with green leaves and red berries. A raccoon was at the foot of the bush, pawing at a cluster of low-hanging berries.

Lee slid a pocketknife from his pocket and flicked the blade open. I glanced at Quincy to see if he had the same reaction I did—I wasn't into killing the raccoon—but Quincy didn't make eye contact with me. He was staring at the raccoon.

I knew that if Lee was going to be stopped, it was up to Quincy to do it. Lee didn't let any kid challenge him except for Quincy. It was like he instinctually knew that his impulses had to be kept in check, but he only let Quincy play that role. Quincy kept him out of the worst kind of trouble—the kind that involved fights with seriously dangerous kids and/or the police.

Lee liked me for a different reason, a reason I didn't figure out until years later. Though Lee was a rough-and-tumble kid, a delinquent in the making, he was also smart, and I validated that part of him. I was his only smart friend, as in a friend who got good grades and was quick to understand anything thrown at him. Our friendship made Lee superior to the other kids who were troublemakers.

Lee raised his arm, the knife poised in his hand. He aimed, then whipped his arm forward. The knife rocketed through the air, its blade spinning so smoothly it was obvious that Lee had been practicing. Still, I was shocked when the blade found its mark and stuck the raccoon right in the back. The wounded creature immediately scurried off.

"Bull's-eye," Lee said, with cold confidence, then raced after his prey.

We followed. "Why'd you do that?" I said.

"That's what we're here for." Lee was pulling away from us. "But I want that goddamn knife back!"

Up ahead, in the underbrush, I caught a fleeting glimpse of the raccoon's gray coat. Crimson blood glistened around the blade, which was still embedded in the poor animal. We zigged and zagged around trees and bushes, trying to keep up with him, but we lost him.

"Do you see him anywhere?" Lee asked.

"Nope," Quincy said.

Lee was scouring the underbrush ahead. "I want that

goddamn knife back."

You should've thought of that before you threw it, I thought.

We spent the next hour or so looking for the raccoon, and just before we were about to give up, we found him.

He'd been gutted.

The raccoon lay on his back, and his stomach had been slit open lengthwise. His gray fur was matted with blood, thick and gooey, and his wet entrails, pink, white, and black, glistened in his open stomach. Just above his head, Lee's pocketknife was stuck in the ground, upright, like a grave marker. It, too, was covered in blood.

"What the fuck?" Quincy said, turning away from the gruesome sight.

Feeling nauseated, I also turned away, but Lee's eyes were filled with morbid fascination as he stared at the display.

"Let's get out of here," Quincy said.

"Let's see if we can find the guy who did this," Lee said, scanning the woods around us, trying to spot the culprit.

"Who cares who did it?" Quincy said, and he started back toward the trail.

Lee approached the raccoon, knelt down next to it, and grabbed some leaves off the ground. He wrapped the leaves around the knife, then pulled it out of the ground.

I took off, following Quincy's lead.

"We should explore a little more," Lee shouted at us from behind.

"We can explore more later," Quincy said without even bothering to turn around. "Let's see if we can find the trail."

I caught up to Quincy. "Can you believe someone did that?"

"Someone put it out of its misery," Quincy said.

"They went overboard."

And the only explanation I could come up with was that it was a warning. Maybe if I'd taken it as such I would've never gotten Dantès's letter twenty years later, because I would've left Cold Falls right then.

I glanced back and saw that Lee had caved in and was following us. When he got closer, I blurted out, "Why'd you stab it in the first place?"

"It's called hunting, not stabbing," he said, and he was right. But he didn't get who was really being hunted. None of us did.

By the time we made it back to the campsite, it was early evening, and we were hungry. But when I unwrapped my sandwich, the image of the gutted, bloody raccoon flashed through my mind, and nausea coursed through me again. I ended up taking just a few bites of my sandwich before wrapping it back up. Quincy ate half his sandwich before stopping. Lee, on the other hand, was ravenous, as if the raccoon had whetted his appetite. He made himself three bologna sandwiches, and he devoured them one right after the other. Then he pulled his knife from his pocket—it was still wrapped in leaves—and washed off the blood using water from his canteen.

When he was done, he announced, "Time to check out the Potomac."

"Cool," Quincy said, eager for a new, and hopefully better, adventure.

I looked up and saw the orange glow of the setting sun beyond the treetop canopy. Nightfall was on its way.

"We should take our flashlights," I said.

Lee shook his head in disgust, as if I'd proposed surrendering to a weak-kneed enemy. "We don't need flashlights." He got up and started through the woods. Quincy and I fell in line behind him.

We hiked to the edge of the precipice, where we all stared down at the long stretch of boulders and the Potomac below.

"Let's do this," Lee said.

My dad's warning was still fresh in my mind, and I weighed whether to say anything. I decided not to—I didn't want Lee getting on my case so early in the trip, calling me a "wimpy pussy," his preferred term for kids who didn't join him on his reckless excursions.

Lee started down the steep decline of boulders, but Quincy hung back. I hoped Quincy would say something, and the longer he stood there, the more that hope grew. But he didn't say a word. Instead he clenched his jaw, braced himself, and started down after Lee.

I looked to the south of where we stood, to the area my dad had pointed out, where the edge of the forest met the banks of the Potomac. No cliff, no precipice. Just a muddy, rocky shoreline. But that option wasn't on the table, so I reluctantly followed Quincy.

It was a steep climb down, and we had to use the ledges

formed between the boulders to find our footing. The problem was that some of those ledges—and they were too shallow to deserve that appellation—were barely wide enough for the tips of our sneakers to grasp. We also grasped onto whatever crevices we could find on the boulders' surfaces, then hugged the rocks with our bodies so as not to tumble down into the river below.

Halfway down, we got a reprieve. Lee found a perch, about forty feet above the Potomac, where a massive boulder jutted out and provided a surface wide enough for all three of us to stand on safely—more or less. We congregated there, and I saw why Lee had stopped. The rest of the climb down was even steeper than the one we'd taken so far. Again I thought about saying something, and again fear of being labeled a wimpy pussy stopped me.

"You guys ready for round two?" Lee said, motioning down toward the river.

Quincy glanced up at the sky; the orange glow had turned to a purplish blue. Evening had arrived, and darkness would soon follow. "We should head back before it gets dark," he said.

Lee's lips curled into his trademark smirk. "Chicken, huh?"

"Nope." Quincy glared at him. "And we should've brought our flashlights."

I was ready for Lee to anoint Quincy a wimpy pussy, but instead he pointed across the river. "Check that out! A fucking wolf!"

On the opposite bank of the river, above us, stood a husky and powerfully built gray wolf. He was staring down at us, and I saw menace glinting in his large black eyes. Just before he turned and started trotting downstream, his eyes flashed gold for a split second.

"It has to be a dog," I said as I watched the animal trot downriver. "There aren't any wolves around here."

"Says who?" Lee demanded.

"My dad checked it out." My dad had called the Park Service to find out if dangerous animals roamed Cold Falls. None did.

"Let's go downriver and get a better look at him," Lee said, and he started climbing back up the cliff.

I was relieved that he'd abandoned this particular expedition, and I took another look at the animal who'd rescued us. The animal glanced back, and this time his large black eyes looked like human eyes—smart, cunning human eyes. I glanced at Quincy to see if he'd caught this, but he'd already started climbing back up.

"Hurry up," Lee shouted from above. "We're gonna lose him."

By the time we reached the top of the cliff—which took much longer than the climb down—evening had turned to early night, and though the real darkness hadn't settled in yet, it suddenly felt like we were far from home, alone.

"Let's get the flashlights before going downriver," Quincy said—a reasonable suggestion.

"We don't have time for that." Lee was angry.

Quincy didn't argue, and neither did I. We both understood that even though flashlights were a good idea, going back to the campsite would put an end to tracking the wolf, our new adventure.

We moved downriver, but there was no trail here, so we had to pay close attention to our footing. And that was why we lost sight of the wolf.

"He's still out there," Lee said. "When we can see straight across the Potomac we'll find him."

Maybe, maybe not, I thought, but at least the farther south we moved, the narrower the river became and the easier it was to see the riverbank on the other side.

When we made it to the flatlands and got a clear line of sight across the river, Quincy concluded, "I think we lost him."

"We got plenty of time to find him." Lee marched forward, following the shoreline but skirting the muddy, rocky bank.

"Maybe he went back into the woods," I said.

"Then we gotta cross the river."

That was absurd. One of his classic, crazy exploits. "This isn't a creek," I said. "We're not going to find some rocks to walk across."

"You think I'm an idiot? Maybe there's a boat pulled up on the shore."

"I don't think there's gonna be a boat around here," I said.

"Why not?" He was determined to track down the wolf.

"There aren't any boat rental places in Cold Falls."

"What if a camper brought one?"

He had a point, and Quincy laughed. "He got ya."

"So the plan is to steal a boat?" I said.

Lee didn't answer, but marched on. Quincy shrugged his shoulders and shot me a smile, as if to say *Let's cross that bridge when we come to it.*

We hiked in silence, concentrating on avoiding the mud while also checking the other riverbank, hoping to catch a glimpse of the elusive wolf.

No such luck.

It wasn't long before a waxing crescent moon brightened the night sky, painting the forest and river with a pale halo. But the halo didn't illuminate the woods. Instead it bathed them in this unsettling, otherworldly hue. I still remember that abnormal tint, and thinking, *Shouldn't the light of the moon make the forest brighter, not creepier?* Not only did I feel like I had traveled far from home, I now felt like I'd crossed over into another world.

"Whoa—" Lee said. "Don't move." He pointed straight ahead. "There he is."

Quincy stepped up to Lee. "Where? On *this* side of the river?"

"Yeah, but what did I tell you, you fucking retard: don't move. He's right by the water."

I scanned the edge of the river up ahead and spotted him. He stood as still as a statue, a silhouette of a magnificent and malevolent wolf. His head was held high, but I couldn't see his eyes this time.

Lee slowly moved forward.

"What are you going to do?" Quincy couldn't hide the fear in his voice.

"Get a closer look." Lee pulled out his knife.

"Why?" I said. The only scenario I could imagine was Lee antagonizing the wolf.

The wolf lifted its head toward the crescent moon and unleashed a piercing howl. The threatening wail cut through the night air, dominating the land.

The hair on my neck prickled and my heart started racing.

Suddenly the wolf charged at us—and we took off, sprinting toward the precipice, stumbling over rocks and underbrush. Somehow we managed to keep our balance and press forward. Lee and Quincy were ahead of me, so I glanced back to see if the wolf was about to pounce on me.

I saw shimmering gold and black eyes in the darkness— animal eyes, but somehow human, too—and then I tripped and went down hard on the muddy shore, body first, followed by my head, which skirted off a large rock. An excruciating pain shot through my skull, but I bit down on my lip and clenched my fists, trying to contain it. Then I furiously scrambled back to my feet and lunged forward.

I looked past Lee and Quincy, toward the precipice of boulders, to see how far I had yet to go, and was dumbstruck by what I saw. It had to be some kind of nighttime mirage— weird shadows cast by that eerie halo. Or was it the blow to my head, which throbbed with every breath I took? The raging pain must've blurred both my vision and my mind, because the precipice now looked like a medieval castle—as if someone had sculpted all the boulders into a stronghold on a hill. The spectacle made me stumble, but this time I had enough sense to slow down, check the ground, and find my footing.

When I looked back up, the castle was gone.

I raced up toward the precipice, gaining ground on Lee and Quincy, driven by the fear that I was going to hallucinate again. We all made it to the top and veered into the forest, toward the campsite. Running through the woods here was both less of challenge and more. The footing was surer than it had been on the shoreline and cliff, but there were many more obstacles: tree trunks, bushes, and clumps of vegetation. Every few yards we were swerving in one direction or another to avoid them.

After a frenzied sprint of zigs and zags, we finally landed in the small clearing that was our campsite. We bent over, hands on thighs, and tried to catch our breaths. My head was still throbbing, but as I caught my breath, the pain lessened. I touched the side of my head and looked at my fingers—there was no blood. That realization was enough to make the pain ease just a little more.

I scanned the woods. They didn't offer up any clue as to whether the wolf had tracked us—no dark silhouette, no gold or black eyes.

"I think he gave up," I said.

"He sticks to the river," Lee responded, as if he was an expert. He was scanning the woods, too, and I saw fear in his eyes, as if he knew the wolf could spring at us at any second. "Let's get our flashlights," he added.

We went for our backpacks and started digging through them. It was then that I came closest to asking them if they'd seen the strange vision—the medieval castle on the banks of the Potomac. But with each second that passed, I was more convinced that the mirage had been the result of the blow to my head. I'd been knocked for a loop, and that, mixed with the fear and adrenaline coursing through my body, had resulted in the weird apparition.

We ran our flashlights back and forth across the woods, and after verifying that we were alone, we sat down and ate again. My appetite still hadn't returned, except when it came to Lee's offering: he'd bought a box of Oreos, which he agreed to share, though not in a generous way. Instead he sparingly dispensed each cookie as if he were a king who'd been forced to distribute some of his gold bullion.

By the time we'd polished off the box—Lee had scarfed down more than two thirds of the Oreos—the creepy halo painted over the forest had turned into a pale fog that clung to the treetops. Tendrils reached down from the luminescent white shroud into the woods below.

"You guys ready to do a little exploring?" Lee flicked on his flashlight and swept the beam around the forest. The contrast between what we could see in the beam of light and what was hidden outside of it was stark. Where there was no light, obscure shapes of black on black loomed.

Lee flicked off his flashlight, and the darkness engulfed us again. "I got a better idea than exploring," he said. "Hide 'n' seek."

The potential for danger made hide and seek the perfect game for Lee. We'd have to avoid getting lost in the fog, avoid becoming dinner for the wolf, and avoid tumbling down into the Potomac.

Quincy didn't respond, and my guess was that he thought it wasn't a great idea.

"You up for it, John?" Lee asked me, probably sensing resistance from Quincy.

"Sure." I was counting on Quincy to talk Lee out of it.

Lee flicked on his flashlight, shining it right into Quincy's face. "You in? Or does the big bad wolf scare ya?"

"Shut that off, you fucker."

Lee did. "You ready to play?"

"Rock, paper, scissors—loser's it," Quincy said. Again, if this decision had gone the other way—if Quincy or I had said *no, this is a stupid idea*—maybe my life wouldn't have been cursed.

"On three." Lee made a fist.

We all pumped our fists and threw down.

Lee lost. "Goddamn it," he said.

I didn't blame him for being pissed. If there was fun to be had, it was in the hiding and not the seeking, which would amount to blundering through the dark.

"I'll close my eyes and count to a hundred," Lee said, and proceeded to do just that.

Quincy took off, but I hesitated. My eyes fell on the

tent—a great place to hide. Lee would never look there. I took a confident step toward it, then glanced at Lee and changed my mind. Even though he wouldn't find me, once I revealed myself, he wouldn't think it was a clever hiding spot. He'd call me a wimpy pussy for hiding there.

I ran into the forest, and was about thirty yards in when I saw Quincy just standing there as if he was lost. He wasn't attempting to hide.

"What's the matter?" I said.

"I saw something out there." He pointed in the direction of the Potomac.

Under the blanket of chirping crickets, I could hear the river gurgling. But I didn't see anything. "Turn on your flashlight," I said.

"No—" Quincy leaned forward, straining to pick out something in the dark. "Lee'll say I'm cheating and force *me* to be it."

And Lee was another sound I heard loud and clear. He was speeding up his countdown, his impatience kicking into high gear. "It was probably a deer or something," I said. *Or the wolf*, I thought.

"There—" Quincy pointed in the direction of the precipice. But there was too much forest between it and where I stood to make anything out. Not only was my view obscured by darkness and branches, but also by tendrils of fog, which had now grown thicker and descended closer to the ground.

I couldn't see anything, and I was ready to find a hiding

place right where we were, when I caught a glimpse of a shape moving swiftly through the night. Whether it was man or animal, I couldn't tell. It appeared to be traveling low to the ground like the wolf, but then it rose, as if unfolding itself, to the height of a man. Then it blended into the darkness—black into black—and disappeared.

Whatever it was, real or imagined, it left me with the creepy sensation of being unmoored from Cold Falls. It was as if I'd traveled far from the campsite and far from my Virginia home. *Too* far. To a different land. Mysterious Native American land. Glorified land. But glorified with what?

"Did you see it?" Quincy said.

"Yeah... I think so." *Hadn't I?*

Lee was now counting louder and faster. Quincy went on the move, though he didn't go far. He crouched down behind some wild berry bushes a few yards away.

I forced myself to move on too, scouting for the closest hiding place. After weaving around a few trees, I spotted a cluster of large boulders, hurried over to it, and crouched down behind it.

Then I scanned the terrain around me, on the lookout for whatever it was I'd just seen.

"Ready or not, here I come!" Lee shouted, sounding angry.

I peered over the boulder, toward the campsite. Lee's flashlight beam flowed between the tree trunks and flickered off the low-hanging fog.

I slid out of sight, turned my back to the boulder, and sat down. At that very second, staring into the misty darkness, I knew that our adventure was doomed. But I had no idea that our lives were also doomed.

I told myself that my sense of foreboding stemmed from the fall I'd taken, and I tried to focus on my surroundings, not on what I was reading into them. The air was filled with the thick blanket of crickets chirping, and with the rustle of raccoons, opossums, and squirrels scurrying though the brittle underbrush. I could also hear owls hooting in the pale fog.

A few minutes later, I heard a loud and rhythmic crunching of leaves—footsteps. Even though I knew it had to be Lee, I tensed up, fearing it was someone or something else.

Lee shouted out, "I know I'm close, 'cause you pussies are too scared to go far!" He was angry, and I was glad to hear it. It meant things were normal.

A minute later, I saw him about ten yards away, heading toward the Potomac. He was sweeping his flashlight across the woods. At one point, he turned around and flashed the beam in my direction. It skimmed the forest this way and that, but missed me.

He continued on, and when he was out of sight, I considered heading back to the campsite. Waiting here like a sitting duck, for whatever danger the fog and night threatened, seemed stupid. If Lee bitched that I'd cheated by going back to the campsite, I would just tell him I thought we were playing with the home base rule—where a player's goal is to get back to base without being caught.

A howl pierced the darkness—the same menacing howl we'd heard earlier. When it ended, I noticed that the crickets were no longer chirping and the owls were no longer hooting. I listened for the rustle of raccoons and opossums and squirrels—but those sounds had also been silenced.

A creepy, unnatural stillness had enshrouded the woods.

Then I heard thumping—it was my heart pounding. I wanted to rush back to the campsite, but I couldn't risk it. The wolf was on the prowl.

After a few more seconds of that deathly stillness, I peered over the boulder. Quincy was walking toward me warily. He flicked on his flashlight.

"We have to see if Lee's okay," he said.

I stood up. "He passed me a few minutes ago. He was headed toward the Potomac."

Quincy pointed his flashlight in that direction. "Is that where the howl came from?"

"I couldn't tell."

"Lee!" Quincy shouted as he scanned the forest with his flashlight. But because the fog had now infiltrated the woods, the light's beam was dull and diffuse. It couldn't penetrate the darkness.

I flicked on my own flashlight and took a few steps forward. "Come on, Lee! No jokes!"

Quincy and I slowly walked forward. "It's like he turned the tables on us," I said.

"What do you mean?"

"We're 'it' now and he's hiding." And we fell naturally into our new roles. Without a word, we slowly made our way toward the Potomac, on the lookout for Lee.

The thickets of fog touched my skin, leaving their clammy, dank fingerprints. In the absence of any other sound, my every step seemed unnaturally loud. Every time I stepped on dry leaves, the resulting crunch was amplified, as if the volume had been turned up to ten. Even my breathing was inexplicably loud, resonating with overtones I'd never heard before.

Why hadn't the crickets resumed chirping?

"Lee!" I called out.

"If he turned the tables," Quincy said, "he's not gonna answer."

We stepped out of the woods and onto the precipice. Here, the fog was so thick that it turned our flashlight beams into glowing shields through which we couldn't see. We both flicked off our flashlights. This was better, but we still couldn't make out much—

Until the fog suddenly lifted, revealing Lee. He was standing way too close to the edge of the cliff, his back to us. And I thought I also saw a tall, thin man in front of him, though it could've been just a black hole in the mist. Before I could tell for sure, the fog once again engulfed Lee and filled the space between us.

"Lee!" I moved in his direction, and Quincy followed. But we both stopped after a few yards. In the fog, it was hard to tell just how close to the edge we were. And there was something else that stopped us. The fog now smelled foul—as if it carried the odor of rotting meat—and it had thickened. I felt like I'd been wrapped in a dank, moldy web.

A gust of wind suddenly swept across the precipice, sending the fog into a wild dance—a dance that cleared away just enough of the mist to reveal Lee again—

Lee pushed the tall, thin man over the cliff.

I was about to race forward and yell out, shocked that Lee had just sent a man to his death, but before the man disappeared over the edge, and before the fog danced back over the scene, I caught a glimpse of the man's face. It was an unearthly, pallid color, not quite white, but not quite flesh-colored either. And even more odd was the expression on the man's face. *Satisfaction*. Of course, I couldn't be sure. I saw his ashen face for only a fraction of second.

The gust of wind died as suddenly as it had risen, and the fog settled back over the scene, obscuring it. A second later, I heard a hard and cruel thud, followed by a splash, as if a body had first struck that ledge below, then continued down into the river. My heart rate increased tenfold, sending blood rushing through my body with such force that my veins felt like they'd explode.

Lee stepped out from the mist. "Let's get the fuck out of here."

I stood there, stunned, as Lee rushed by me into the woods.

Quincy took off after Lee. "What the hell, Lee?" he shouted.

I followed them both. Lee had flicked on his flashlight and was making his way through the forest back to the campsite.

"Lee!" Quincy shouted.

I was replaying what I'd just witnessed, and I was left with the same question Quincy had shouted out: *What the hell, Lee?* Why had Lee just killed that man?

While those questions roared through my head, I noticed the sudden change in my surroundings. The fog had lifted, and the chirping of crickets once again blanketed the woods.

I picked up my pace and heard the owls hooting and the raccoons, opossums, and squirrels rustling in the underbrush. The creepy, unnatural quality of the night had lifted. It no longer felt like I had crossed over into a world far from home. The wilderness was normal again.

When I made it to the campsite, I found Quincy face to face with Lee. A thin sheen of sweat covered Lee's face, and he was breathing heavily. He had a panicked, wild look in his eyes.

"Why'd you push that guy over?" I said.

"He tried to kill me."

"That's a bunch of crap," Quincy said.

From what I'd seen—which, granted, had been fragmented, hazy, and unreliable—the one thing I could say for sure was that the man hadn't been trying to kill Lee.

"The guy was hunting me down," Lee said, "and I couldn't shake him."

"So you cornered him and pushed him over?" Quincy wasn't going to let Lee skate.

"The fucker had me by the throat!"

I shook my head. "He didn't touch you."

"You don't know what the fuck you're talking about. He would've killed us all."

"We've got to go the ranger station." I knew that was the only option. "Tell the ranger what happened. Maybe the man is still alive." If cell phones had existed, I would've called the police right then and there, and that would've been the end of it.

"What the fuck is wrong with you?" Lee stepped closer to me. "We're not gonna blab to a ranger."

I moved past him, dipped into the tent, and grabbed my backpack. I stuffed my empty food containers inside, then zipped it up.

Lee popped into the tent. "What are you doing?"

"Going to the ranger station, then calling my dad and going home." I grabbed my sleeping bag, brushed past Lee, and emerged from the tent.

"Are you coming with me?" I asked Quincy.

Before Quincy could answer, Lee burst out of the tent and grabbed my arm. "You're not gonna talk to the ranger."

I shook him off and stared Quincy down. "Are you coming with me or not?" Lee couldn't stop both of us. "Maybe the man made it to shore and they can help him," I said, trying to convince myself that the man had survived— that there'd been no murder.

Lee smirked and wiped the sweat from his face. "Can you believe this guy?" He was addressing Quincy.

Quincy took a step toward Lee. "What the fuck is wrong with you?"

"Fuck you! I told you. He came after me."

"Let's see if we can help the guy," I said.

Quincy glared at me. "News flash! We can't! No way he survived!"

I headed toward the trail, but Lee lunged forward and grabbed my arm again. "You can go, but first we get our stories straight."

I tried to shake him off again, but this time his grip was firm.

"If our stories are different," he said, "it's not gonna help any of us."

"I'm not going to lie about this."

"Neither am I," Lee said.

"Great. Now get the fuck off of me." I whipped my arm out of his grip and marched toward the trail. If he wanted to fight me, then that's what he'd have to do.

"I'm telling them exactly what I saw," Lee said. "*You* pushed that guy over the edge."

I whipped around.

Lee was grinning. "You did it accidentally. You two were horsing around, but still..."

I looked over at Quincy for support. His mouth was agape—he, like me, couldn't believe Lee would stoop so low. "Lee—this is real," Quincy said. His tone had shifted—upset, not angry. "This isn't like the trouble you usually get into."

Lee didn't even look at Quincy. He stared at me. "That's

why we're sticking together. You got that?"

I got it all right. If I wasn't willing to cover this up, he was going to pin the murder on me. And if I told the truth, it'd be his word against mine. *Except* there was Quincy's word, too. His word would tip the balance.

"Quincy, you'll tell them what really happened, right?" I said.

Quincy shifted uneasily. Then his body sagged as if the weight of the world had been dropped on his shoulders.

"Quincy doesn't know what happened," Lee said, "because he didn't see anything. Right, Quincy?"

"Why the fuck did you do it in the first place?" Quincy shot back.

"I told you—the weird motherfucker attacked me!"

Quincy needed to stand up to Lee now more than ever, but he was more panicked than aggressive, which wasn't going to help.

"I'm not going to cover it up," I said, hoping this would give Quincy the courage to stand up to Lee—and head with me to the ranger station.

Lee reached out and thumped me hard in the chest. "It's not up to you, buddy."

I didn't say a word, but I glared at him and stood my ground, which made him angrier than he already was.

"We could say it was an accident," Quincy said. "That we saw the guy fall off the cliff. That he must've gotten lost in the fog."

Lee's face hardened. "We're not gonna say anything."

"If they find the body tomorrow, they'll question us," Quincy said. "But if we go to the ranger now, it's not so suspicious."

"If we go now, we'll have to answer a ton of questions," Lee said, his attention now solely on Quincy. "Let's just camp tonight, like nothing happened, and go home in the morning."

"It they find the body tomorrow, they'll track us down and question us at home." Quincy was pushing back hard. Of course, I didn't really know if he was looking for a way to get to the ranger station in peace so he could tell the truth, or if he was negotiating a compromise.

"So what?" Lee said. "We tell them we don't know anything and didn't see anything."

Quincy looked over at me as if he wanted my help. But I didn't want to negotiate a compromise. A compromise was a cover-up. "You're not going to back me up if I tell the truth?" I asked him.

He didn't answer. Instead he looked into the woods in the direction of the Potomac. His eyes betrayed defeat and resignation.

"Quincy, you're going to back me up, aren't you?" *Had I lost him?*

"I don't know what I saw out there."

"He admitted he pushed him over!" I blurted out.

"*And* he said the guy attacked him!"

"He's lying."

Quincy turned from the woods to me. "What did *you* see?

Think about it. It was hard to see anything at all, wasn't it? That's the truth. And whatever you *did* see, it didn't make sense, did it?"

I knew what he meant—the bizarre texture of the entire incident. Dank, wet, foul, misty—a distorted, creepy nightmare that didn't quite seem real. And the man's pallid face. The expression it bore. How was I going to explain any of this to anyone? No doubt Lee's version, his lie—laying the blame on me—would be straightforward and easy to follow.

I needed Quincy to back me up, but it was becoming clear that he wouldn't.

Lee seized the momentum. "So it's a done deal. We keep our mouths shut." Again, he was focused on Quincy. And so was I.

Quincy stared at me for a couple of beats, resigned, then looked at Lee. "… Okay," he said, in almost a whisper.

I should've stood my ground, but I was fourteen, easily influenced, and trying to shake off a feeling of foreboding, which had returned with a vengeance. The horrific scene from the precipice—part hallucination, part nightmare, and part brutal reality—replayed itself in my head, unwanted. I just wanted to go home and forget about the entire night.

Lee laid down the law: if anyone asked us any questions tomorrow, or next week, or next month, or even a year from now, we'd say we hadn't seen anything or heard anything. And if no one ever came around to ask questions, we'd never bring it up, *ever*.

Quincy took it one step further. "We shouldn't talk to

each other again either."

"About this?" Lee asked, but I knew what Quincy meant.

"About anything. After tonight, we go our separate ways." Quincy was adamant, as if he was sure this was the way to make the murder go away.

Lee looked taken aback—he'd been in control, exerting his will, but now Quincy was making the rules. "Is that the way you want it?" he said.

Quincy nodded.

Lee didn't ask me if that was the way *I* wanted it too.

"Then you got it," he said, and stormed off into the tent.

"Quincy—" I said, but he cut me off before I could finish. He must've thought I was going to try to talk him into going to the ranger station.

"I don't want to talk about it anymore," he said. "Let's get through the night and get the hell out of here."

And that's what we did. Quincy and I unrolled our sleeping bags, outside the tent, crawled into them, and waited for dawn. We didn't say a word to each other; we just stared at the crescent moon as it moved through the sky. There was no hint of fog the rest of the night.

Lee slept in the tent.

When dawn broke, Quincy was asleep. I quietly rolled up my sleeping bag, grabbed my backpack, and hiked the trail back. The entire way, I was reconsidering the deal we'd made the night before—the unholy pact. But only when I got to the parking lot and saw the ranger station did I make my decision.

Leaving the trail behind and stepping onto the parking lot's blacktop was my reentry into a familiar world. That, plus the clear light of day, was more than enough to transform my chaotic, shrouded vision of a man tumbling to his death into a nightmare best forgotten. It was as if I'd awakened from a troubling sleep.

I went to the bank of pay phones, called my dad, and told him I was feeling sick and wanted to be picked up early. While I was on the phone, the ranger on duty stepped out of the ranger station. I'm sure I'd caught his attention because I was the only living soul around at that early hour.

I wanted to run, but I knew that would be suspicious, so I wrapped up my call in what I hoped was a nonchalant manner. But when I hung up, I was positive the ranger could see the guilt on my face. Or worse: he already knew about the dead body and suspected me.

"Everything okay, son?" he said.

"I feel kind of sick, so I called my dad to pick me up."

"What's wrong?" He moved closer to me.

For a second I thought he was referring to my guilt, but I caught myself before I confessed. "It's a stomachache," I said. The words came out stilted because my throat was constricted with panic.

"You think you ate something bad?"

I shook my head, then realized I should've just said yes. Too late. "I think maybe it's the flu," I said.

"Any vomiting or fever?" He was doing his job, figuring out if I needed immediate medical attention.

I shook my head again, wanting him to just leave me alone. I couldn't go on lying without giving myself away. I wasn't built for it.

"Did anything happen while you were camping?" he said.

So he *did* know. My throat constricted even more, and I weighed whether to confess. Then Lee's threat reared its ugly head—he'd pin the murder on me if I answered the ranger's question with anything other than one simple word.

"No," I said, shaking my head to emphasize it.

"You didn't get bit by a raccoon or anything?"

With that question, I understood where he was going. He wasn't trying to connect me to the dead body—he was just focused on my illness. "No," I said.

"Good."

Please leave me alone, I thought, suddenly overcome with the fear that Lee was racing up the trail and would catch me talking to the ranger. His impatience would kick in, not to mention his anger, and he'd think I was spilling my guts. That would be enough for him to run up to the ranger and carry out his awful threat—blaming the murder on me.

I tried to think of a way to extricate myself from the ranger's questions. "I'm going to sit down and wait for my dad," was the best I could come up with.

"You can wait inside," the ranger said.

No, I can't. If Lee saw me heading inside, it would be an invitation for him to ruin my life. "I'm okay out here," I said, and pointed to the picnic table nearest the parking lot. "I'll wait over there where my dad can see me."

"All right, son. I'll keep an eye out for you in case you feel any worse," he said. Then he headed back into the cabin.

I started toward the picnic table at a fast clip, but quickly slowed down—I didn't want the ranger to think I was well enough to hurry anywhere. At the picnic table, my fears continued unabated. First, that the ranger would get a report about a dead body that had just been fished out of the Potomac and would rush out of the cabin to question me. And second, that Lee would appear and interpret my early departure as evidence that I'd ratted him out.

Neither happened.

My dad picked me up, and I told him that I was already feeling better, which was true. I was feeling better because I was leaving Cold Falls forever. Or so I hoped. But that would turn out not to be the case. In two decades, I'd return to the scene of the crime, and maybe in the back of my mind, or in my gut, where a dull ache had started to grow, I knew those woods and that night would draw me back in.

In the days that followed, I could've told my dad the truth about Cold Falls and gotten his advice about going to the police and combating Lee's version of the story. My dad and I had a close relationship, so confiding in him wouldn't have been as hard for me as it might have been for some kids.

But I didn't confide in him. Instead, I watched the local news every night, flipping between stations, expecting to land on a story about a man who'd recently disappeared, or about a man who'd been fished out of the Potomac, or about a man who'd washed up on the riverbank with his head cracked open. In the mornings, I'd search the *Washington Post* looking for a headline about a man who'd drowned in the Potomac, or about a man who'd been found bruised and battered in Cold Falls State Park.

Days turned into weeks, and I never saw or heard anything about any such man. And when weeks turned into months, not only did it seem foolish to confess, I also became more convinced that the incident hadn't unfolded the way I'd originally thought. I replayed it over and over again, in great detail, to confirm that, indeed, it had been a nightmare of shadows, fog, and fear.

But there was a huge kink in that interpretation. Lee had *admitted* to pushing the man over the cliff. And obsessively reliving that night didn't wipe out that kink. More times than not, when I was caught up in that loop of creepy, unsettling images, it triggered a clawing guilt, accompanied by a physical reaction. My skin felt clammy and dank, as if the fog were touching it again, reaching out from Cold Falls to haunt me. It took me a long time to stop reliving that night. Only when months turned into years was I able to bury it in a hard-to-reach corner of my psyche.

Chapter Five

"I remember it all," I said. The dreadful images from that night may have been buried deep in my psyche, but they were perfectly preserved, ready to be recalled at a moment's notice.

Lee was looking at the mantelpiece as if he was studying the vases of dead flowers. "But you never believed me," he said. "That that guy was hunting me down."

"It doesn't matter now, does it?" There was no point in debating the past. And there was no time. This was all about saving Nate's life.

"If you really remember that night," he said, "you'd remember it was fucked up."

That much we agreed on, but I still wasn't sure if he was referring to the surreal elements. "So?"

"No one reported the man missing," he said. "It was like he disappeared."

"We got lucky."

"And now you think our luck finally ran out?" His question dripped with disdain, as if he was daring me to agree with something absurd.

"Someone discovered what we did and is getting revenge."

"No one found out."

Anger suddenly boiled up inside me. "What are you talking about?"

"It's him."

"Him? You mean the guy you killed?"

He didn't answer my question, but he held my eyes, resolutely and confidently, meaning "yes" and also calling me out as a fool for not believing him.

"That's ridiculous," I said. "You're the one who doesn't remember that night. He couldn't have survived that fall. I heard his body hit the boulders."

"But what did you *see*? Actually *see*?"

"Just because I didn't see him hit the rocks and float on downriver, doesn't mean it didn't happen."

"That's not what I'm talking about. I mean what *did* you actually see?"

If he wanted me to talk about the dank, foul fog, or the wolf, or the castle, or the unearthly pallid shade of the man's face and the strangely satisfied expression it bore, he was barking up the wrong tree. When it came to covering up the murder—now that it might cost the life of my son—that creepy, otherworldly vibe from that night didn't matter. Lee had killed a man, and someone was getting revenge for that sin.

"I didn't see anything else," I declared without disguising my anger.

"You know what? It doesn't really matter," Lee said.

"We're both after the same guy, no matter who the hell you think it is."

There was no question about that. We had to make the connection between that night and the murder of our wives if we were going to find Dantès.

Lee reached for the letter. "Let me take a look at that again."

I handed it to him, and as he scanned it, he said, "Why didn't Dantès send *me* the letter?"

Lee was clever to probe in this direction. He was analyzing our dilemma with precision, getting to know our enemy. If I had thought to ask him more questions—and if I had believed at least some of his answers—he might have opened up right then about what he knew, rather than later. There was more going on than what the letter implied, and he knew it. But he also knew that I wouldn't buy it. Not yet.

"Is there a connection between your wife's death and Cold Falls—anything from our camping trip?" Lee said. "I'll tell you this, it'd be tough to make a connection to what happened to Grace."

"Nothing jumps out at me. Not anything from the police report. But I think I know where we should start." My suggestion came straight from the letter. "'The past isn't dead. It isn't even the past.' Cold Falls."

"You want to head to Cold Falls?" Lee wasn't bothering to disguise his doubt.

"You have a better idea?"

He looked down at the letter, scanned it for a minute or

so, then conceded. "No. But there's one person we should talk to first."

"Quincy," I said.

"Did you track him down already?"

"Just his address and phone number."

"You want me to call him, or do you want to?"

"You call him while I talk to Nate." I gave him Quincy's phone number.

"Are you going to send Nate to his grandmother's?" Lee said, and I thought I heard concern in his voice.

"I can't. You're right. Dantès knows too much about us."

"Take it for what it's worth, which isn't much. Don't send him to any relative. The guy behind all this is gonna track him down. Send him to someone who's not too connected to you." This time the concern in his voice was evident, and I liked him for it.

I nodded, acknowledging his good advice, and immediately thought of Jenna Corcoran. A few years ago, Lucy had helped Jenna. She'd taken on Jenna's case, pro bono, and saved her from doing time for a minor drug offense. Afterward, Jenna had turned her life around, gone back to school, and earned a nursing degree. She had been eternally grateful for Lucy's help.

Nate would be safe with Jenna. At least, that was my thinking then.

But it wouldn't take me more than a day to realize that Nate wasn't safe with anyone.

Lee ducked into another room to call Quincy while I

called Jenna on my cell. I lied to her, telling her I'd been asked to go to a conference at the last minute as a replacement for a sick colleague, so I needed someone to take care of Nate. She was more than happy to help out. Within minutes, it was all arranged. I'd drop Nate off at her place and he'd spend the weekend with her.

In the kitchen, Nate had finished his sandwich and chips and had the TV on. He was watching another Nickelodeon animated show.

"Do you remember Jenna?" I said.

He smiled, which made me feel good about my decision. "Yeah. Mom was proud of her."

"That's right." I was surprised he'd understood that. Jenna had come over for dinner a few times, and Lucy had praised her dedication. Jenna had gotten her nursing degree in record time, landed a good job, and received a promotion. I had assumed Nate was too young to have picked up on how proud Lucy had been of Jenna.

I kneeled down beside him. "You're going to be spending a couple of days with her."

He looked up from the TV show. "What about my birthday party?"

How stupid could I be? Naturally that'd be his first question, and because I wasn't prepared for it, I doubled down on my stupidity.

"You'll be back for that," I said, instead of warning him in advance that the party might have to wait until another weekend. Now he'd be even more disappointed if Sunday came and he was still with Jenna, with no party on the horizon, which was the mostly likely scenario.

He cocked his head, narrowed his eyes, and shot me a curious look. "I know what you're doing."

My pulse quickened. Had he been eavesdropping on Lee and me before turning on the TV? I braced myself.

"You don't want me around, so you can get me a surprise for my birthday!" he said. He was so excited that he abandoned the TV show and turned his attention to me. "Tell me what the surprise is!"

I'd managed to make things even worse. His expectations were now sky high.

"Please tell me, Dad!" He couldn't contain himself.

"Honey, there isn't a surprise. I just found out that I have to be at work for most of this weekend, and I don't want to leave you alone."

"Okay..." he said, grinning, as if he was still expecting a surprise. "I can hardly wait until my birthday party."

I felt awful, but there was no time to fix this. If I had any chance of ensuring he'd have many more birthdays to celebrate and that he'd grow up to lead a full life, I had to focus on the real horror I'd brought into his life: Dantès.

"Go ahead and finish watching your show," I said. "I'll be back in a few minutes, and we'll go home and pick up some of your clothes, then head to Jenna's."

When I walked back into the living room, Lee was just stepping out of the hallway. "Quincy is dead," he said. "A drowning accident a few days ago."

I didn't quite feel the shock I should've, nor sorrow. Probably because I was still reeling from the revelation that Dantès had murdered Lucy. My reaction was cold and analytical. "It's another clue from Dantès."

"How?"

"I don't know." And I didn't, but I was sure it was.

"So, do we go down to North Carolina and check it out?"

"We need to find out more about it first." I already had the sense that the web of clues I'd have to follow to uncover Dantès's real identity would be dense, so no stone could be left unturned. On the other hand, we also didn't have time for a wild goose chase to North Carolina.

"While I'm taking Nate to Jenna's," I said, "will you find out everything you can about Quincy's death? I'll be back in less than an hour, and we can head to Cold Falls."

He nodded, and our unlikely partnership was born.

*

At the house, I packed some clothes for Nate and asked him to grab a couple of his toys and books. Then we headed to Jenna's.

I didn't take the most direct route in case Dantès was watching us. My circuitous course took us into the parking structure for the Ballston Common Shopping Mall and through a neighborhood that was packed with dead end streets. If you didn't know the neighborhood well (and I did), even with navigation in your car it was almost impossible not to get to lost.

But the whole ruse made me feel like a fool. Lee had summed it up best. Did I think I worked for some kind of covert ops outfit? Did I think I could outwit a killer who knew so much about me? And even those thoughts themselves seemed absurd. How could things in my life have changed so much in the course of a couple of hours?

The past isn't dead. It isn't even past. That's how. My long ago transgression had come back to haunt me.

Nate didn't say anything about the long and winding route to Jenna's, and I was glad I didn't have to explain it. But I wasn't glad about his demeanor. He seemed lost in thought and didn't chatter at all. I hoped he hadn't picked up on the fact that I was in crisis mode again, like I'd been right after Lucy's death. Of course, I had never really shifted out of crisis mode, had I? Wasn't that why I'd become a distant father?

Jenna opened the door to her townhouse and greeted us warmly. In that instant, I knew I'd made the right decision. She was a petite brunette who radiated enough positive energy to light up any room—and Nate would be bathed in that positive energy instead of in the gloom that emanated from me.

She showed us to a spare bedroom, which Nate immediately liked. The walls were light green, his favorite color. Lucy and I had promised to paint his room green, but we'd never gotten around to it. I unpacked Nate's suitcase while he laid out his toys and books on a dresser. Then he went on to explore the rest of the townhouse while I filled

Jenna in on the one thing that might cause a problem, using another lie to do it.

"I'm having a hard time getting a flight back from the conference on such short notice," I said. "So I may not be back by Sunday."

"That's okay," she said. "He can stay here as long as you need him to."

"I appreciate it, but it might not be okay with him. His birthday is on Sunday and we planned a big birthday party. If I can't get a flight back, I'm going to cancel it, and he's going to be crushed. He'll be inconsolable."

Jenna didn't hesitate with a solution. "Don't worry about it. If you can't make it back in time, I'll be glad to run the party. Just tell me what needs to be done." Her gracious offer was given with cheer.

I was so thankful that I almost said yes before remembering the reason Nate was staying with her. He couldn't go back to the house for the party on Sunday—he'd be a sitting target for Dantès.

"Thank you," I said, "but I can't impose on you like that. I'm going to try like hell to make it back in time." And if there was any chance of that happening, I needed to get on the road. It was time to excuse myself and say goodbye to Nate.

But just then, Jenna's cheer dimmed. "How are you doing, John?" she said.

"Okay." I didn't want to open up about Lucy, so I just told her the only truth that mattered. "I miss her." Even with that simple statement, I couldn't stop the tears from welling up in my eyes.

She hugged me. "I'm so sorry."

I accepted her embrace for a few seconds, but had to pull away for fear of breaking down.

She had tears in her eyes, too. "Every week since the funeral," she said, her voice cracking, "I'd tell myself to call you, to see if you needed to talk, but I never did. I guess I didn't know you well enough and thought I'd be intruding."

"Don't worry. I wasn't much into talking." And I still wasn't. I wanted to change the subject. "Besides, helping me out with Nate means a lot more to me."

"I'm glad I can help. But if you ever need to talk, please call me. I'm not a professional counselor, but nurses make pretty good listeners."

She was a kind soul. No one—not my colleagues at work, nor my friends, nor my neighbors—had asked me how I was doing after the first couple of months. It was like everyone assumed that after the initial trauma, you stepped right back into your normal life as if nothing had happened. At that moment, I understood more than ever why Jenna was a good nurse. Not only had she thought to ask how I was doing, but the little wrinkles of concern at the corners of her teary eyes revealed she also cared deeply.

I felt compelled to tell her what was going on—that it had nothing to do with my grief, overwhelming as it was, and everything to do with a sin from my childhood, which, at least according to Lee, had literally risen from the grave.

But instead I said, "It's all fine," and covered up this lie with a feeble grin. Then I added, "I should hit the road."

I joined up with Nate in the living room and knelt down in front of him. "So I'm taking off now. You set?"

"Yeah," he said. "You'll come back before the party?"

"That's right. Give me a big hug."

He did, and I hugged him back, tightly, and tried to push away the thought that this might be the last time I'd ever see him. "I love you, honey."

"I love you, too," he said, then smiled. "Tell me what the surprise is."

"Sweetie, there is no surprise. It's just work, really." I stood up. "I want you to listen to Jenna and do what she says. Okay?"

"Okay."

"I'll be back soon." I had to kneel down and hug him again. When I pulled away, I took a couple of seconds to take him in. He was smiling, and his blue eyes were sparkling with anticipation—about the surprise.

In the car, I sent out an email canceling the party. There was no way this was going to be wrapped up by Sunday. I also called the magician and canceled, apologizing for the late notice and offering to pay him for the gig regardless. He refused at first, but I insisted until he accepted.

When I pulled up to Lee's house, he stepped outside, ready to go. He'd shaved, combed his hair, and changed into a denim shirt and dark jeans. Whatever battle lay ahead, he wasn't going to march into it looking defeated.

As he climbed into my car, I also noticed that his skin, which had been pasty and lifeless, had gained a little pinkness, as if this mission had revived him. I should've guessed that kindling his anger would be a boon to his well-being.

"I never thought I'd be going back to Cold Falls," he said.

"That makes two of us. Did you find out anything more about Quincy?"

"Yeah—it happened on Roanoke Island. He was vacationing with a girlfriend, and the couple of articles I dug up said that he went out for an early morning swim and disappeared."

"I thought you said he drowned."

"That's what they think happened, but they didn't find the body."

"So he disappeared? From Roanoke Island?" I glanced at Lee to see if he'd make the same connection I had.

"If you're getting at something, just spill it," he said.

"The Roanoke colony—never heard of it?"

"No."

He would have if he'd been a halfway decent student. "It was the first English colony in the New World. And to make a long story short, three years after it was set up, the entire colony—every man, woman, and child—disappeared without trace. It's called 'The Lost Colony,' and there are all sorts of theories about what happened."

"The fact that everyone disappeared... you're saying that's the connection?"

"Could be. Quincy disappears without a trace from a place infamous for that, and we're searching for a body that disappeared."

"And how does that help us?"

I glanced at Lee again. His hollow eyes, like his formerly pasty skin, had also joined the world of the living. They had the weighty look of thought behind them now. Lee was alert.

"I have no idea," I said. "At least, not yet. But I have a feeling it's all going to add up."

And it would. But we'd have to follow a long and winding road of clues to find out how.

Chapter Six

It was Friday evening, and rush hour traffic was terrible. It took us more than an hour and a half to get to Cold Falls. As soon as I pulled into the parking lot, I noticed the changes. The parking lot had been expanded, and the trees around it had been cut down to make room. Also, land had been cleared to make room for three sprawling picnic areas equipped with tables, barbecue pits, and trashcans. But the picnic areas and the parking lot were practically empty; the park was a daytime attraction.

I parked near a large, rectangular park map—a map made of wood and meticulously painted and carved, a work of art compared to the paper map under glass from the past. Painted yellow lines represented the trails; swirls of green and brown, in relief, represented the forest; and orange circles represented the campsites. The names of the trails and campsites hadn't changed—the Gray Owl Trail still led to the Clear River campsite—though judging from the map, it appeared that the trails no longer stretched as far into the forest as they once had. I took that to mean that huge swaths of trees had been razed in the far reaches of this wilderness, just as they had been razed for the picnic areas and parking lot.

We started hiking to the campsite, and as we got closer, I noticed another change: the trail had been widened to allow for more pedestrian traffic. And when we made it to Clear River, I saw that it, too, had undergone a transformation. There were many more campsites, and they were grouped in clusters, as opposed to many years ago when each individual campsite had been isolated. Again, trees had been cut down for the expansion. There was also now a trail from the Clear River campsites to the Potomac.

Our first order of duty was to locate the campsite where we had spent that ill-fated night. Very few campsites were being used, and I suspected that since Cold Falls was now in the heart of Virginia's expansive suburbs, rather than on the edge, the campsites were only in demand during the summer, when they provided a cheap place to stay while visiting D.C.

We headed over to the cluster closest to the Potomac, the most likely location of our campsite from that night. There were now half a dozen campsites there.

"Any idea which was ours?" I asked.

"Hard to tell." Lee was staring at the one closest to us. "We're going to have to check each of them out."

And that's what we did. We walked through each campsite—none were occupied—until we got to the smallest one. The one closest to the river.

"This is it," Lee said immediately.

One side of the campsite was connected to the other

campsites by a dirt footpath, but the other three sides were surrounded by untamed woods, woods that made my blood run cold. Though other parts of Cold Falls had changed, this part looked exactly the same.

I didn't want to be here.

Lee began walking the perimeter of the site, checking it out more closely. "What do we do now?" he said.

"I don't know."

"Then tell me again why you wanted to come here?"

He was already agitated, so reminding him that we were here because of a Faulkner quote wasn't going to help. He'd blow a gasket if I told him I'd resorted to a failed strategy to deal with this crisis—that even though novel therapy had failed me after Lucy's death, I had latched on to a Faulkner quote as my lifeline.

Just then, the crackling underbrush caught my attention. Soft footsteps, measured in even strides, were approaching us from the woods, not the trail. The footsteps sounded like those of a lithe animal.

Both Lee and I turned. A beautiful woman was gliding through the woods toward us. Her stride was graceful and confident, and her beauty was striking: long and lush blond hair, radiant ivory sky with a touch of rose, and emerald eyes so vibrant I was mesmerized. She stepped into our campsite.

Neither Lee nor I said anything, and from the knowing smile that flickered across her lips, it was obvious that she knew how her beauty affected those who saw her for the first time. She was wearing slim-fitting blue jeans and a thin black

T-shirt, both of which showed off her figure. Her thong sandals, which featured fiery red toenails, were a clue that she wasn't a hiker.

"You're clever," she said, looking at me. "You followed the breadcrumbs like—"

Without warning Lee reached into his jacket and whipped out a gun. I was stunned, though I shouldn't have been. Not only should I have suspected that he owned a gun, I should have also suspected that he'd bring it with him and would use it the first chance he got.

The woman wasn't stunned in the least. She flicked her blond hair away from her face and shot him a sneer. "Your anger isn't going to help. But it never does, does it?"

"It'll help me end your goddamn life." Lee trained the gun on her.

"You shoot me, and you'll never find out who murdered the only good thing in your life."

"Fuck you." Lee started to squeeze the trigger.

"No!" I lunged at him. "We need her!" She was my only lead to Dantès's identity—the only way to save Nate.

"That's right," she said calmly, then stepped up to Lee. "Listen to John. After all, isn't he the one who got you this far? Isn't he the one who followed the breadcrumbs? Isn't he the one who discovered Grace was murdered?"

I couldn't tell if Lee was convinced, but for the moment he wasn't pulling the trigger.

The woman turned from him to me. Even with the gun trained on her, she was in control. Her captivating green eyes were pools of self-assurance.

"Who are you?" I said.

"Otranto."

"That's not a name," Lee said.

"Oh, I think it is," she said to me, not him. "What do you think, John? Does it sound like a name to you?"

It did. It was another clue, another breadcrumb. *The Castle of Otranto* was a novel from the 1700s, the first Gothic horror novel and the first modern work of supernatural fiction. She'd pulled her name from its title, and by using that name had immediately tied tonight to my first night here so many years ago. She'd tied herself to my unsettling apparition, the castle that had appeared on the precipice in the glow of the crescent moon.

"Are you Dantès?" I said.

"Is that what you think?"

Absolutely not. She was the messenger. "Tell me why he's playing this game."

She nodded toward Lee. "*He* chose the game."

Lee still had his gun trained on her, but the urge to shoot her had passed. "I didn't choose anything. You're a goddamn nut job."

"Hide and seek," I said. Again she'd gone back to that night. We were still playing the game. And this time I was "it." I had to find where Dantès was hiding.

She looked pleased with my deduction. "And the stakes are life and death. The only kind of game worth playing."

Her knowing smile pranced over her lips again. She turned

back to Lee and faced his gun with no fear. "Can you stay the course long enough to play the game? The guy who's never held a job for more than two years? The guy who got a fresh start, a lucky break, when Duncan, his buddy, asked him to help run a new burger place? You did well for a little while, the place did great, and how did you repay Duncan? By skimming some of the profit off the top—"

"You don't know shit," Lee said, but the slight tremor in his voice said she did.

"I don't know shit, huh? Then how about this? When Duncan fired you, you took it like a coward—you set fire to his place. But you got away with it. And then you got lucky again. Grace came along, and you promised you'd shape up. But look at you now. A loser with a gun in his hand. You can't stay the course. You can't even keep your promise to Grace, and that promise is the only thing you have left."

Lee's grip on his gun loosened, his resolve weakening.

Otranto turned back to me. "Good luck," she said, and she started toward the forest.

"Wait!" I was desperate for a real clue. "Why did Dantès send you here?"

"To tell you to face your fear."

"Is that the next breadcrumb?"

"Yes."

"It's too obscure." And it was.

She glanced back. "You came back to the scene of the crime tonight. Isn't there another scene of the crime?" And with that, she retreated farther into the wild, veiled by the trees as if she were an animal who had blended naturally into its habitat.

"I'm going after her," Lee said.

Without having to think about it, I knew that following her was futile. But logic dictated otherwise. She was our link to Dantès, so when Lee started after her, I joined him.

"She's headed toward the Potomac," he said.

Her movements were graceful and fluid, and she easily put distance between us. Though night had fallen, the going was easy for her, as if she could see in the dark. For us, it was like navigating an obstacle course.

"Let's use that new trail," I said. "We'll get there faster."

"No—we'll lose her."

Lee was determined to keep up with her, but she was so far ahead of us, moving with the speed of a winged creature, that we had no chance of catching of her.

Finally, he caved in. "Where's the trail?" he said.

"This way."

A minute later we were on the trail, hurrying toward the Potomac. We made it to the riverbank, but the trail hadn't led us to the precipice. Instead we found ourselves on the rocky, muddy shore, downstream from the cliff of gray boulders. When I saw the precipice—the reality of it looming over me—it instantly resurrected my memory of it, and with that memory came a powerful vortex of fear and dread. While Lee scanned the shoreline in both directions searching for Otranto, I couldn't pull my gaze away from the boulders, almost expecting the fictional castle of Otranto to appear and validate my fear.

"She's not here," Lee said, already hurrying back toward the trail. "Once she lost us, she must've doubled back."

I didn't believe that, but I followed him anyway, glad to get away from the precipice. When we hit the Gray Owl Trail, Lee started racing toward the park entrance. "We'll catch up with her in the parking lot," he said.

My bet was that this part of the game was over. We'd found what Dantès had wanted us to find: Otranto and the next breadcrumb. Now it was time to follow that breadcrumb—to face my fear.

When we got to the parking lot, there were still a few cars scattered about. Lee wanted to wait and see if any of them belonged to Otranto.

"She's gone," I said.

"She drove in. She has to drive out."

"She did her job, and I guarantee you she's not going to screw it up by letting us follow her out. Don't you think Dantès thought of that?"

"I don't know what the fucker thought."

"You did before. You know he's not going to make a stupid mistake."

He didn't respond. He turned his attention to the trailheads.

"I've got forty-eight hours," I said, "maybe less, to save Nate, and I'm not spending them sitting in this parking lot." I headed to my car.

Lee shook his head. "So if you don't want to wait her out,

what's the next step?"

"Face my fear," I said, and it was a fear I didn't want to face. Wasting time following Otranto through the woods had been a way to avoid it. A way to avoid visiting another scene of the crime.

"We're going to my wife's office," I said.

Chapter Seven

I drove out of Cold Falls and headed toward Lucy's former office, a law firm in Tysons Corner.

"Do you think one of her cases was related to Dantès?" Lee said.

That thought had never crossed my mind. When Lee wasn't angry, he was sharp. That was something I'd forgotten about him. It was one of the primary reasons we'd been friends when we were kids.

"It's possible," I said, but I wondered if he actually thought that was a possibility, considering he believed we were chasing down a man from twenty years ago who'd basically come back from the dead.

He took a couple seconds before asking his next question. "Do you want to tell me why you're scared to go to her office?"

I took a couple seconds myself. "She was murdered there."

"Oh," he said, nodding as if he understood.

But he didn't understand, so I explained. I figured he should know that I'd developed a psychological block about going to her office. A block Dantès obviously knew about.

He knew my psychological state, which seemed like something he couldn't possibly know. But he did.

"A month after she died," I said, "her firm asked me if I wanted to come down and pick up her stuff. They hadn't asked me to come down earlier because they'd wanted to give me time to mourn—they hadn't touched anything in her office. I said yes and scheduled a time to go, but I never went.

"After about another month, they called again. That time, I got as far as loading up my car with empty boxes, but I never pulled away from my house. I told myself I didn't want any more reminders of her around. I already had a house full of reminders... But the truth was that I didn't want to pack up her office because I had this ridiculous idea that her office was waiting for her to return. And if I packed everything up, she couldn't return. I mean, I'd already packed up her stuff in our house and stuck it in the basement—so she wasn't coming back home."

I was like one of those kids who didn't understand that death was permanent. I had expected Lucy to walk right back into her office as if nothing had happened.

"Anyway, when her law firm realized I wasn't ever going to show up, they packed up her stuff and sent it to me. I carried those boxes down to the basement and stacked them up next to the rest of her stuff."

I stared ahead into the traffic, which had thinned out, and out of the corner of my eye I saw Lee glance at me. He didn't say anything, as if he was waiting to see if I'd finished my tale of woe.

"You probably went through the same thing," I said.

"Yeah, and I'm still going through it."

Me too, I thought. But his loss was recent. I had no excuse. I should've stabilized by now, instead of turning into a distant dad who couldn't build a new life for his son or himself.

"If that bitch—Otranto or whatever her real name is—had told me to face my fear," Lee said, "I wouldn't know where the fuck to begin."

I'd never thought of Lee as a person who'd open up about his feelings, but he'd just done it. Only for a second though. "Who do you think Otranto is in relation to Dantès?" he said.

Good—at least one of us was sticking to facts. I hadn't told Lee where the name Otranto had come from because that would've put us in the realm of fiction. On the other hand, I wondered if he should know, because it once again confirmed just how much Dantès knew about us. Not only did our enemy know intimate details about our lives, as Otranto's diatribe had proven, he knew about my Achilles' heel, novel therapy, and he was exploiting it.

"Maybe *she's* Dantès," I said.

He shook his head. "You're not getting who he is, are you?"

I didn't answer because I didn't want to argue with him.

"It's *him*," he said, raising his voice, arguing with me anyway. "And the sooner you get that, the faster we find the bastard." He took a breath, then continued in a calmer tone.

"She's too young to be his sister, but she could be his daughter. Or she could be a hired gun. Not related to Dantès at all."

I tried to come up with an answer based on the source of her name, but then told myself to stop—no novel therapy—and that led to another question.

"Why are we doing what they want?" I said, hoping to escape the world of fiction.

"You mean following their breadcrumbs?"

"Yeah. We're playing his game, but isn't it going to take a lot more than that to have a chance at beating him?"

"It's all we got," Lee said. "That's why I went along with your lead back at the house. My uncle was in the army, and he said the army taught him a bunch of ways to fight the enemy. But he always remembered one tactic because it came in handy in his own life—especially when things are going against you. He said, 'Play the cards you're dealt.' If you don't have a good strategy to fight the enemy, you go with what you got. But you don't just do nothing. If you got crap, you use crap. If you got bad targets or bad leads, you use 'em. Sooner or later, the tide will turn." He looked over at me. "We keep going, and we're gonna find the right trail."

"I need the right trail by Sunday," I said. "What do you think your uncle would say about that?"

"He'd have some story to tell you."

"What?"

"My uncle made his points by telling stories."

I supposed that could've been the end of that

conversation, since Lee didn't go on. But he'd hit too close to home for me to not follow up. His uncle made his points by telling stories, and though stories didn't necessarily mean novels, it was damn close. It was like Dantès was forcing my hand—so I followed this breadcrumb.

I asked Lee about his uncle, wondering if there was a clue there, and Lee obliged my curiosity.

"I spent a lot of time at his house," he said. "My parents would drop me off when they wanted to go out drinking. Uncle Harry was in a wheelchair, so it was a two-fer: they'd get rid of me, and I'd take care of Harry so my dad wouldn't have to. He was supposed to take care of him, but he always snaked out of it. He got my mom to do it, or one of Harry's neighbors, or me—whoever he could rope in."

"Harry is your dad's brother?"

"Yeah, but much older. When he and my dad were kids, my dad worshipped him. Absolutely thought he was the greatest. Until Harry got his legs blown off. When Harry came home from Walter Reed, a cripple in a wheelchair, my dad didn't like him so much anymore. And my dad was the one who had to take care of him. Their parents were in bad shape and were barely able to get around themselves. Problem was, my dad couldn't even stand the sight of him anymore. Harry went from hero to zero for my dad. So when I was old enough, my dad started taking me over to Uncle Harry's place and showing me how to wash him and change him and do all sorts of shit for the guy. I was the answer to my dad's prayers. I'd take care of Harry."

"How old were you?"

"Six."

Wow. That was an eye-opener—rough-and-tumble six-year-old Lee with this huge responsibility. "You never said anything to us back then."

"Why should I've?"

"No reason, I guess."

After a couple of minutes without Lee volunteering any more information, and the lights of Tysons Corner—home to Lucy's office—almost upon us, I piped up again. "Do you remember any of your uncle's stories?"

"Yeah—some of them. But the guy had thousands of them. War stories, civilian stories, stories about himself, stories he'd heard." Lee turned away and stared out the side window. "You know, taking care of him was hard. Especially those first years when I was a little kid. But I liked the stories. He used to say that stories tell you all you need to know."

He stopped talking again, but this time I didn't press him—I guess I thought he'd opened up more than he'd wanted to. I sure wanted him to go on; I sensed he was leading us down the right path—that he'd mentioned stories for a reason—and my instinct would turn out to be right. But the time had come to face my fear.

*

The building where Lucy had worked was almost completely dark. The only light came from the east end, from the vestibules where the elevators were located. I drove around to the back of the building and parked in the lot. I was within yards of the spot where Lucy had breathed her last breath and thought her last thought, which must've been about leaving Nate alone, forever, abandoned without the love of his mom.

I looked up to the floor where Brown & Butler, Lucy's old firm, was located. Not one light burned there tonight. Apparently this was one of the rare nights when no one was working late.

Lee climbed out of the car and started toward the building, but I stayed put. When he saw I wasn't going anywhere, he walked back.

I swung my car door open, but still didn't make a move to get out.

"If you want, I'll snoop around and see what's up," Lee said.

That's exactly what I wanted, but I got out of the car, ready to face my fear. I had to—if I didn't, it meant I was already conceding the game, and Nate's life. I should've come here months ago. I should've weathered the storm of emotions the visit would have unleashed. I should've cleaned out Lucy's office. I should've been a better father to Nate. Instead I had sought shelter from the storm. A shelter I never found.

We stepped up to the glass doors at the back of the building. They didn't slide open. "It's locked for the night," I said. Through the doors, I saw the dark hallway that ran to the lighted lobby out front. "Let's see if the security guard is still on duty."

I headed to the path that ran along the south side of the building.

But Lee glanced to the back of the parking lot like he'd spotted something, so I took a look, too. Two parallel rows of privacy hedges separated the lot from the back yards of the houses on the other side. A bulky man wearing a grimy knit cap was pushing his way through a gap in the row that bordered the lot. When he stepped onto the blacktop, I saw that he was bearded—a scraggly nest of steel wool—wild-eyed, wobbly, and covered in layers of ragged and dirty clothes.

Lee and I continued around the southern corner of the building without commenting on him. Over the last two decades, the homeless had become as big a part of the Northern Virginia landscape as the relentless sprawl of homes, shopping malls, and business parks. Nate was terribly frightened of the homeless. When we'd pass a homeless man or woman on the sidewalk, he'd avert his eyes and circle as far around them as the width of the sidewalk would allow. And if he was holding my hand, he'd squeeze it more tightly.

Lucy had patiently explained to him who the homeless were, hoping to ease his terror. I remembered her compassionate descriptions. They were pour souls down on their luck, or they suffered from mental illness, which she explained to him as the inability to distinguish between make-believe and reality, or they were addicts, which she said was another illness, one where a person couldn't stop doing things that made them sick.

But I never said a word about the homeless to Nate. Because, in a way, I felt the same way he did. Not that I was afraid of the homeless—but I was afraid of what they represented: the reality that life could easily descend into despair, as mine had.

We rounded the front of the building and headed to the lobby. Through the large glass doors, I spotted a heavyset security guard, late thirties, with thinning, sandy hair, sitting behind a marble counter. He must've been engrossed in something because he didn't look up until Lee and I had been standing there for a few seconds.

When he finally noticed us, he shook his head, donned an annoyed expression, and mouthed, "We're closed."

I waved him over, but he shook his head again and reiterated his mantra: "We're closed."

"It's important," I said, loudly, so it'd carry through the glass.

He frowned and stood up slowly, as if it took an impossible effort, then made his way around the counter. He took his damn sweet time walking over to the glass doors. So much time that I thought he must have been trained by Andy Callen, the security guard on duty the night of Lucy's murder. The police report had stated that good ol' Andy, ensconced behind the marble counter in his own world that night, hadn't seen or heard a thing.

I leaned close to the doors and didn't raise my voice this time. "I work at Brown & Butler, but I forgot my pass card," I said.

"Name?" the guard said, and he moved close enough to the door for me to read his nametag.

Andy Callen.

I was face to face with the man who could have saved Lucy. The man I'd purposely not confronted. What good would it have done? Detective Wyler had hammered that into me. He'd said over and over again, *It's not going to change what happened*, and he'd also said, *It's just going to make you angry.*

He was right. It did make me angry. But I kept my anger in check and forged ahead with the mission at hand.

"Rick Serway," I said. Rick had been one of Lucy's colleagues. He'd started at the firm the same month Lucy had, five years ago. He'd been so broken up at her funeral that I hadn't been sure he'd ever recover. I hoped he had. I hoped he hadn't ended up like me.

"Rick Serway, huh?" Callen said. "Hang on to your horses." He moseyed on back to the counter, leaving Lee and me to stare at our reflections in the glass. It took him forever to look through whatever he was scrutinizing behind the counter. It was probably a directory, but now that I knew who he was, I couldn't help but think it was porn. And that it'd been porn he'd been engrossed in on his cell phone before we'd interrupted his night, and that it'd been porn he'd been watching the night of Lucy's murder, so absorbed by it that he couldn't pull himself away to escort Lucy to her car.

Finally, he strolled back to us. "You got ID?"

"I don't. I left my wallet up there and it's got my driver's license *and* pass card in it. It's got pretty much everything in it—credit cards, you name it. That's why I had to come back."

He looked me up and down without bothering to hide his sneer. Then he shook his head again. "Can't let you in without ID."

"If I had ID, I wouldn't be here, because I'd have my wallet. You get that, right?"

Lee flashed a grin, apparently pleased by my aggressiveness. But Callen wasn't so pleased. His face reddened and his nostrils flared.

"Listen, buddy," he said. "Without ID, you're not coming in." He headed back to the counter.

I pounded on the door.

He whipped around, the fastest he'd moved since we arrived. "Keep your hands off the door!"

"I have to get in there and get my wallet!"

"I just told you: You're not coming in!" He headed back toward the counter.

I pounded on the door again—and he whipped around again, but he also made the effort to march up to me. "If you don't get the hell out of here," he barked, "I'm calling the police."

"The police? Are you kidding me? *This* is why you call the police?" I was shouting now. "My wife was executed right under your fucking nose and you just sat there on your butt and did nothing! Why the hell didn't you call the police then? Why the hell didn't you walk her to her car? *Why the hell didn't you do a goddamn thing?*"

Callen's mouth was agape and the color had drained from his face. He was no longer annoyed. He was frightened.

Lee was staring at me, wide-eyed. "Didn't think you had that in you," he said.

What I had in me was grief and pent-up anger. And I had spewed it all out at a convenient scapegoat. "Let me into the goddamn building," I added as a coda.

Callen didn't react. He stood there like a frightened animal, unsure what to do next.

Out of the corner of my eye, I saw Lee reach into his jacket pocket—he was going for his gun. Did I want to go that far? If not, I had to stop Lee now.

"What's all the racket about?" The raspy voice came from behind Lee. We turned toward it. The homeless man was ambling toward us, a mobile heap of ragged clothes. As he approached, I heard a repetitive ripping sound that matched his footsteps. It came from one of his filthy high-top sneakers, which was fortified with duct tape. In the wake of every step he took came the crackling of tape peeling off concrete.

"Can you help me out with a little change?" he said, bringing with him an odor so rancid I had to step back. "It's been two days since I got some food."

"Go back where you came from," Lee said.

"I'm from here." The man was staring at me instead of Lee, as if I'd been the one who'd told him to take off. His skin was weather-beaten and coarse. His beard was a mixture of matted clumps and wiry projections.

I had to turn away from him, as Nate would have done, and now I was facing Callen again. He no longer appeared frightened. His arms were folded in satisfaction as if he was glad to be off the hook.

Lee took a menacing step toward the homeless man. "Get the hell out of here."

The man didn't budge. "Can you help me out?" he said behind me.

"No," Lee said.

"Come on. A man's gotta eat."

Callen started to walk away, but not before I saw the sneer return to his face. He was getting the last laugh, leaving us to deal with what was probably one of his own recurring problems: a pain-in-the-ass homeless man who accosted the tenants of the building, begging for handouts.

"Hey! We're not done here!" I shouted, and pounded on the door.

"You touch that door again, and the cops will be all over your ass," Callen said. So he had a short memory. He'd already forgotten my tirade.

"Open this goddamn door or I break it down!" I said, reminding him that I had every reason to do something violent and stupid—that I held him partially responsible for Lucy's death.

"Don't cause trouble here," the homeless man said. "They don't need no more trouble."

I glanced at him.

"Just give me a little change," he said and moved toward me, accompanied by the sound of duct tape peeling off the pavement. *Skrrritt, skrrritt, skrrritt.*

I pulled out my wallet, grabbed a couple of dollar bills, and thrust them at him, hoping to send him on his way. As he took the money, I realized my incredibly stupid blunder.

I looked back into the lobby. Callen was staring at my wallet—the one I'd supposedly left upstairs. Then his eyes met mine for a beat. His smugness was blatant. He walked back toward the counter.

"Thank you, mister," the homeless man said, and began his retreat. "God bless you. This ain't no place for trouble. Somethin' wicked this way comes."

What the hell? The homeless guy was throwing off Ray Bradbury titles? Was this novel therapy or just a coincidence? For the second time in less than a few minutes, I didn't react the way I normally would have. First I had stepped out of character and unleashed my anger at Callen, and now I was going to hold a conversation with a homeless man.

"What you do mean, 'something wicked this way comes'?" I said.

The homeless man stopped his retreat, turned back, blinked two or three times, slowly, as if he was rebooting himself, then stuffed the money into his soiled and ripped navy pea coat.

"I told them already," he said. "Yep, they know." He shivered, then started to amble away, accompanied by the duct tape symphony. *Skrrritt, skrrritt, skrrritt.*

I went after him. "You told who *what*?"

"Let him go," Lee said. "He's off his rocker."

Lee might have been right, but I was conjuring up a scenario where Lee was wrong. Perhaps when Otranto had said face your fear, she meant *this* fear. The fear of descending into despair, which the homeless man represented for me. Did she want me to talk to this man?

And then came the answer to that question: I glanced back once more toward Callen, and in the glass door, I saw my reflection and Lee's reflection—and *no* reflection for the homeless man.

Sure, it was possible that he was standing in a dead spot, or at the wrong angle, but I knew that wasn't so. My pulse raced and the night rushed in on me. I looked back at the man, then again at the glass. There was no doubt: he wasn't casting a reflection. My chest tightened as I realized that the netherworld of Cold Falls was exerting itself right here, right now.

"Tell me what you mean by 'something wicked this way comes,'" I said, "and I'll give you more money."

The duct tape symphony stopped, and the homeless man turned back to me. I pulled out my wallet and fished out a couple more dollars.

He stared at the cash, then looked at me and blinked that slow measured blink again. A second later, he plucked the money from my hand and stuffed it into his pea coat.

"I mean that lady who was killed in the parking lot," he

said.

I swallowed. "… You saw it?"

He nodded. "Yep."

I was flabbergasted. My anger rushed back, but this time my fury felt like molten steel burning in my gut. It was so painful that it hindered my breathing. There had been no witnesses to Lucy's murder.

I forced myself to breathe. "Why didn't you tell the police?"

"I told 'em."

That couldn't be right. Detective Wyler had told me there had been no witnesses. I pulled out my cell phone, ready to call him right then, my rage dictating my actions, but then I glanced at the glass door and saw the man's lack of a reflection again and realized that this wasn't under Detective Wyler's jurisdiction—it was under *my* jurisdiction. I tried to push my rage away.

"Please tell me what you saw," I said.

He blinked a few times. "He was back there, in the bushes. Right outside my place."

"Your place?"

"I got a good setup back there. A nice tent. He was looking to steal it."

"Who's he?"

"I'm telling you that. I looked out of my tent and saw him. He was crouched down, or kneeling down or something. It was hard to tell. And I couldn't really see his face neither—like it was covered or something. But it wasn't.

'Cause I saw his eyes. They were black, with some gold in 'em, too."

That hit a nerve, and I glanced over at Lee to see how he was reacting to this man's tale. He was already riveted by it.

"Then he goes over to the opening in the hedges and crawls through. That was *my* door. *I* made it. They closed it now. They put new bushes there. I see him go out into the parking lot—but he doesn't walk normal. Like he don't wanna stand up or something. Maybe he was staying low so no one would see him. I don't know. But when he gets near the building, he stands up. He's tall. Real tall. Then he kinda disappears in the shadows or something."

The vagrant stopped talking and stared at me. He wasn't blinking slowly anymore. He wasn't blinking at all. It looked like he was studying me, gauging my reaction to his story, as if he was expecting me to cut him off. I wasn't going to, though—not yet, anyway. His story tracked, but just barely.

"Then I see him again. Close to the building. But he wasn't moving, and I got to thinking it wasn't him. It was just a shadow. A dark one. So after I stare it awhile, and it don't move—at all—I go back into my tent and fall asleep. Not sure for how long. But I wake up and hear a click, click, click. Someone's walking across the lot. Click, click, click, you know, like ladies' shoes."

Lucy's shoes.

"So I get out of the tent and look through the bushes. There's a lady walking across the lot. And then I see him again. It had to be him, but he looked different."

"How?"

"This time I see his face. It's kinda white, but not white like paint—white like maybe he's sick. Like maybe he got a disease. But she didn't see him. Or I'm guessing she didn't see him. Or she woulda run. She's just walking to her car. Click, click, click. The only car in the lot. He's moving toward her, fast. Only he isn't running, he's kinda gliding. I crawl through the bushes—I'm gonna warn her. When I get out, I see him wrap around the lady, kinda like a blanket. Except this blanket is as black as the night. Like she'd walked out of the light. Or he blocked the light or something. She screams, and then he comes at me. But he's hunched down again—like an animal coming at me and—"

"The lady—what happened to her?"

"She was on the ground—not moving—didn't know if she was—"

"He didn't shoot her?" Though his story was far-fetched, almost hallucinatory, I'd been following along, sucked into it, until this detail.

"He came after me and I ran. I had to run—"

"Did he shoot her?"

"I headed for Ma—"

"Did he shoot her or not?"

"No—I told them no—"

"Told who?"

"The cops."

"You told them no shots?"

"I didn't hear nothing. No gun."

Maybe this guy was off his rocker after all. And that was why Detective Wyler hadn't told me about this supposed eyewitness account. Or there was another possibility—

"So the lady you saw that night *wasn't* the lady who was shot?"

"I'm telling you about something wicked this way comes. That's what you wanted me to—"

"This happened back there. In the parking lot. In the middle of the night." He must've been talking about Lucy, even if this detail wasn't right.

"Yeah."

"Okay… What happened after he came after you?" Maybe he'd give me something to verify that he was talking about Lucy. Or that he wasn't.

"I run outta here, down Maple Avenue. I get to Jefferson. It's all lit up there. So I finally look back. He's gone. All I see is some dog, one of those big ones. You know, kinda wild, but smart-looking. That dog mighta scared this guy away."

"Then what?"

"I stay there in the lights. Near the Best Buy sign. Don't know for how long. Then I hear sirens and see cop cars coming. So I go back and tell 'em what I saw."

He stopped and stared at me intently for a few seconds, then concluded: "You don't believe me, do ya?"

He may have been off his rocker, but he was reading me perfectly. I was thinking that he'd come up with this story *after* he'd heard what had happened in the parking lot, and that he'd added his own bizarre elements. I'd have to see if

Detective Wyler or another officer had interviewed him on the night of the crime.

Lee hadn't said a word up to this point, but now he passed judgment. "Let's move on. You threw your money down a rat hole."

If this vagrant was the reason Otranto had sent me to Lucy's office, then I wasn't picking up on the next breadcrumb yet. Oh, I got that he was connected to Dantès. If the lack of a reflection wasn't enough to make that point, his story about a black-eyed man with white skin and the big, smart-looking dog on Maple Street—which I took to be a wolf—clinched it.

"You don't believe me, 'cause you can't see it," the homeless man said to Lee.

"See what?" I said, not ready to give up.

"You're stuck in the cave. That's why you can't see."

Lee shook his head and smirked. "Enough already."

"I'm stuck in a cave," I said, "but what can't I see?"

"Everything," he said, and started to walk away. *Skrrritt. Skrrritt. Skrrritt.*

My anger boiled up again. The homeless man—my lead—had gone from recounting a semi-coherent story to spewing crazy talk.

"Did Dantès tell you to say that?" I said, harshly.

Skrrr—he stopped in mid-step. "Dantès?" he whispered, almost to himself, then glanced back at me. "Are you looking for Dantès's Firegrill?"

Lee's eyes went wide, surprised by this reversal of fortune.

"Yes. Yes I am," I said. *Wasn't I?* "Where is it?"

"I don't remember."

"What do you mean you don't remember?"

He shook his head. "I don't got too good a memory when it comes to the good times."

"You had a good memory when it came to what happened in the parking lot."

"Bad times got a way of sticking with me."

I couldn't argue with that—the same was true for me. "So what's Dantès's Firegrill?" I said.

"It's where the good times roll." He walked away again. *Skrrritt. Skrrritt. Skrrritt.*

I was about to start after him when Lee said, "Let the good times roll—it's some bar. It's a place where he used to get drunk."

I pulled out my cell phone, looked it up, and hit my first snag with this clue. There were pages of Google hits for Dante's Firegrill, but not one of them was in Virginia. Granted, I hadn't looked up the name with the spelling D-a-n-t-e-s-apostrophe-s, because I made the assumption that whichever bar used this name was playing off of the name "Dante" as in Dante's *Inferno*, so that's the way I spelled it.

Dante's *Inferno* was a celebrated work of fiction, part of the trilogy known as *The Divine Comedy*. In it, the Roman poet Virgil guides Dante through hell. There was no doubt the bar owner had replaced "Inferno," the fires of hell, with "Firegrill" and thought himself or herself clever.

As for me, I realized that this meant Dantès had changed

the meaning of his pen name. Rather than referring to Dantès in *The Conte of Monte Cristo,* the master of revenge, he was now referring to Dante from Dante's *Inferno,* as if he was now guiding me toward hell.

But since there were no Dante's Firegrills in Virginia, I took a chance and tried searching with the spelling D-a-n-t-e-s-apostrophe-s. As I'd expected, I came up empty. Not one hit.

"What you got?" Lee said.

"Nothing in Virginia. Maybe we're going to have to go down to North Carolina. There's one there. Or maybe it's not the clue."

"We should check out your wife's office. That's why we're here, right?"

"Dante's Firegrill," I said, wondering how it could not be a clue.

"He didn't say Dante's Firegrill," Lee said. "He said *Dan T.'s* Firegrill."

"Are you sure?"

"I wasn't the smartest kid in the class, but I wasn't the dumbest either. I know the difference between 'Dante' and 'Dan T.'"

I typed *Dan T.'s Firegrill* into the Google search bar, and the first hit was a bar in Alexandria, less than twenty minutes away.

Chapter Eight

After I got onto Leesburg Pike, heading toward the GW Parkway, which would take us into the heart of Alexandria, I told Lee why I had jumped on this lead. Because of novel therapy. I explained that Dantès was plucking his breadcrumbs from fiction. From Dante's *Inferno*, to *Something Wicked This Way Comes*, to *The Castle of Otranto*, to William Faulkner's quote.

Lee listened more patiently than I would've expected, so I went on to tell him how novel therapy had started. How I'd lost my dad. How my dad had been rambling with me at the dinner table one night, and was gone the next, the dinner table silent, cold, and distant.

"I liked your dad," Lee said. "I know that sounds stupid, since I met him only four or five times. But he seemed like a nice guy."

"He was," I said, but I didn't as feel sorry for my sixteen-year-old self as I usually did. My childhood been a blessing when compared to Lee's. He'd had indifferent, selfish parents, and his dad had turned him into a home healthcare worker at the age of six.

I also told Lee what worried me about using novel therapy to uncover Dantès's identity: "Garbage in, garbage out."

"Yeah—but you're going with the cards you're dealt," he said.

"Dealt by Dantès," I countered.

"But that's exactly the point of my uncle's advice. The cards are coming from the enemy, and somewhere along the line, he's gonna make a mistake. One of those clues is gonna have his fingerprints on it. It's going to tell us more than he wanted it to."

I supposed that was possible, but it seemed like a long shot, especially when Nate's life was riding on it.

"Let's say the Firegrill is the right move," I said. "How did he pull it off? Did he pay the homeless guy to say that? To tell us that whole story?"

"I don't know."

But that wasn't totally true. Lee knew more than he let on, enough to want to follow some of these breadcrumbs, no matter how outlandish they were. And maybe if he'd told me just a bit more—even though I still wouldn't have believed him—I would've felt better about this lead. Instead, the closer we got to Alexandria, the more I felt we were off course. I stared at the lights of Rosslyn, and at Key Bridge, crowded with cars, each hauling scores of revelers into Georgetown's nightlife, and I wondered if I should turn around and go back to Lucy's office.

Out of nowhere, Lee said, "Was there something else that made you want to talk to the homeless guy? I mean, I get the

Something Wicked This Way Comes part, but was that it?"

I weighed whether to tell him about the vagrant's lack of a reflection. But this peculiar phenomenon seemed more in line with the madness of the vagrant's story, not a part of the harsh reality of Dantès's three murders. Lucy, Grace, and Quincy. It was insanity to bring it up.

But Lee did. "He didn't have a reflection, right?" he said.

I glanced at him. "It must've been because he was standing too far away from the glass."

"Yeah," Lee said, not quite sarcastically, but his tone said, *If you want to believe that, go right ahead, but you're lying to yourself.* He didn't explain why he was so calm about meeting a man who didn't cast a reflection, and I didn't press him. If I had, he might've tried to get me to believe more than I was willing to. Instead he went on to another observation.

"The breadcrumbs are designed for you. Novel therapy— even though you hate it—is *your* deal."

His insight would turn out to be perfectly timed. In a way, he had just predicted Dantès's next move. Dantès was about to integrate Lee fully into his game.

Gliding along the GW parkway, I took in the Potomac, which ran wide and calm here, bordered by bike paths and monuments instead of rocky, muddy shores and cliffs. This didn't look like the same river that had come back to haunt me.

*

Friday night wasn't the best night to be headed into Old

Town Alexandria, where Dan T.'s Firegrill was located. Old Town boasted an even more active nightlife than Georgetown, so its bars and restaurants were packed every weekend.

I'd never been one to partake in D.C.'s nightlife—not during high school, not during summers back from college, and not even during my post-college years. That didn't change when I met Lucy. We were cut from the same cloth. Neither of us was big on Georgetown or Alexandria or any other popular nightspots. Our favorite outings consisted of dinner out at one of the small Vietnamese restaurants in Arlington, then a movie.

Our first date was dinner at The Four Sisters, a Vietnamese restaurant just off Wilson Boulevard. That had started our tradition of Vietnamese dinner and a movie. On that date, we'd been so intrigued by the exotic appetizers—from the quail dipped in lime sauce to the baby clams—that we'd ordered all eight appetizers on the menu as our dinner. Ironically, our last date—Nate was at a sleepover—had also been at The Four Sisters. But that time we ordered normal entrees, and it still depressed me that we didn't go for the smorgasbord of appetizers. Who could've predicted that this date and the first date would be the bookends to our life together?

A wave of nausea hit me as I realized that this rhetorical question actually had an answer. Dantès could have predicted it.

I closed in on King Street, which went through the very

center of Old Town, and traffic came to a standstill. Lee pulled out his cell phone and mapped out a new route to the Firegrill, one that skirted Alexandria's main arteries.

We circled around a bevy of bars, restaurants, boutiques, and galleries, which together added up to the gentrified parts of historic Old Town, and ended up on a street lined with rundown brick townhouses. This was a neighborhood of glum facades and understated signage, a neighborhood that didn't cater to the nightlife a few blocks away.

With one exception.

At the end of the block, a large red neon sign publicized Dan T.'s Firegrill. The sign ran along the top of a squat, two-story building, painted red.

We found parking a couple blocks away and walked back. The front of the building boasted a mural that conjured up hell—at least, it did for me. It was a straightforward but enormous painting of a barbecue pit. Huge red and orange flames lashed up from deep inside the pit. If the mural was supposed to advertise the Firegrill's culinary treats, it did a bad job of it: the pit didn't have a grill on top, nor any food barbecuing in the flames. Instead, it advertised the blazing flames themselves.

I wondered how many other Firegrill patrons saw those flames as the flames of hell. Of course, I had a reason to—I'd been descending closer to those flames ever since I'd received that letter. And even before then. Since Lucy's death.

Inside, the bar was packed, loud, and oppressively hot. As you'd expect hell to be. And Lee and I were in the thick of it.

"So what now?" Lee said.

I hadn't really thought about it. I guess I thought the breadcrumb would appear in the bar. And maybe it would, but it was still likely that we'd have to look for it.

"We talk to Dan T.," I said. That seemed like a logical place to start.

"Okay." Lee nodded toward the large bar in the back. "Let's ask a bartender if Dan's around."

With that shaky plan in mind, we started inching our way through the crowd. Sweat immediately formed on my brow. I wiped it off and took a deep breath. It felt like I was stuck in an overheated swamp. I took a closer look at my surroundings, hoping this would ground me and keep me from racing outside.

Tall bar tables surrounded by patrons formed small islands in the otherwise free-floating crowd. Booths ran along the walls, providing more havens from the unmoored mass. Waitresses, in short black skirts and tight white blouses, swam through the crowd, delivering drinks and food.

The Firegrill's patrons were surprisingly varied. There were hipsters, the men in skinny jeans and Buddy Holly glasses, the women in floral, vintage dresses and costume jewelry; young professionals, the men in suits, ties loosened, the women in sleek dresses, their hair down; faux cowboys in boots and bolos, and faux cowgirls in wide skirts; college kids in T-shirts and jeans; and old-timers, also in T-shirts and jeans.

As Lee and I moved closer to the bar, dishing out *excuse*

me's right and left to get through the throng, I wondered if the varied clientele was a clue in itself—a message that hell didn't discriminate, that everyone was welcome.

Including and especially me.

We made it to the bar area, where every stool was taken and the hordes massed around the seated customers, ordering drinks, paying, and then retreating. Lee forced his way closer to the bar, cutting past people who shot us dirty looks and barked out *what the hells*. Lee didn't care and continued to steamroll his way forward.

I held back, sure that his aggression would end in a confrontation. And I wasn't the only one who was thinking that; a waitress came up behind me and asked, "Can I get you and your friend something to drink? He seems mighty thirsty." A kind way of saying he was too pushy.

"Is Dan T. around tonight?" I asked.

"He's around every night." She motioned to the far end of the bar. "That's him. Behind the bar."

She'd singled out a dramatically handsome man with a square jaw that was covered in a three-day stubble. He was talking to a patron who was sitting at the bar finishing off a draft beer. From this vantage point, their conversation—in contrast to all the other conversations swirling around me, overly animated and bursting with exaggerated laughs—looked easygoing, two guys calmly shooting the shit as if they were sitting on a back porch far from the madding crowd.

I raised my voice. "I found him, Lee."

Lee stopped his steamrolling, looked back at me, and the

waitress gave out a little sigh of relief. "Good," she said. "It's too early for trouble. So what can I get you to drink?"

Lee stepped up to me. "Where is he?"

I pointed out Dan T., then thanked the waitress and started toward the end of the bar with Lee in tow. But that didn't last long. When Lee saw that I was politely making my way forward, he cut in front of me and muscled himself a path. He was still pissing people off, though not quite as badly as before, since now he wasn't actually cutting in line.

Just before he made it to Dan T., he stopped and waited for me to catch up. When I did, he said, "You're up."

So even though he'd led me through the swamp, he expected me to take the lead when it came to interrogating Dan T. Of course, he had every reason to expect me to—so far, this night had been my show.

I stepped up to the bar and made eye contact with Dan. He stopped his conversation and flashed me a friendly smile. "What can I help you with?" he said.

It was only then that I realized I hadn't thought this through. I didn't know the homeless man's name, and he was my only connection to the Firegrill.

"I'm sorry to butt in," I said, "but I wanted to ask you a few questions." Was there any other lead I could ask him about? Anything that didn't make me sound like a lunatic?

He grinned. "A few questions? Am I in trouble with the law?"

"No—not at all—but you might know someone who is," I said, regretting it immediately. I couldn't jump right into asking him about Lucy's or Grace's murders.

"Are you serious?" His grin disappeared.

"It's a long story, but—"

"Listen, if you've got a beef with me or my place, you need to talk to my lawyer." He was calm, but his friendly demeanor had turned ice cold.

His buddy at the bar glanced at me with narrowed eyes, as if he was ready to defend Dan T. using his fists. With his leathery skin and thick neck, he looked more rural than suburban. He was wearing a T-shirt with the motto *Virginia Is For Lovers* on it, but the word *Lovers* was crossed out and *Americans* was stamped over it, declaring his bigotry to the world.

"I'm doing a crappy job of explaining," I said. "I just wanted to ask you a few questions about a former customer. He said you could help us."

"Who's the customer?" Dan said, still cold, but also still calm.

"I don't know his name."

"That's a bad start." He turned his attention back to his buddy. "You ready for another beer, Frank?"

Lee lurched forward, brushing up against Frank, who instantly leapt off his stool with a "What the fuck?" Frank was ready to brawl—his chest was puffed out and a blue vein bulged in his forehead.

Lee ignored him and focused on Dan. "Listen, we don't want to be here as much as you don't want us here. But I got a problem. A big problem. My wife was murdered and I want to know who did it."

Frank retreated a few inches, not so eager to brawl anymore. His eyes began to dart back and forth between Dan and Lee as if he was now expecting Dan would be the one getting into a brawl with Lee.

"Why the hell would I know who did it?" Dan said.

"I don't know why, but I know you do," Lee barked out, exaggerating the lead we had beyond recognition. "One of your former customers told us you do."

Dan shook his head, disgusted, pulled out his cell phone, and began typing a text. "I got some friends who are going to help you find your way out."

Lee leaned across the bar. "I don't need your goddamn bouncers to show me the way out."

"Then get the fuck out yourself."

This venture had turned into a bust, built on imaginary connections. It wasn't worth salvaging, and my thought was that we *should* get the fuck out.

Dan looked over at Frank. "So—can I get you that refill?"

"That's what I been waiting for," Frank said, and sat back on his barstool.

Dan grabbed the empty beer mug and was about to turn away when Lee put all our cards on the table. "Some homeless drunk told us you could help us out. He said we can't see things. We're stuck in a cave or some shit like that, and we can't see the killer. He told us we'd find something here."

It was clear from the curious expression on Dan's face that

Lee had hit a nerve.

"Do you know what any of that means?" I said.

"I know what part of it means," Dan answered.

"Then tell us," Lee said. His tone was still belligerent, so I added: "Then we'll be out of your hair."

"Your homeless drunk was talking about the Allegory of the Cave," Dan said, then walked away with the empty beer mug. I stood there dumbfounded, taken aback at hearing a reference to the Allegory of the Cave in a bar in Old Town Alexandria. Dan dumped the mug into a plastic bin filled with dirty glasses and dishes.

I was sure that the Allegory of the Cave fell far down the list of usual discussion topics at a place like the Firegrill— below work, gossip, relationships, sports, politics, and at least several hundred other more common topics of conversation. But I remembered the reference from a college philosophy class—it came from Plato, that much I knew—but I didn't remember the allegory itself.

Dan plucked a fresh mug from a rack of clean ones hanging over the bar and stuck it under a tap. As the beer flowed into the glass, he sent another text, which I assumed canceled his request for bouncers—for now. Then he grabbed the mug, wiped the foam from the top with a small wooden paddle, and headed back our way.

He plunked the beer in front of Frank and looked to Lee. "I'm sorry about your wife," he said.

Lee nodded, but it wasn't gracious gesture of peace. It was a gesture that said *Let's get on with this*, and Dan responded in kind: a flicker of hardness covered his face and his jaw tightened. So I said something to keep the lead alive. "Can you just take a minute to tell us why you think your former customer wanted us to know about this allegory?"

"I have no idea why."

"Can you just tell us the allegory then?"

"How the hell is my little bar story going to help you with a murder case?"

"Who knows?" I said, and that was the truth—though I had to admit that when he had used the word "story," it had given me a slight bit of hope.

"Why aren't the cops involved?" he said. A reasonable question.

"They are," I said. "But so are we."

He stared at me a beat, then smiled. "Good answer." He looked over the Firegrill as if he was surveying his kingdom, then said, "Okay. No skin off my back."

Frank grabbed his beer and slid off his stool. "I'll check back in later. I heard this one already." He retreated into the crowd.

"I'm giving you the bite-size version," Dan said, and dove right in, clearly ready for us to be on our way. "There's a bunch of people who live in a cave, and they've lived there all their lives. They're chained down, sitting on the ground, like prisoners. So they can't move. *And* they're facing this blank wall. It's the only thing they can see.

"Now, behind them, there's a fire. They don't know about it, and they don't know there are other people in the cave walking in front of that fire. Those people are carrying these wooden figures—figures of all different shapes and sizes. And because of the fire, the figures are casting shadows on that blank wall. So to the prisoners, those shadows are the real world, because it's the only thing they've ever known. They've never seen anything else. But if someone freed them, they'd see that the shadows are just shadows. And that the real world is something else."

Dan folded his arms. "So that's my little story, boys. Sometimes I stretch it out if people aren't getting it."

I got it. It all came back to me from that college philosophy class. I looked over at Lee to see if he got it. His brow was creased, and I thought it was because he was thinking about it. But I was wrong.

"So what?" he said, confronting Dan even though Dan had obliged our request.

Before Lee pissed him off again, and in case there was more information to be gleaned, I ignored Lee's belligerence and answered his *so what*. "It means what we think is real isn't real. It's just a shadow of what's real."

"I got that," Lee said, and before he said anything more, I interjected.

"Why do you tell your customers that story?" I asked Dan.

"It does some good for some of them," he said.

"How? Why that story?" I was pressing him because I had nothing. No breadcrumb.

"I came up through the ranks, and any bartender who does has got to be a psychologist," he said. "That story is part of my go-to advice."

"I don't get it." I didn't see how the allegory would help his customers, and I certainly didn't see how it would help us.

"I'll bottom-line it for you. If someone has a problem they're obsessing about, sometimes it's all in their head. The reality they're seeing isn't real at all. It's just a shadow on a wall. If they get out of their cave and look behind them, they'll see another reality. The one outside their head."

Lee grunted—annoyed and dismissive. "When your wife dies, that's fucking reality."

I couldn't have agreed more.

"Of course," Dan said, "I get that. If the problem isn't in your head, then I got other advice. For example, *you* need to calm the fuck down."

I was sure Lee was going to leap across the bar. But he didn't. He actually took Dan's advice. He shook his head, not so much disgusted, just ready to give up. Then he glanced at me and said, "Let's go."

But I wasn't ready to give up. We didn't have another lead, and I didn't understand why Dantès wanted us to hear the Allegory of the Cave, if indeed he did.

"What about Plato?" I blurted out. "Why bring up Plato?"

Dan raised his eyebrows, amused. "You mean why would some dumb fuck bartender know about Plato?"

"You own this place, so that makes you a hell of a lot smarter than me," I said.

He grinned, glanced at Lee, then came back to me.

"You're lucky I'm used to loudmouth customers."

Lee just shook his head again and didn't attack. I was grateful for it.

"My dad was a philosophy professor at Georgetown," Dan said, "so he was always talking philosophy. He made sure I knew what each big-name philosopher had to say. Locke, Nietzsche, Rousseau, all of them. But Plato was the one that stuck with me." He leaned back and folded his arms, and a wistful look crossed his face. "My dad told me that when you got right down to the nitty-gritty, Plato and his crew had some crazy ideas. Ideas that got buried by Aristotle and were never recovered. Plato and his crew thought science and magic were part of the same world. Equal. That fact and fiction came in the same package—that everything was kind of like a giant shake and bake. I always liked that idea."

Fact and fiction came in the same package—a giant shake and bake. Was that the breadcrumb we'd come for? It felt like Dan had confirmed something, but I wasn't sure what that something was. It had the flavor of novel therapy, but no specifics. It would've been so much better if our conversation had yielded something specific—somewhere to go, someone to see—but it didn't. The best I could come up with was that if fact and fiction were the same, then attention had to be paid to the bizarre and unexplainable elements of the past and present—from the strange, dank fog and the husky wolf, to the homeless man's missing reflection and his strange story about the man who'd turned into a blanket of darkness.

Lee said, "Are we outta here?"

"Sure." I didn't know where to go next, but I thought our trip to the Firegrill had run its course. I couldn't have been more wrong.

Lee took off, using aggressive *excuse me's* to once again cut a path through the throng of patrons.

"Thanks for your help." I stuck out my hand to shake, and Dan took it.

"Don't see how I helped," he said, "but you're welcome. And do me a favor. Make sure your chum there doesn't get himself into any trouble until after he gets out of the Firegrill."

I nodded and turned to go, but I couldn't locate Lee up ahead. I scanned the crowd from left to right and back again. There was no sign of him. He couldn't have gotten through the crowd so fast, but he must have. I moved forward, zigzagging through the crowd, toward the doors, assuming that Lee was well on his way out. As I was making my way around one of those islands in the swamp, I finally spotted him.

He was a few yards away, standing still between two clusters of people, focused on something or someone near the booths. I made my way over to him.

"I don't fucking believe this," he said.

I followed his gaze and saw a man in a dress shirt and loosened tie gesticulating wildly to a group of men also with loosened ties. I saw two young women, nodding to a third, as if they were agreeing with her about some profound insight. I saw three guys barely above the drinking age, laughing uproariously. But I didn't see the reason for Lee's incredulity.

"What's up?" I said.

"I know why we're here."

"Fill me in."

He didn't. Instead he plunged forward, dispensing with the aggressive *excuse me's* altogether and letting his hostile pace do the talking. Which it did—people scooted out of his way.

He made his way to the booths that lined the wall. Every one of them was jam-packed with people—all except for one. There, two men in their sixties were drinking bottled Budweiser and eating barbecued ribs.

Lee had slowed down, and when I caught up to him, he motioned toward that booth. "The one on the left—that's my dad. Macon. The last time I saw him was ten years ago. He came over to Uncle Harry's place on the day I was moving Harry out. I thought he'd come over to help me pack. It turned out he wanted to see if Harry had anything worth selling. He wanted to pocket the cash."

I was already predisposed to dislike Macon, and his appearance didn't do anything to change that. He was wiry, with a sharp, rat-like face, and narrow lips that were currently wrapped around a greasy rib. His hair was gray, thin, and slicked back.

"You think we're here because Dantès wanted us to run into him," I said.

"Yeah." Lee headed to the booth.

Macon spotted Lee, and while still gnawing on his ribs, he

grimaced as if he'd seen something troubling.

Lee stepped up to the booth, and Macon let out an unfriendly, "Speak of the devil."

Again, hell.

"Great to see you, too," Lee said, without disguising his sarcasm. To the other man in the booth, he said, "Can you give us some space?"

The man looked to Macon for guidance. Macon waved his hand, shooing the man away. "Go on, give us a minute here."

Displeased, the man snorted, grabbed his bottle of Bud, and slid out of the booth. Lee slid into the vacated spot, scooted down, then motioned for me to take a seat next to him.

I didn't hesitate. Like him, I didn't think this was a chance meeting. This was part of Dantès's game. Whatever we'd learned from Dan T. was either bonus material or gobbledygook.

"Why's he part of this reunion?" Macon said, nodding in my direction.

"Whatever you got to say, he needs to hear." Lee wasn't going to take any crap from his dad.

"I don't got nothin' to say." The old man took a swig of his beer.

"Why are you here?" Lee was getting right to the point. "And don't tell me it's for drinking. I got that part."

"I don't gotta give you answers."

"If you want me to leave, you do."

Macon glanced around the Firegrill as if *he* was the one considering leaving.

"Don't even think about running away," Lee said. "You've done enough of that to last ten lifetimes." He wasn't pulling any punches. "You're not going anywhere till you give me some answers. Now, why are you here?"

"What's it to you?"

"Maybe something. Maybe nothing. Just spit it out and I'll tell you."

Macon put his bottle of Bud down on the table. "I got a goddamn gift certificate. Free drinks and food—"

"Free drinks are always a good motivator for you."

"Yeah, but if I'd known they'd come with meetin' your good-for-nothin' family, I woulda stayed away from this shithole."

They were both brutal.

Lee leaned back from that blow and took in a breath. Macon did the same. Time out.

I shifted uncomfortably and started to think that this was going to be a dead end, too.

"You still living on Route 50?" Lee asked, softening a bit.

"Nah—I got a mansion in McLean now." Macon scoffed, picked up his bottle, and took another sip. "Yeah, I'm still there."

"What about Mom? Do you know where she is?"

"The no-good bitch is long gone."

Lee suddenly slapped the beer bottle from his dad's hand—it smacked hard into the old man's chest, splattering beer all over his shirt, then fell into his lap. He scrambled to grab the bottle, snatched it up, and put it back on the table.

"You goddamn punk," he said, scooping up napkins. He started mopping his shirt and pants. "Since when do you give a crap about your mom?"

"You screwed up her life just like you screwed up mine."

"When are you gonna learn? It's the fucking Bellington curse."

"That bullshit again? You're blaming mumbo jumbo for your shitty life—but hey, I guess that's your style, right? Blame someone else."

"You don't gotta believe me, but the proof's in the pudding. How's things been going for *you*, huh? Everything hunky-dory? Or did the shit hit the fan?"

Lee glanced at me. I saw unease flicker across his face and thought, *Score one for the old man*. And Macon knew he'd scored, so he rampaged on. "The Bellington curse caught up with you, huh? Outta nowhere, it smacked you right down, didn't it?"

"We're done here," Lee said, then gestured for me to slide out of the booth.

I complied and stood up, but wondered if this encounter had ended too early. Had it generated our next lead, or was I going to have to make something out of Plato's Allegory of the Cave?

We snaked through the crowd and out onto the sidewalk. Cool, fresh air greeted us, and I was glad I'd emerged from the hot and crowded swamp that was Dan T.'s Firegrill. We headed toward the car, but Lee's stride dragged, as if any confidence he'd had was gone. He was running his hand through his hair and staring down at the ground. The encounter with his dad had left him shaken.

"Where to?" he said.

Chapter Nine

"We have to figure out where the Allegory of the Cave is supposed to lead us," I said, hoping the cool night air would bring with it some clarity.

"I don't see how that's gonna help us track down a killer." Lee no longer sounded sure of himself. "I say we go back to basics: search the web for a lead about a missing man from that night. When was the last time you did that?"

"A hell of long time ago—maybe fifteen years."

"Me too. Figured there was no need to connect myself to that. But who knows what's online now? There might be an article or some police report from back then about a missing man."

We decided to drive back to Lee's place and scour the web, but I told myself that I would spend the drive there trying to figure out if there was a breadcrumb to be had from Plato. If I understood one thing, it was that Dantès's game involved more than online research.

First I texted Jenna to see if Nate was okay. Though I tried my best to hide my worry from her, she must have picked up on it, because she texted me back immediately with details. She said she'd read Nate a story that she'd loved as a kid, *Big Mack and the Mountaintop*, and that Nate had loved it, too, and now he was sound asleep.

On the road, I racked my brain trying to connect the allegory to something we could follow up on—looking to novel therapy again, my default mode. But I couldn't come up with anything. The only thing that resonated was that fact and fiction were a giant shake and bake.

"What about your dad?" I said. "Are you sure he didn't give us something to go on?"

"He's never given me anything to go on."

"There's always a first time."

"The guy's a loser. And I know what you're thinking: that I was just like him until I met Grace. But that's not right. I have one thing on my dad: he always blames other people for his problems. And if he can't pin the blame on someone alive, he blames it on a three-hundred-year-old dead relative. You won't catch me doing that. I never blamed my shitty life on anyone but myself."

He was baring his heart, opening up again, and I should've responded to it, but his mention of a three-hundred-year-old relative triggered the quote *The past isn't dead, it isn't even past,* and I responded to that instead.

"What do you mean, a three-hundred-year-old relative?" I said.

"It's just bullshit. His excuse."

"Tell me about it."

"Why? You think that's going to get us somewhere?

Believe me. My dad isn't going to get us anywhere."

He wasn't going to dig into this unless I pushed. "What's the Bellington curse?"

"I told you: an excuse."

"I got that part. But what does it have to do with your relative from three hundred years ago?"

"It's a dead end. Drop it."

I was on the GW Parkway, headed back to Arlington. "If it gives me any chance of saving Nate, it's not a dead end."

"It's a waste of time."

"Dantès *wanted* us at that bar. I have no idea how he got a gift certificate into your dad's hand and got him there tonight, and I have no idea how he could be so sure we'd end up there too, but as soon as you saw your dad, you knew that was Dantès's plan."

"I was wrong—it was a coincidence."

"Like novel therapy? Dantès made breadcrumbs from what I hate. Well, it looks like he made breadcrumbs from the thing *you* hate, too."

Lee cocked his head, then looked out to his right, at the Potomac. He stared at the dark oasis. I knew he was about to cave in. My logic wasn't the greatest, but it was close enough.

"You know how you said the leads were about me?" I said. "Guess what? This one's about you."

He continued to stare at the river. Or maybe he was staring at he monuments of American history on the other side. They were lit up as if to say the past isn't dead—you can bring it back to life by shining a spotlight on it and making it blaze brightly in the night.

After another minute or so, Lee opened up. "... My family goes way back," he said. "All the way back to the Plymouth Colony. Our ancestors came over here on the Mayflower. You wouldn't know it to look at us, right? We never got any special privileges as far I can tell. Hell, I don't really know if *any* Mayflower descendants did, but a lot of them hit it big. You got John Quincy Adams, FDR, Marilyn Monroe, Humphrey Bogart, Alan Shepard, and too many rich businessmen to even count—like Eastman, the film guy.

"But my family... We're descended from John Bellington. Mayflower passenger, original colonist, but what he's known for..." Lee glanced at me, then looked back at the Potomac. "He's the first murderer in American history."

Lee took a breath, and I said, "Never heard of him."

"Why would you? He's a footnote. An answer to a *Jeopardy!* question. John Bellington was hanged for killing someone who trespassed on his property—at least, that was the charge. The case was murky. Uncle Harry told me that some historians think Bellington was provoked into shooting the trespasser, or maybe even framed. On the other hand, good ol' John Bellington already had a track record. It turns out he'd been a troublemaker from the get-go. On the Mayflower, he led a mutiny that failed."

"A mutiny? He must've been pretty pissed off about something."

"He was. The way Harry tells it, the Mayflower passengers were divided into two groups: the Puritans and the Strangers.

The Puritans were coming over to start a new religion. The Strangers were basically everyone else: families looking for a new start, servants of rich passengers, workers on the ship, Catholics, et cetera. Anyway, Bellington was one of the Strangers. A guy looking for a new start. But the trip was nasty. He suffered, and so did his family. People were dying left and right. Harry said historians think that that's why some of the passengers mutinied. But other historians had a different theory. And Harry liked one of those theories: the Puritans were pricks and they bossed the Strangers around, until the Strangers got fed up."

"Sounds like Harry did his homework."

"It made for a damn good story—and the man loved stories."

"So the mutiny was a bust?"

"Yeah, but that didn't stop Bellington when he got to Plymouth Rock. He didn't let up—he was always getting into trouble. A few years after the colony got going, the leaders accused him of being part of a group that wanted to overthrow them. But Bellington somehow talked them out of arresting him."

I was listening for any connection between Lee's story and Dantès, but even though my instinct was telling me that this was the right trail, following it in search of a clue was beginning to feel as futile as following the Allegory of the Cave trail.

"After that," Lee said, "Bellington kept out of trouble. Until he shot that trespasser. For that, he was tried and hanged. But according to Uncle Harry's version of American history, Bellington was railroaded—because the other settlers didn't like him."

I turned off the GW Parkway and glanced at the speedometer. I was speeding and realized this was because I was impatient—so I got to the central question: "What exactly is the 'Bellington curse'?"

"It turns out that a lot of Bellington's descendants ended up being troublemakers. Swindlers, con men, and outright criminals. So the Bellingtons started to believe that our entire line was cursed."

"But—"

"Don't say it. I'll say it for you: being a troublemaker and having bad shit happen to you are two different things."

"Exactly."

"Evolution," he said and shot me a grin.

"What?"

"The curse. It evolved. It went from Bellingtons doing bad things, to bad things happening to the Bellingtons. And then you start to look for examples. Like your baby girl gets hit by a car—that's what happened to my grandma's first kid. Or you get married and two days later your wife runs off with your best friend—that's what happened to one of my great-great-uncles, Jeremiah. Or you drown in a lake even though you're a damn good swimmer—that's what happened to one of my great-aunts. Or just nothing at all goes your way at all, like my dad." Lee let out a little chuckle. "But the most famous example is James Garfield."

"The U.S. president?"

"Yeah. He was a direct descendant of John Bellington."

"And he was assassinated."

"You got it—the Bellington curse."

"But he was president. That's not bad luck."

"That's how Uncle Harry sees it, too. And you know what? I've always liked that about Harry. He never blamed his legs getting blown off on the curse. He says bad shit happens to everyone."

I was in Harry's camp; I didn't believe in curses either. But as I pulled off the GW Parkway and onto Lee Highway, I could identify with Lee's dad. Nothing was going our way. For one thing, a psychopath—who knew way more about us than was possible—had murdered both our wives. But the idea that this was the result of a curse was still too far-fetched for me.

On the other hand, it was no more far-fetched than everything else that was happening. And I should've made a connection based on that. But I wasn't ready yet. I hadn't traveled far enough yet. My view of the world was still limited, just like the prisoners in Plato's cave.

Without any other leads to go on, the idea of scouring the web was looking better and better, so I proposed going to my place instead of Lee's. On my computer, I already had open access to research sites provided to librarians and not available to the general public. At Lee's place, I'd have to find those sites and remember my dozens of passwords.

Lee agreed, so I headed for home. Still, I didn't give up

trying to tease out a lead from Lee's story. It's just that I was coming up with zilch.

*

As I rounded the corner onto my street, I saw flashing red lights pulsing across lawns and houses. Down the block, fire trucks and police cruisers were clumped together in front of one house.

My house. Ablaze in flames.

Dantès had struck again.

I slowed down and gaped at the sight. It didn't take but another few seconds for Lee to figure why I was in shock. "I'm sorry..." he said.

I pulled over, and we both climbed out and joined the gaggle of bystanders. Yellow emergency tape separated them from the inferno. Lee didn't say a word. There wasn't much to say about the growing dismantling of my life.

While Lee hung back, I made my way past the gawkers, most of them my neighbors. Vicky and Jim, who lived next door, were staring at my house, wide-eyed and utterly flabbergasted. I was about to move past them and duck under the tape when Vicky spotted me.

"Oh my God," she said. "Nate isn't with you? They said it didn't look like anyone was in the house."

"Nate's fine," I said. "He's good."

"Thank God!" She hugged me tightly. "I'm so sorry. I just can't believe it." She didn't have to say any more than that. The rest was implied. *How could God take Lucy from you and then your home?* I wanted to tell her it wasn't God. It was Dantès.

But instead I asked, "What happened? Do they know?"

She shook her head. "The place went up like that. The fire department got here fast, but the fire was faster." She squeezed my arm. "Whatever we can do, please let us know."

"Thank you," I said, then ducked under the yellow tape.

The firefighters were battling the flames with water cannons, but it didn't look like it was doing much good. The flames were raging on both the first floor and the second, and thick black smoke was billowing from the windows. The place was a disaster.

I swallowed and stood there for a long beat, accepting that nothing of my former life was going to be salvageable. Then I hurried over to a fireman who had taken off his headgear.

"That's my house," I said. "Can you tell me what happened?"

"You need to talk to Captain Bowman." He pointed toward a firefighter perched in the cab of a fire truck, door open, speaking intently into a dispatch radio. It was then that I realized I could feel the heat from the fire even at this distance. I was back in hell, in Dante's *Inferno*, only this time it wasn't courtesy of Dan T.'s Firegrill. It was courtesy of my own home.

I headed over to Captain Bowman, pulling out my wallet on the way and removing my driver's license. As soon as the captain saw me approaching, he lowered the dispatcher handset. That and the concern on his face told me he already knew I was the distressed homeowner.

"I'm John Gaines," I said, and passed my driver's license up to him. "That's my house."

He glanced at my license and handed it back. "I understand that you have a son—"

"He's safe. He was with me."

"Great. Good." The captain's concern softened. "That's the best news I've heard tonight."

"Do you know what happened?"

"Not yet. That may take a while. When did you leave the house?"

My life had gone so far off the rails that it seemed like an eternity ago. "About four-thirty," I said, hardly believing it.

"Did you notice any strange odors before you left?"

"No."

"Were you storing anything flammable in the house? I don't mean liquor. I mean something highly combustible."

I shook my head. "Nothing."

"Nothing at all? Nothing in the basement? Sometimes people forget they stuck a propane tank down there. Or gas for a leaf blower."

"No."

"What about supplies for a renovation project?"

I shook my head again.

"Well, it's too early to say for sure what started it, but I gotta tell you it's a bad one." Bowman stepped down from his perch and surveyed his battlefield—my house. "When we got here, your place was already too far gone. We got inside, but had to retreat after a few minutes." He turned to me. "Whatever it turns out to be, I'm betting that fire had help— a lot of help."

"Help?"

"An accelerant. That fire didn't go from zero to sixty by itself. When the first neighbor called, she said she saw smoke coming from a downstairs window. Our trucks were on the scene twelve minutes later. The A-side and C-side of the house—the front and rear—were almost lost already."

"You're saying someone set the place on fire," I blurted out.

"We'll investigate. So will the police. And there's always the possibility that there was an accelerant in the house that you weren't aware of." Then Captain Bowman asked me, point blank, "Do you know or suspect someone who might've done this?"

Did I? Not by his real name. Not even close. "No," I said. I didn't want to be interrogated by him, nor by the police right now. Not while the clock was ticking on Nate's life.

"If you have a lead, or suspect someone," he said, "you should walk over there to Lieutenant Wilson and tell him." He nodded over to one of the police cruisers.

I have dozens of leads, I thought, *and none of them make sense*. They were the leads that a crazy man, a conspiracy theorist would string together: a mysterious woman in the woods, a homeless man living between the hedges, a Mayflower passenger hanged for murder, the castle of Otranto on the banks of the Potomac.

"I wish I had a lead," I said.

"If you *do* have one, let the police know. If a fire's the result of arson, it's usually obvious." He looked back at the house. "I'm sorry we couldn't do more."

Dantès made sure you couldn't.

"Do you have a place to stay for the night?" Bowman said.

"Yeah... thanks."

"If you need anything, we have a coordinator that can help you."

"I'm okay... I mean, under the circumstances."

"Good. Give Lieutenant Wilson your information and we'll talk tomorrow."

I walked toward Lieutenant Wilson as if I intended to talk to him, and I checked out my house on the way. The first floor was a crispy wreck of smoke and charred walls; the second floor was a stronghold of flames refusing to simmer down. But there were a couple of areas where the firemen were successfully beating back the flames with the water cannons.

Staring at the jets of water pounding those areas was sobering, because it made Captain Bowman's battle strategy perfectly clear: he was using the water cannons to keep the flames from jumping from my house over to my neighbors' houses. This was a reaffirmation that my house was a total loss. The best-case scenario was that no other houses would be damaged. Dantès had taken the love of my life—Lucy— and now he'd stripped my life of any semblance of normalcy.

I veered away from Lieutenant Wilson and headed back

toward the yellow safety tape and Lee. I was now more desperate than ever to find the next breadcrumb. Without it, I'd lose Nate as surely as I'd lost everything else.

I ducked under the tape and hurried past the gawkers, fielding a few *I'm sorrys* and a couple of neighbors' offers to spend the night, which I politely declined.

Lee was lingering at the back of the crowd, on his cell phone, which he lowered when he saw me.

"Checking on your house?" I said.

"Yeah. It's fine."

"Good, because that's our next stop."

We headed back to my car, and as soon as we'd left the crowd behind, a woman's voice rang out: "Having trouble finding the next breadcrumb?"

It was Otranto. Lee and I both whipped around to face her.

She flicked her blond hair away from her face, and this time her beauty hit me as otherworldly. She was too beautiful to be human. She was a seductive demon from hell enjoying a night out on the town. But I pushed that insane thought away and focused on this woman in front of me, clearly of flesh and blood.

"You're still fighting it," she said, then glanced back at the flames. "I think Churchill said it best: 'If you're going through hell, keep going.'"

"Why all this bullshit?" Lee said. "Get to the goddamn point."

"Still angry." Her smirk came back. "How's that working

out for you? Dantès handed you the next breadcrumb. Had your papa deliver it to you in a nicely wrapped package. But you're blinded by the same baggage your papa carries. You can't escape the tyranny of your emotions. You haven't learned to control them. They're always there, weighing you down. If John hadn't walked back into your life today, you'd be huddled in your house, crushed by grief. It would've killed you."

Lee didn't have a response. It was as if Otranto had punched him right in the gut. His big body slumped, beaten down by her words.

Otranto then set her green eyes on me. "Help him figure it out. You've got more at stake."

If she was saying Lee's dad had delivered the clue, then it meant I'd been on the right track. "The Bellington curse," I said.

"Warmer." She was pleased, her smile full of mischievous pleasure. "Think about the pieces in the game. What are they made from?"

Another obscure clue. Was she referring to novel therapy? Were the pieces made from books? That couldn't be right. This was about Lee.

She put her hand on her hip, stood up tall, and flicked her hair away from her eyes, striking the pose of a runway model. For a few seconds—during which I supposed she expected the lead to miraculously dawn on me—she stood like that, radiant.

But then she darkened with disgust. "How do you know

about the Bellington curse?" she demanded.

"Lee told me."

Her eyes went to Lee. "How do *you* know about it?"

"My whole fucking family knows. That's how."

"Suit yourself," she said, and she started to walk away, back toward the crowd.

"Wait!" I wanted more help, but even as I yelled out "wait," I knew that each visit by Otranto was perfectly calculated. I wanted to chase her down, but that wasn't part of Dantès's game.

So instead of going after her, I pressed Lee. "How *do* you know about the Bellington curse?"

"Just like I told her: my entire family knows about it."

"That's not the right answer." So what *was* the right answer? *What are the pieces of the game made from?*

And this time the answer came to me. Lee had told me half a dozen times how he'd learned the details of John Bellington's life. He learned it from one of the pieces in the game. The pieces in the game were made from people. Lucy, Grace, Quincy, Nate, Lee, the homeless man, Dan T., Macon, Otranto, and me.

"I know where to go." I headed around to the driver's side of my car.

"Where?"

"To meet a new piece in the game—your Uncle Harry."

"That's a long shot."

"Just get in and tell me where he lives."

Before I climbed into the car, I took a final peek at

Otranto. She was gliding through the gawkers, toward the burning house, as if she was a supernatural creature drawn to the blazing inferno. But there was also clear evidence that she was real, and that came in the form of the stares she drew from my neighbors as she walked past them. They were taken by this stunning woman, just as I had been the first time I'd seen her.

In the car, Lee spoke first. "You sure Harry's the next stop?" he said.

"'Sure' is an awfully strong word. Where does your uncle live?"

"Head to Lee Highway and get on 66."

Chapter Ten

I could tell by the way Lee was fidgeting with his hands that he didn't want to visit Uncle Harry, and the reason—guilt— became apparent after we'd gone about twenty miles on Route 66.

"He should be in an assisted living place," Lee said, "but his VA benefits don't even come close to paying for a place like that. So he lives in a crappy apartment. I didn't have extra money or I would've done better by him… but hey, at least it's not right next door to a power plant. The last place I got him was next to one of those electric substations, so even though it was a decent place, the rent was cheap because no one wanted to live there. Everyone's scared those substations will give 'em cancer."

Then Lee told me his uncle's apartment complex was another ten miles out, in Chantilly, which made sense. There were no cheap rents close to D.C. If you wanted to save some cash, you needed to travel to the far edges of the suburban sprawl.

Unprompted, Lee went on to add more details about Harry's living arrangements, as if he felt he had to justify them even more. "I got him a caretaker," he said. "She's from Guatemala. Sweet gal. She goes to his place in the morning, helps him out of bed, makes him breakfast, and helps him get ready for the day. Then she comes back at night, cooks him dinner, and helps him get ready for bed."

"You mentioned your uncle was a big storyteller," I said. "What did you say he said about stories?"

"Stories tell you all you need to know."

That was the connection that couldn't be denied. "There's a story Dantès wants us to hear," I said, "and your uncle is going to tell it to us."

"Don't hold your breath—the guy's got a million stories."

"Is there a story he already told you that applies to any of this?"

"Not one that I can come up with off the top of my head."

"What about a story about the Bellington curse?"

"I already told you what he said about that."

Right now, as it stood, there was just no way for me to fathom that Dantès's game could encompass the Bellington curse, the Allegory of the Cave, Uncle Harry, and a new story—a story that Harry had never told Lee. But Dantès knew I'd eventually put it all together. I was playing checkers, and he was playing chess. I was moving from square to square, barely able to pick out my next move, in need of coaching from Otranto—while Dantès was moving effortlessly across the board, planning far ahead. He understood me better than I understood myself.

*

We drove through one of Chantilly's low-income neighborhoods, which consisted of a string of rundown, four-story apartment buildings. They were probably once respectable places, but no longer. Even under the streetlights, their fall from grace was obvious: gouged wooden walls and peeling paint, cracked cement walkways, and landscaping that had deteriorated into dirt lawns with random patches of weeds here and there.

After driving seven blocks, passing buildings that got progressively more rundown, with graffiti added to the mix, Lee told me to turn in to one of the extremely narrow driveways between buildings. Driving down this constricted gauntlet felt like a test to see if you could make it through without hitting either wall. And my headlights revealed that some drivers hadn't passed the test: there were long scrapes along both walls.

The gauntlet opened onto a dimly lit parking area filled to capacity. Lee told me to head down to the third row. As I did, a distant barking filled the air. It sounded vicious, and that brought with it an image of skinheads in some nearby apartment, training their pit bull for mayhem.

Lee pointed to an empty space halfway down the third row. "Looks like we're in luck. That's Harry's spot. Sometimes his dirtball neighbors snag the spot since he doesn't have a car, and that leaves Marta, the gal who helps him, with no parking. The poor woman has to drive the streets until she finds one. That's why I bet she quits on me soon."

I pulled into the tight spot, cut the engine, and opened the door. There was barely enough room to climb out, and when I did, the first thing to hit me was the barking—louder and more malicious. The second thing was the pungent scent of roasting sweet peppers, which conjured up the image of a South American woman preparing a late dinner for her family—a contrast to the disturbing image of the skinheads with their menacing dog.

Lee must've been thinking along the same lines because he said, "You know, the Hispanics never take Harry's parking spot. Not once. It's always the goddamn white-trash lowlifes." He chuckled, the first laugh from either of us since the start of our warped journey. "Makes me ashamed of my own kind."

"Every kind has bad apples."

And what kind was Dantès? It didn't matter, did it? He was the bad apple, rotten to the core.

As we approached the building, the vicious barking got even louder. So much so that Lee and I both scanned the windows to see where it was coming from.

If we'd been looking down instead of up at the apartments, we might've seen the person who sicced the nasty creature on us. But we didn't.

The huge black dog vaulted toward us from between a couple of cars. It was snapping and snarling—spittle flew from its mouth.

Lee and I immediately took off, heading to the back of the

lot, scrambling between parked cars. I followed Lee's lead, figuring he knew the area a hell of a lot better than I did. After running through a couple rows of cars, we hit an alleyway. We began to race down it, and I took the lead, but neither of us was going to win any sprinting contests. The dog was hurtling toward us, barking madly, its paws clicking on the asphalt.

The alleyway was lined with dumpsters and discarded furniture. There was no place to hide. I glanced back. Lee was ten yards behind me, closely trailed by the dog, a massive animal that looked as much like a wolf as it did a dog—no surprise there. Its canine teeth were white and spiked, and its black snout was pronounced.

Lee suddenly stopped, and for a second I thought he was giving up, but he opened a dumpster and jumped in. I wasn't looking over my shoulder long enough to see it, but I heard him slam the lid down over himself, then noticed that the paws were no longer clicking on the asphalt.

When I looked back again, the dog was growling menacingly at the dumpster. It stood on its hind legs and attacked the lid's metal lip, savagely snapping at it. But watching this unfold slowed me down, and the dog quickly caught on and bolted toward me. Instead of picking up my pace, I followed Lee's lead, lunged for a dumpster, opened it, scrambled inside, and pulled the lid closed.

I gagged from the stench of putrid food and dog feces. The plastic trash bags surrounding me were leaking, and their juices were already seeping into my clothes, coating my skin with stench. The rancid stink was unbearable. My stomach clenched, and I willed myself not to puke.

A heavy thud landed above me, followed by clawing and snarling. The rabid dog's scraping was so powerful that I actually thought he might be able to claw through the metal. Anything was possible in hell.

Then there was another heavy thud—and another—and another. The dog was throwing himself against the metal lid. I could hear him growling every time he righted himself. With each blow, he became stronger and more fierce, until he was rocking the entire dumpster.

My nausea worsened, and just as I thought I was going to vomit, the impossible happened: the lid started to warp under the dog's relentless assault. The metal was somehow *buckling*. And if that wasn't enough to make me believe I was no longer in a world where reality mattered, I suddenly remembered one of the rings of hell in Dante's *Inferno*—a river of feces—and I realized that that was exactly where I was now trapped.

I vomited. The retching was deep and painful. The contents of my stomach added to the already unbearable stench. My retching ended with a couple of dry, agonizing heaves, which left me sweaty, aching, and sore.

I was so dazed that it took me a minute or more to notice that the dog's assault had stopped. Maybe he'd retreated, pleased that he'd driven me so deep into hell, or maybe he was waiting me out.

I debated whether to make a run for it or stay put, but

soon the decision was made for me. The dumpster lid whipped open—revealing Lee, breathing heavily. His eyes looked dead, as they had when I had first seen them. His cheeks were pale. The life had been chased out of him. He didn't say a word as I climbed out, and I figured he was too shell-shocked to talk and left it at that.

I was in bad shape, too, in pain from retching, and shaken by the damage the dog had inflicted on the dumpster's lid, which was even more apparent from the outside; the metal was dented as if someone had repeatedly smashed it with a sledgehammer. But I still should've realized that Lee's demeanor wasn't quite right—that his zombie-like state didn't stem from shock and fear.

When we stepped up to the back of the apartment building, I finally spoke. "Do you think that Dantès sicced that dog on us?"

Lee was wearing a hollow, blank expression, as if he wasn't all there yet. He shook his head—that was his only response.

Inside the building, we walked down a cinderblock hallway, past apartment doors, distressed and scratched, and into a dingy lobby. The lobby had no furniture, and there weren't even any cheap paintings hanging on the walls, the usual go-to adornment when attempting to add some cheer to an otherwise dreary environment.

Lee pressed the elevator call button, then stared at the numbers above the door. The elevator motor started up, grinding loudly, straining to do its job. Along with the motor's mechanical squawking, I heard what sounded like growling.

I glanced around the lobby, but it was empty. I glanced at Lee to see his reaction, but he was just staring up at the numbers, lost in his own world. Maybe I'd imagined the growling.

Then I heard it again, this time more guttural and raw, and my heart skipped a beat, because it was close. *Real* close. But there was no one and nothing else in the lobby except for Lee and me. Lee still hadn't reacted, nor said anything, and I found myself suddenly taking a step back from him as if he was the source of the growling. But he just continued to stare up at the numbers, which now indicated that the elevator had arrived.

The door slid open, squealing as it did, and as Lee finally looked down, I heard the guttural growl again, this time mixed in with the door's squealing. It sounded like it was coming from Lee, but he stepped into the elevator before I could be sure. I followed, telling myself that I was still unnerved by my stay in the dumpster.

The elevator was spare and sad, its steel walls buffed to a flat dullness by repeated attempts to remove graffiti. Of course, the delinquents had battled back by engraving their markings right into the steel—sharp cuts forming curse words and threats.

We creaked to a stop on the fourth floor. Lee led the way down a hallway more ugly than the one downstairs and stopped in front of apartment 4E, where I expected him to pull some keys from his pocket—but he didn't. Instead he stood there for a beat, as if he couldn't remember where he was, and then he did something weird. The motion was so slight, I couldn't swear I'd actually seen it. He appeared to crinkle his nose as if he was sniffing the air. A second later, he bent down, lifted the corner of the plastic doormat, and picked up a key from underneath it.

He unlocked the door, and we entered the apartment. The odor of the place hit me first: a mixture of body odor, dirty clothes, mildew, and rotting food. It wasn't as bad as the stench in the dumpster, but if left to ripen for a few more days, it would be.

I unintentionally winced, then glanced at Lee, hoping he hadn't seen my reaction. He already felt guilty enough about his uncle's living conditions, and I didn't want to pile on. Still, I had to wonder why the caretaker wasn't doing a better job. But then I realized she must have quit, as Lee had feared she might.

Lee didn't notice my reaction. He'd already made it across the living room and was walking down a narrow hallway toward the back of the apartment. Rather than follow him, I took in the furnishings of the shabby room: a well-worn plaid couch, either salvaged or really old, and covered with dark stains; an easy chair; and a plastic coffee table.

"Get the hell outta here!" A voice—rich, deep, and southern—thundered from down the hallway. I scooted over to check it out and saw Lee stepping back out of a room at the end of the hall.

"I ain't gonna tell ya again!" the voice said.

Lee continued to back away, and Harry came following after him in a wheelchair.

Even though he was seated, I could see that Harry was a big man, bigger than Lee, with a barrel chest and broad shoulders. If Lee had the build of a linebacker, Harry had the build of an All-Pro linebacker. And if that didn't make him intimidating enough already, the rifle lying across the armrests of his wheelchair would have.

Harry took his hands off the wheels, grabbed the rifle, and tucked the butt firmly into his shoulder, like he knew exactly how to wield the weapon. He trained the rifle on Lee. "I knew you'd be comin'," he said.

Maybe that was why instead of wearing pajamas, he was dressed in street clothes—a gray sweatshirt and a pair of jeans. The jeans were cut off at the knees and sewn up to encase his thighs, which were all that remained of his legs.

Lee wasn't responding to his uncle, and I weighed whether to chime in and tell Harry that Lee was in shock.

"You ain't gonna get me," Harry said, then skillfully and quickly placed the gun back on the armrests, grabbed the wheels, rolled the wheelchair forward, and snatched the gun back up. He trained it on Lee once again.

Lee was now backed up into the living room.

Harry's wheelchair rolled to a stop at the mouth of the hallway, and now he aimed the gun at me. "If you're helpin' him, I'd just as soon put a bullet in you, too. I can get off two shots before you know what hit ya."

He aimed the gun back at Lee. "I been waiting for you. I

knew he'd send something my way. I been on the lookout."

I looked at Lee. Why wasn't he responding?

His response came just then. It took the form of a step toward Harry. One step.

A shot rang out, quick, sharp, and with no fanfare.

Lee's head snapped back and his body crumpled to the floor. Part of his forehead had been blown off, leaving a gruesome cavity of flayed flesh and bone over his right eye. Dark, crimson blood was oozing from the cavity and pooling around his head.

Stunned, I sucked in air and looked away from the disturbing sight. Unfortunately, my eyes fell on the bits of skull and gray matter littering the plaid couch. My throat went dry and my stomach clenched. The nausea was returning.

"Go on, get out," Harry said.

I looked over at him. His rifle was trained on me.

"Go on," he said.

"You killed him…" I couldn't accept that this had actually happened. *Fact and fiction. A giant shake and bake. Please let this be fiction.*

Harry drew the rifle butt more firmly into his shoulder and aimed the barrel at my head. He was ready to squeeze off another round.

I wasn't going to challenge him, so I headed toward the door. But when I glanced down at Lee, I stopped in my tracks. I was staring down at a huge black dog lying dead in a pool of blood. The very same dog that had been hunting us down in the alley. It was *his* head that was missing a chunk of flesh and bone. Not Lee's.

Confused, I turned back to Harry and stared at him. What the hell was going on? Harry had somehow seen that Lee had been a shadow. And he'd somehow seen the rabid dog *behind* the shadow. *But how?*

Though Harry hadn't lowered the rifle, I wasn't going to run. I was standing in front of the only person who might be able to help me. Harry wasn't chained down in Plato's cave. He wasn't a prisoner facing a wall of shadows.

"How did you know it wasn't Lee?" I said, and I stopped there even though I wanted to unload a barrage of questions.

"You just got to look," he said. A straightforward answer that echoed the homeless man, but was still of no help.

"I've been with him all night and I didn't know."

"Then you're a dumbass." He finally lowered his gun, as if he'd concluded that this dumbass was too stupid to pose a threat.

"What do you mean, 'You just got to look'?"

With his rifle, he motioned to the dog. "If you've got something to do with that, then you gotta be on the lookout."

"And what exactly am I supposed to be on the lookout for?"

"Why'd you come here?" he demanded.

"Lee and I were looking for the person who murdered our wives. We thought you might have a lead."

"You're a lying son of a bitch." Immediately he aimed the

gun at my head again. "Grace died in an accident. She wasn't murdered."

"Lee found out tonight that it wasn't an accident."

"And where *is* Lee?"

"I don't know." But I did know this: the dead-eyed thing who'd opened my dumpster wasn't Lee. Lee was still out there somewhere—in a dumpster, or worse. "Listen, Harry," I said. "When Lee—I mean whatever that thing is—walked in here—"

"It's a goddamn dog—plain and simple."

"Okay, but you said you knew something would be coming. You knew someone would send it. Who? Who would send it?" I wanted him to say Dantès, but I knew the answer wouldn't be that simple.

Just then the front door lock rattled. Harry instantly swung his gun around.

The door swung open and Lee stepped inside. His eyes immediately fell on the dog. "Holy shit!" he said. "How the hell did it get in here?"

"It morphed into you and walked in," I said, accepting as fact something I would've dismissed as fiction just hours ago.

Lee cocked his head. "What are you talking about?"

"I don't get it either," I said.

Lee approached his uncle. "Harry—what's going on?"

"We gotta get out of here. Right now. That's what's going on."

"What's the rush? It looks like you took care of business."

"Business ain't over."

"Okay, then fill me in."

"We gotta get outta here first."

"What the fuck is going on, Harry?" This time I was happy that Lee's anger was calling the shots. I wanted answers too.

"It's a long story," Harry said.

And that was my cue to chime in. "My bet is that it's the exact story we came here to hear."

"Well, you ain't gonna hear it now, boys." Harry rolled his wheelchair across the room. "We're sitting ducks." He stopped in front of a closet and opened it. "Now get over here, Lee, and grab the guns." He pointed to a metal box at the back of the closet. "And the ammo."

"We need to hear that story now," Lee said.

"I told ya—we don't got time."

Lee didn't push it. He walked over to the closet and dragged the box out.

"Harry," I said, impatient and starving for information, "you were waiting for something to show up. How did you know it would?"

"I got lucky—I don't wait every night. Maybe ten times a year. Tonight was one of those nights. I guessed pretty good, huh?"

Lee opened the box and grabbed a rifle and pistol from inside. He tried to hand me the pistol, but I wouldn't take it. I just shook my head. You'd think by now I'd be ready to dish out some vigilante justice, or, at a minimum, use lethal force to protect Nate, but I had been bred to have an aversion to guns, and it was going to be hard to overcome it.

Lee grabbed two boxes of ammo, then went into Harry's bedroom and returned with an army duffel bag. He stuck the rifle, pistol, and ammo inside.

Harry thrust his own rifle toward Lee. "Stick this in there too. Can't be wheeling through the hallways with it. And gimme the pistol."

Lee loaded the pistol, then handed it to Harry, who stuffed it between his thigh and the wheelchair. "Okay—let's go," Harry said.

"Where to?" Lee stuck the duffel bag on Harry's lap and pushed the wheelchair toward the door.

"There's a place that's kinda safe."

"Kind of?" I didn't think that sounded too promising.

"It kept me safe," Harry said. "But you boys are in all sorts of trouble, aren't ya?"

On the way downstairs, and in the elevator, Lee gave Harry a CliffsNotes version of our fateful night at Cold Falls. He told it as a tale of self-defense, explaining that the strange man had hunted him down through the foggy night.

"I had to push him over or he would've killed me," Lee said.

"Don't make no difference," Harry said.

"What are you talking about?" Lee voiced my exact thought.

Harry didn't bother to answer. We were now in the parking lot, and he was focused on our surroundings with keen concentration—every muscle in his body was taut. Lee helped him into the back seat of my car, then folded his wheelchair, which I put in the trunk along with the duffel bag.

As I backed out of my parking space, Lee asked Harry where the place was that he wanted to go, the place that was safe. *Kind of.*

"My old place—on Glebe," Harry said.

Lee shook his head. "We can't. Someone's living there."

"Nah, that's not what I mean. Just go to that block. He don't like it there."

"Who's *he*?'" I said.

"*He's* what my story's about."

"Let's hear it, Uncle Harry," Lee said, then gave me my marching orders. "Head to Glebe and Columbia Pike."

"What happened to the third boy you said was camping with ya at Cold Falls?" Harry asked.

"Quincy's dead," Lee answered. "Drowned."

I looked at Harry in the rearview mirror. "Do you know who killed him? Who killed our wives?" My patience was running thin. Probably because my belief system was cracking. After all, it was hard to admit to myself that a rabid dog had fooled me into thinking it was Lee.

"Let him tell the story," Lee said. "Stories tell you all you need to know."

"Damn right," Harry said.

I took a deep a breath and let it out. Apparently Lee was now the patient one. At least, patient enough to sit through one of Uncle Harry's stories rather than get right to the point.

"Lee, first I gotta fess up," Harry said. "I didn't lose my legs in combat. I told you that 'cause there was no reason to tell you any different. You were a kid and you didn't need to know the truth. But I told your daddy the truth. He didn't believe me, but I can't really blame him. He thinks the curse is just some kind of bad luck. He don't understand the curse, because it's got nothing to do with him."

"I thought you didn't believe in the Bellington curse?" Lee said.

"Not in the way your daddy does."

"But you always told me it was bullshit."

"It's bullshit when it comes to thinking of it like bad luck."

"You're saying you believe it?"

"Listen, I didn't tell you nothing before because I was hoping you'd get off scot-free. Your daddy did."

"But his life is a mess."

"That's just it. His life is a mess because he made it that way. The curse ain't about that. It's more like the Hatfields and McCoys. But one side, one family, is always on the run. We're that side. And it's not all Bellingtons that get messed with. Like I said, your daddy got off scot-free. His problems ain't nothing but his own fault. For me—well, that ain't the case. And from what I'm hearing tonight, it ain't the case for you either."

And why am I involved? I thought. I wasn't a Bellington. I wasn't a Hatfield or McCoy. Was it just because I'd become friends with the wrong kid in middle school? Had my parents been right when they'd warned me, "Don't hang out with the wrong kids"?

"When I was young, I was strong as an ox," Harry continued. "I was captain of the football team. And it wasn't just any team. We were state champs, and that was something back then. This was prime football country, and our team— the Washington-Lee Generals—we were the best of 'em.

"But I wasn't dumb like most of the other players. I knew that football was gonna end. Even if you got a couple more seasons of glory in college, it was gonna end. So I didn't see no use in puttin' it off. I had a hell of a good run with the Generals, so I figured I might as well start in on a career. I signed up for the Marines."

We were back on Route 66, where the glow of the vapor lights along the freeway became the campfire around which Harry told his story.

"That turned out to be the right choice," he said. "They told me I had the brains to be an officer, and that was good enough for me. They sent me to boot camp in South Carolina. For everyone else, that part was hard. For me, it was a piece of cake. I set records on some of the obstacle courses. Yeah—I did real good."

I glanced in the rearview mirror and caught Harry looking down at his legs. I didn't see regret on his face, but I thought I saw a flicker of determination. As for myself, I felt a pang of sorrow.

"I did so good in fact, that I got sent up to Quantico

when I was done. That's where the smart ones got sent—for more specialized training. If I had stayed in South Carolina, would it've made a difference? Maybe I would've been safe. Who knows?

"Anyway, at Quantico, I was getting trained in targeting. My days were jam-packed. Both classroom learnin' and practice. No boozing for me. No women neither. Just didn't have the time. But I felt good. Better than I ever had.

"Then one night Art Craig—he was my best buddy at Quantico—and me drove out to Dumfries for a bachelor party. It wasn't a big deal kinda party like ya see nowadays. We're talking a hotel room, a couple of strippers, and drinking. And even that wasn't as bad as it could've been, because most of the fellas were married and had to work the next day. Art and me had to report at oh six hundred, so we headed back about one in the morning. Art was drunk, and I was pretty wired up too, but not as bad as him.

"Art was drivin', and back then no one gave a rat's ass about drivin' drunk. But that ain't what did us in. What did us in was Art's clunker. That car wasn't fit for the road. But it was never a big deal until that night. It wasn't like we really needed cars. Like I said, our days were jam-packed, so there was no time to do nothing else or go anywhere. And everything was on base. Still, I guess you wanna have some freedom. Too bad."

Harry paused, and I glanced at the rearview mirror again. This time we made eye contact, and he turned up the corners of his mouth in a *what the hell can you do* grimace of disgust at himself.

"Anyway, we were driving down Joplin Road through Prince William Forest Park," he said. "It's old land. They keep it wild. *Untouched*, they call it. They say it ain't changed since the start of our country. It was Chopawamsic land back then."

Lee looked over at me. As I said, the guy was smart. I knew he'd just made the same connection I had, even though it wasn't a strong connection—at least not yet. Cold Falls was old land, prime Native American land, glorified land. Or so we'd believed as kids.

"The clunker started huffin' and puffin' like it was gonna conk out and die," Harry said. "Then it did, right there on goddamn Joplin. *And* it didn't wanna start up again. So we got out and pushed it over to the shoulder, then talked about hitching a ride back. But we decided against it. What if an officer from the base pulled over? He'd see we were drunk. There was no hidin' that. He might do nothing, or he might report us, dependin' on the officer and the mood he was in. So we decided to walk back instead.

"Now, that wasn't such a bad idea. The bad idea was the next one. We decided to cut through Prince William Forest. That way there'd be no chance an officer would spot us. Yeah, that was a dumb move. So we started through the woods, and it was dark as hell. But we didn't think about that until we were too far from the road. And by then it was too late. We were lost. All your training goes out the door when you're drunk.

"But after wandering a little ways, the dark sobered us up—just enough that one part of our training came back. We found a patch where we could see up through the trees to the sky, and we picked out some constellations. Then we were able to figure out what direction the base was in.

"It was slow going at first, but we sobered up some more and got on track. And that was when we heard someone followin' us. It could've been an animal. But if it was, it was a mighty big one. We could tell by the footfalls. So we figured it was a man, and we stopped to check it out—which ain't easy in the dark, no matter what your training is. But we didn't hear nothin' and we didn't see nothin'. The guy only moved when we did. He wasn't stupid.

"So we kept going, and then it started to get a little foggy, which wasn't helping none. So we sped up the best we could to get away. Now, don't get me wrong. It wasn't like we were scared, but something didn't feel right, you know? Like this woods wasn't our place. Like we were trespassing or something.

"Anyway, because of the noise we were making in the brush—louder now 'cause we were going faster—we couldn't hear if he was still followin' us or not. And we were good for a while. I was in the lead. I was better at navigating, checking the constellations and adjusting our direction. But it was gettin' harder. The fog was gettin' thicker so it was harder to see the sky. And then the woods started to stink, like there was a rotting animal around.

"A few seconds later, Art screamed out. I looked back,

figuring he tripped or ran into something, but he must've been hurt bad for him to be yelling like that. Turns out Art was down on the ground and another man was standing over him. Art was floundering around, tryin' to get up, but he just couldn't do it. The fella standin' over him had already taken him down. But the thing was, I could see the guy wasn't beefy. He looked skinny and weak. Sure, he was tall all right—real tall—six ten, maybe seven foot. But I didn't see where the strength was from. He'd put Art down, which wasn't an easy thing to do. And the weirdest thing: he was wearing camo, like he was a marine. But no one on base was that tall.

"Course, that wasn't going through my mind right then. The only thing I was thinking was to go help Art. And that's what I did. But when I got close, close enough to see Art's face—it wasn't a pretty sight, crushed and bloody—the tall man swung his arm at me and sent me smashing into a tree. His arm was like a goddamn club.

"I picked myself back up, ready to jump him, but it was too late. I heard a nasty cracking sound—bones breaking— and Art wasn't trying to get up no more. The tall man stood up from Art, and I saw that Art's head was sideways. His neck was broke.

"Then I looked at the man, and caught sight of his face for a second. He's as calm as the night. His face is kinda soft, and there ain't no sign that he's upset or angry or nothing. He's as calm as an animal going about its life. A well-bred animal. And that calm tells me what I should do next.

"I ain't never run from anything, but this guy's got a look that's tellin' me to get the hell out of there. Besides, Art was already dead. No question about that. So I ran. Didn't get but three yards away when I felt him grab my legs. I went down hard, face first. Didn't know how he caught me so fast. He just wasn't close enough. But I didn't have time to worry about that.

"He was pressin' down on the back of my legs, and I was sure he was gonna move up and snap my neck. I tried to twist around to fight him face to face, but he kept pressing on my legs. A raw sting—burning hot—shot through them, God-awful, and so bad that I screamed out, and then it got worse, shooting through all of me, like lightning made of pain. I heard a cracking sound before I even felt it. He was crushing my legs, and I was screaming so loud that I couldn't think straight.

"I didn't know how long that lasted. But I stopped screaming because I felt like I was gonna pass out. I told myself not to pass out, and I tried to twist around, to look back, to see if he'd gone—but it was too hard to move. The pain was shooting through me and I was throbbing, like I was one big heartbeat. I wasn't really thinking and I just started dragging myself. Maybe back to the road. I didn't really know what I was doing or where I was going. It didn't matter anyway, 'cause I didn't get far.

"I was about to pass out for sure this time when I saw him again. He was standing over me. He said one word, not a word you usually hear, and then he was gone—or I passed out—it was hard to remember.

"The next thing I knew, I woke up in a hospital bed. The nurse ran out to get the doctor, and the doctor came in and told me I was lucky to be alive. Ha! Lucky! I mean, yeah, I was luckier than Art. But if you're young and healthy, it ain't lucky to become a cripple.

"Now I'm going to skip over the parts where I felt sorry for myself—no one needs to hear that crap—and get back to the part you all want to hear. I told the police what happened. And I told the MPs. They were all gung-ho to get the guy. And I made sure to tell them everything. I replayed the whole thing in my head over and over again, so I wouldn't forget nothin'. It was the only way to catch that guy. I talked to the police a lot. Same with the MPs. But months go by and they don't find a thing. Not even one damn lead.

"So when I got better, I got some buddies to take me into the woods, so I could look around. It didn't do any good, except for one thing: I remembered that word. *Bloodlines.* And it don't take a genius to figure out that bloodlines means family. So I dug into our family history. Ya see, my parents, your grandma and grandpa"—in the rearview mirror, I saw him nod over to Lee—"they didn't raise your dad and me tellin' us much about the curse. Sure, they told us we were descendants of the Mayflower colonists. They were proud of that, 'cause we were poor and it was all we had to separate us from the other poor kids. But when it came to the curse, they only talked about it 'cause they had to. 'Cause other relatives brought it up.

"So I looked at the family history myself, and I saw that pattern. You know those stories, Lee. From Jeremiah to Aunt Selma to your poor grandma losing her firstborn when he got hit by a car. But she never blamed it on the curse—"

"My dad did," Lee said.

"Yeah, well, as soon as I told Macon there's something to the Bellington curse, he grabbed on to it like a drowning man grabs on to a life preserver. It means bad luck for all of us, he said. Hell, I was now the prime example. But that's not what I saw in our family history, Lee. What I saw was ancestors getting killed. Accidents, murders, disappearances. And not just Bellingtons, but some of their buddies. Of course, there was that criminal crap, too—the hoodlums and con men— but when you looked at it real close, that part was nothing. I saw a bigger pattern. The Hatfield and McCoys. Maybe I saw it 'cause I lived it. It wasn't bad luck that crushed my legs. It was a goddamn *person*. What if someone drowned Selma or ran down your grandma's firstborn?"

Harry stopped with that question, and I looked in the rearview mirror, waiting for more.

Lee provided more in the form of his own question. "If we're the Hatfields, who are the McCoys?"

"The man who crushed my legs."

That hung there, and I wondered if Harry meant it the way it had sounded. Was he saying there was only *one* McCoy? As the phrase goes, the *real* McCoy? He couldn't possibly expect us to believe that. He had to mean the man who had attacked him was *one* of the McCoys and that other McCoys were responsible for the attacks down through the generations of Bellingtons.

At first, in the silence that followed, I thought Lee must've been thinking the same thing I was. Then I realized he was already predisposed to believe this outlandish idea. After all, he already believed that the man we were tracking was the same man he'd pushed off a cliff twenty-five years ago.

"Harry," I said. "You're not saying there's just one guy responsible for everything that's happened to the Bellingtons." *The guy would have to be hundreds of years old.* "If it's the Hatfield and McCoys"—I looked over to Lee for support, even though I knew it probably wasn't coming— "then it's generational. It's not the same guy battling it out over hundreds of years."

Lee didn't offer his support, and Harry made his case. "You saw that thing come into my apartment and turn into a dog, didn't ya?"

Harry's theory seemed absurd, regardless of what I'd seen. *Fact and fiction. A giant shake and bake.* Sure, those words went through my mind, but it didn't mean I believed them.

"Can we kill him?" Lee asked.

"I don't know, but I know he's got weaknesses."

"Like what?" Lee had lasered in on what I should've been focused on if I wanted to protect Nate.

"Like power plants."

I remembered Lee had said something about his uncle living next to a power substation where the rent had been low.

Lee turned to his uncle. "You think this guy doesn't like power plants?"

"Well, I ain't positive," Harry said. "But I thought I saw him sixteen years ago. Remember Martha? She was my helper back then? Well, she was pushing me back from the drugstore. We shouldn't have gone out at night in the first place, but I'd forgotten to ask her to pick up my blood pressure pills on her way over. The pharmacy had 'em ready. So after dinner, I said let's go get 'em.

"On the way back, this fella started following us—real tall fella. I wanted Martha to slow down so I could get a closer look at him, but I told her just the opposite: speed up, because I got to go to the bathroom. I didn't want her to end up like Art. So we get halfway down my block and the man stops followin' us. He stops in front of Mrs. Barnwell's oak tree, about a hundred yards from the power plant."

"How do you know it was the same guy who attacked you?" I asked. It didn't sound like a positive ID to me.

"I told ya already—I couldn't be sure. I know you ain't really buyin' this, but you wanted my story, so I'm giving it to you."

Lee shot me an annoyed look, then turned back to Harry. "There was more to it, right? There was something that made you think it was him."

"Yeah. There was fog near the drugstore when we got there. Not heavy or nothing, but it was there, and so was that rotten smell. Martha rolled me through the fog and into the store. Inside, I remember thinking, why the hell didn't I just wait on the pills? Skipping one dose ain't gonna kill me, but going out tonight just might. And when I saw him, it confirmed what I'd been thinkin'.

"Then it happened again three years later—same thing. Only this time, I didn't go out for any pills. This time, I went out 'cause I knew. I knew he was waitin'. But I had to see for myself. I had to know for sure. I told Martha that I wanted to get some air. Just a stroll around the block. So she pushed me outside, and we got halfway down the block, and there he was, waitin' for me. In the same spot. Next to Mrs. Barnwell's oak tree. Just waitin' there. About a hundred yards away from the plant. That's why I think he don't like the plant."

"Why didn't he kill you?" I said.

"I'm telling you—because he don't like the plant."

"No—I mean why didn't he kill you near the drugstore? Or why didn't he kill you in Prince William Forest? Or why not before you even moved to the apartment by the power plant?" I found his eyes in the rearview mirror. "And what about Lee? Why didn't he kill Lee when we were kids, back in Cold Falls?"

"It's a game," Harry said.

I shook my head at the absurdity of that answer. But if I'd been clear-headed, and if I'd remembered that we'd come to Harry because he was the next lead, and if I'd been able to break free of the chains that held me down facing the shadows on the wall, I would've made the connection that

Lee made.

"That's what she told us," Lee said. "That's what Otranto said."

And the stakes are life and death. The only kind of game worth playing. It was exactly what she'd said.

Harry added, "If you live hundreds of years, I'm guessing *everything* becomes a game."

I believed that. But don't think I'd accepted that our enemy was hundreds of years old. No—that part I wasn't buying. I was only buying the part about the game. It was the game which dictated who Dantès killed and when. And there was something else I was starting to buy into: the idea that there were unexplainable elements to this game, elements that appeared to be supernatural. But I knew these elements had to have an explanation—one far better than the notion that fact and fiction were one and the same.

Was this the first step in the process of believing it all? How could it not be? Yet I didn't see it that way. Not then. Of course not. In the same way that I couldn't accept that novel therapy was the way through this, I couldn't accept what I was seeing or hearing. If I had, I might have been closer to understanding that Harry's story, like all the stories so far, was leading me deeper into another story—one of the most famous stories of all time.

Chapter Eleven

Harry's former neighborhood consisted of a dozen blocks of red brick, two-story apartment buildings. Decades ago, the area had been a low-income section of Arlington. I remembered it because my mother used to drive through it with me in tow on the way to Seven Corners, a shopping area that bordered Falls Church. The neighborhood had long since been gentrified, as denoted by the faux, old-fashioned streetlamps.

Amid the quaint buildings and landscaped ground, the electric substation stuck out like a sore thumb. It was an ugly island of massive cylinders, grids, and wiring, surrounded by tan, cinderblock walls that were topped with coils of barbed wire. A small parking lot ran alongside the substation, but a metal arm, chained shut, barred entry.

So I couldn't park there, nor could I park in the neighborhood; street parking was restricted to permits, another mark of a gentrified neighborhood. But the drugstore from Harry's story was close by, so we parked there and hoped we wouldn't get towed.

The neighborhood was then treated to a strange sight:

three disheveled men, one being pushed in a wheelchair, moving rather quickly at this late hour, well past midnight, a most unlikely time for a stroll. And if someone in the neighborhood decided to call the police, which in this neighborhood was a real possibility, and if the police were to make a timely appearance, which was also a real possibility, the officers would discover that the man in the wheelchair had a handgun tucked into his waistband.

"So what's the plan?" Harry asked as we approached the substation.

"Your story is supposed to give us the plan," I said. "It's supposed to tell us where to go next."

"So what does it tell you?"

"I don't know yet. I have to figure it out."

"That's kind of tough, ain't it, since you're having a hard time believing me?"

"It doesn't matter whether I believe it or not," I said. "I'm sure the next lead is buried in your story."

"Because that woman told you so."

"That's right," I said. Lee had filled him on Otranto.

Harry was warily eyeing everything we passed, from the apartment buildings, their windows dark, to the hedges, trees, and parked cars. He was on the lookout for the real McCoy. But as we got closer to the substation, he relaxed a bit. He truly believed we had entered some kind of safe zone. A Dantès-free zone.

I began to hope that his unwavering belief in his story would inspire me to uncover the clue buried in his tale—or that somehow the clue would just come to me in one of those light bulb moments. But as it stood, finding such a lead felt like a task of Sisyphean proportions. *Was* there a breadcrumb hidden in Harry's story? I didn't know. What I *did* know was that the most distinctive, and most disturbing, element of his story was this:

Dantès was immortal.

And if Dantès truly had the gift of immortality, then this game of life and death turned on another reality. The shadows on the cave wall, the ones that were *my* reality, might not be of much help, because those shadows didn't allow for immortality. Nor did they allow for a dog to appear as a man, or for a man to have no reflection. For any of that to be real, fiction would have to be exactly like fact. *Wouldn't it?*

But I wasn't ready to accept that. Just because Dantès was a ruthless predator playing an elaborate game didn't mean that he was some kind of immortal being who had lived for centuries. It didn't mean that there wasn't some logical, reasonable explanation for everything I'd seen. For me, the real McCoy was someone who knew about that night in Cold Falls. The real McCoy was the person getting revenge for Lee's crime. The real McCoy was a flesh-and-blood man seeking retribution on all of us. Not some immortal bogeyman.

I focused on my surroundings—the manicured lawns, the golden glow of the streetlamps, the quaint, red brick buildings—to get a handhold on reality, the reality I saw around me, rather than the reality in Harry's story. *This* was my world, and I told myself that I needed do my best to stay firmly in it.

We made it to the substation, where we picked Harry up and lifted him over the parking lot's metal bar, followed by the wheelchair. Then we all headed to the back of the parking lot, hoping no one would notice the three strange men loitering at the substation. The place was lit by vapor lights, and though one side of the lot was nothing but the concrete wall that penned in the station, the other side and the back were lined with privacy hedges.

"There were no hedges when I lived here," Harry said, then motioned to the apartment building next to the substation. The building's second story was visible above the hedges, and every window facing us was dark. "The back apartment there—that was my place. A damn fine place, too—"

Harry suddenly stopped in mid-sentence, and peered anxiously at the building.

I looked in that direction but didn't see anything suspicious. As I was trying to figure out what Harry had latched on to, I realized that I was hyperaware of the sounds around me. The buzzing of the vapor lights wasn't just one solid drone—I could hear each light sizzling and crackling as if they were individual campfires. And the chirps of the crickets were more than a blanket of undifferentiated noise— I could hear distinct groups chirruping as if I were listening to individual sections of an orchestra. Even the distant sounds were coming in loud and clear: cars whooshing down Glebe Road a few blocks away, an owl hooting—and another, farther away, hooting back—and a dog baying glumly, as if pining for his owner to come home.

A beat later, my eyes caught up to the sensitivity of my ears and I saw why Harry was anxious. At the far end of his former building, one of the residents was looking out of a second-story window.

"We should go," I said. "They probably called the cops already."

"We got to stay here until we know what we're doing," Harry said. "This plant is what's keeping him away."

Lee turned to me. "You've got nothing, right?"

I shook my head, and wanted to add, *I got nothing, so why don't* you *come up with something for a change?* but didn't—he was on my side.

"Harry—I don't like taking off, either," Lee said, "but I know it's not going to look good if the cops find us here. You got a gun on you, and that'll lead them to the rifles in the car, and they're not going to let that slide. They're going to make a few calls and find a dog lying dead in your living room, shot in the head, and that's not going to go over too good either."

"Then let's just get our butts to another power station," Harry said without missing a beat.

It was great that one of us was thinking straight. Harry's mind wasn't clouded with trying to distinguish between fact and fiction. His goal was simply to survive.

Lee and I used our cell phones to search for other substations. We didn't just pick the closest one, though—instead we picked one that was isolated, in a neighborhood with big lots, so there wouldn't be a lot of neighbors. And it abutted Windy Run Park, so there were no neighbors at all on that side of it.

Lee wheeled Harry across the parking lot, and I fell in line. We passed Harry over the metal gate, placed him back in his wheelchair, then headed toward the car. My hypersensitivity was still in full swing. The roar of a plane descending into Reagan Airport was so loud that my bones vibrated. Water flowing in the sewer pipe below the sidewalk babbled so clearly, it was as if I were lying in the gutter listening through the storm drain. And I could hear, emanating from deep inside an apartment, the haunting laughs, compressed and tinny, from the laugh track of an old TV show.

The sights were magnified, too. The street's granular surface glimmered brightly under the pools of light cast down from the streetlamps—every tiny grain of asphalt sparkled. The pitting in the concrete sidewalk formed thousands of distinct little black wells. And each of the blades of grass that made up the broad lawns reflected its own slice of the moonlight above.

I wondered if my keen awareness was more than that. Was I seeing another world? Another reality? I didn't have an answer, but I did tell myself that whatever was happening was a good thing. This was the road that would lead to Dantès. He was hiding in this other world.

Of course that's crazy talk. Crazy talk bubbling to the surface right after I'd made a decision to steer clear of fiction and steer closer to fact.

We made it back to the car, got in, and drove off. It was late enough now that the streets had little traffic, and the way to Windy Run was familiar territory—Shirlington to Glebe to Lee Highway to Lorcom Lane. I went on autopilot so I could concentrate on Harry's story.

This time I accepted the help of my crazy talk—I didn't try to separate fact from fiction. Instead I just searched for clues, connections, and leads. I turned Harry's story over, this way and that, looking for a detail that might lead somewhere—and I came back to the connection between Cold Falls and Prince William Forest. Then I followed this a little farther down the trail.

Harry had said that Prince William Forest was originally Chopawamsic land, and I knew that Cold Falls had been prime Native American land. The Potomac itself was named after the Patawomeck Indians; I remembered that from my Virginia history class. All of Northern Virginia had once been prime Native American land—glorified land.

Okay... so how was this helpful? I glanced at Harry in the rearview mirror and made another connection. The Bellington genealogy stretched all the way back to that period of American history. Plymouth Colony was the beginning of American history, *and* it was also the beginning of the end of Native American land.

But what did this mean? How was it related to Dantès? I

didn't have an answer to those questions—*what a surprise*—but I had found the right trail, just as surely as those first colonists had entered a new world. And in a way, I had entered a new world, too. But I couldn't yet make out exactly what this new world looked like—and I had no idea that I was closing in on Dantès's identity.

But Dantès must've known. He must've known me so well that he'd calculated exactly when I'd find this trail into the new world. He knew that right about now I'd start to pull against my chains and try to look back at the fire to get a glimpse of the real figures, the ones casting the shadows on the wall.

He must've known, because he made his game-altering move right then.

We were close to Windy Run, not more than a half dozen blocks away, and I was stopped at a stop sign. Our car was the only car at the intersection, and we were the only souls here. The houses up and down the street—large, beautiful homes set back on outsized pieces of property—were dark, shuttered for the night.

I was just about to pull forward when out of the corner of my eye I caught a glimpse of someone rushing the passenger side of the car—nothing more than blur of pale skin. I took my foot off the brake, but before I could punch down on the gas, the passenger window shattered in a spray of glass.

Lee reacted instantly, jerking away from the attack, but the glass shards had already done their damage: his face was streaked with bleeding cuts.

A pair of hands—long and bony—reached into the car, seized Lee's head, and pulled it toward the window. Lee grabbed at the hands and tried to pry them off. I lunged at the thin arms belonging to those bony hands and punched at them. But the man behind those arms was too strong.

He hauled Lee out by the head, and Lee's torso was through the window so swiftly you'd think neither of us had offered up any resistance whatsoever. I grabbed at Lee's legs, but they slid through my hands before I could get a grip on them.

Then the sharp sound of gunfire suddenly erupted, shattering the back passenger window. It was Harry—he'd gotten off two shots.

But if those shots had hit home, there was no sign of it. Our attacker—a thin man dressed in black—had Lee's head in a death grip and was now dragging him across the asphalt toward the sidewalk. It was too dark to make out the man's face, but I could see Lee, his legs kicking and his arms desperately trying to grab at his assailant.

Harry aimed the gun through the shattered window and fired another shot.

The man stopped, and for a second I thought Harry's bullet had hit its target. But that wasn't the case. The man had made it to the sidewalk, where he lifted Lee's head, then whipped it hard into the curb.

Lee's body went limp.

I was slack-jawed, overwhelmed with disbelief, but Harry fired off another round. If his shot struck the man, the man showed no sign of it. He just turned from Lee's body and walked away, in no hurry, down the sidewalk.

Harry threw open the back door. "Get me over to Lee!" he said.

I slammed the car in park, jumped out, and circled around. But I didn't go over to help Harry. Instead I raced straight for Lee. It crossed my mind to pursue the man—but that option was taken off the table as soon as I glanced down the block. The man was gone as if he'd somehow folded himself into the darkness.

I kneeled down beside Lee. He was out cold. I reached out and turned his body over—and gasped. The blow he'd suffered was brutal. The edge of the curb had opened a deep, bloody gouge in his forehead. Down to the bone. His eyes were open, glassy, and lifeless. Blood oozed from his gaping wound into his eyes, over them, and down his cheeks onto the street.

"Get him back in the car!" Harry yelled from his perch in the back seat.

I pressed my middle and index fingers against Lee's wrist, hoping to feel his pulse. I waited for the soft thump—the sign of life. When I didn't feel anything, I closed my eyes and held my breath and pressed a little harder.

A few seconds went by. Nothing.

Eyes still closed, I stuck with it for another half minute. There wasn't the slightest hint of a pulse.

I remained kneeling over Lee's body. I wasn't exactly praying, but I wasn't exactly not praying, either. Lee's death was a culmination of sorts. My sympathy for Lee was deep, and the pit of my stomach ached. It ached for Lee, and also for Nate—because at that moment, I realized that there was no way to win this game. That was where this trail was leading.

Where else could a trail into hell lead?

Yet, somehow, for Nate's sake, I had to move forward anyway. I had to lie to myself and tell myself I could win this game. Against all odds, I had to believe I could win. *They call that faith*, I thought. And that's why I'm saying I wasn't exactly praying, but it was close.

Finally, I opened my eyes and looked back at Harry. When I met his gaze, I saw fear in his eyes. He hadn't betrayed *any* fear all evening. He'd been cool when the dog had entered his apartment and calm when he'd executed it. But facing Lee's death was something altogether different. Lee had been Harry's lifeline.

I stood up.

Harry slid back from his perch on the back seat and pulled his car door shut.

Chapter Twelve

"We can't go to the Windy Run substation now," I said, accelerating down the block and around the corner. "I'm sure one of the neighbors heard the gunshots and the cops are on their way." Lights had already come on in a few of the houses.

I glanced in the rearview mirror. Harry didn't respond. He was staring out the shattered window, and the fear I'd seen in his eyes had spread to the rest of his face. It was drained of color.

"When we get far enough away, I'll pull over and look up another substation," I said.

Harry wasn't adding his two cents' worth. Not that I blamed him. He was shaken by Lee's death.

We drove for about ten minutes in silence. The entire time, I tried to keep my mind off of Lee's murder and on my route. I wanted to avoid main streets and even those side streets where police cruisers would be on the lookout for anyone associated with the dead body—which by now they'd certainly found. Luckily, Arlington was my home turf and I knew what streets to avoid.

"Lee wasn't like his dad," Harry said, his shaky voice breaking the silence. "He had some rough patches, but he never made excuses. And he got it all together when he married Grace. She was a sweetheart. So was he. Hot head and all."

His eyes watered up, so I looked away from the rearview mirror to give him some privacy.

"Goddamnit," he said. "Why the hell didn't this fucker go for Macon? I know that's an evil thing to say of your own brother, but it's the damn truth. If he wanted another Bellington, he shoulda taken Macon. That boy ain't never gonna turn his life around."

I couldn't help but glance at the rearview again. Harry was wiping tears from his cheeks when he suddenly turned to the mirror and caught me looking at him. "Why you?" he said.

"Why me what?"

"Why did Dantès—ain't that what you call him?—pull *you* into this?"

"I don't know," I said. This was the very same question I'd been asking myself since the moment Harry first presented his Hatfield and McCoy theory. "I'm not a Bellington, so why'd he add me to his list?"

"You wanna know what I think?"

"Of course."

"Are you gonna believe me?"

I glanced over my shoulder and met his gaze. The fear on his face was changing back to confidence; his jaw was taut and his brow was stern. So was I going to believe him? I didn't know, but I said yes, and I did my best to look like I meant it.

"I know you ain't gonna believe me," he said. "At least not yet. So why don't we start with what *you're* thinking? Why do *you* think he's playing his games with you?"

"I was there that night at Cold Falls with Lee," I said. "Wrong place, wrong time." That was the only explanation I had.

"Nah. You're thinking small. That ain't the reason, and you know that in your heart. Do you really think this guy is playing that simple a game?"

Harry was right. I already understood that Dantès was playing chess while I was playing checkers.

"He killed Art Craig, my buddy," Harry said, "and I never did figure out why. And it's not like I haven't had the time to think about it. I've had years to think about it and I still haven't come up with a damn thing. But I know it wasn't random."

"What about chalking it up to collateral damage?"

"Don't you worry. I thought of that. But this guy don't do collateral damage. He's laser-guided, not a daisy cutter."

I couldn't have agreed more. Dantès's modus operandi wouldn't allow for randomness. His games were too elaborate, too planned, spanning decades—even centuries if Harry was to be believed. Dantès was doling out breadcrumbs, but the breadcrumbs were part of this elaborate game. And this game was the key to fighting him. This game was the big picture. It was the loaf of bread from which

Dantès was plucking his breadcrumbs.

And what *was* the big picture? Why *had* I been drawn into this?

"As far as we know," I said, "there are five people who aren't Bellingtons that are part of this. Grace—Lee's wife—and Lucy—my wife. Then Quincy, Art, and me."

"Nah, take it from me. Lee's wife counts as a Bellington. Dantès don't discriminate. I saw what he done going way back, and marrying in counts."

So that left Lucy, Quincy, Art, and me—and I got it right then and there. The big picture suddenly came into focus. The light bulb moment was shining bright. My heart started racing and my chest tightened. I was elated, frightened, and even more baffled than before. Baffled because even though I had just now graduated from checkers to chess, moving forward with this clue meant I'd have to trust more in the very thing I was running from.

Novel therapy. The one place I didn't want to look for leads. The place that had failed me. But novel therapy now pointed to one book. One very specific book.

Lucy, Quincy, Art, and me—John. Those were the names of the four main characters in one of the most famous books of supernatural fiction: *Dracula*. Lucy Westenra, Quincey Morris, Arthur Holmwoode, and Jonathan Harker.

"I have a lead," I said, though I had no idea how to interpret the lead, or what Dantès meant by it.

I laid it out for Harry, explaining that Dantès's primary way of playing his game with me was through books and stories. Stories were how I'd gotten to Harry in the first place, so it was hard to argue against following this new lead.

As usual, Harry's reaction was direct. "Are you tellin' me that this thing is Dracula?"

"I'm telling you that the next lead is in that book."

"What kinda lead is gonna be in that book?"

"I don't know." I pulled the car over. It was time to find another substation and dive into this new lead. We were in one of Arlington's densely populated corridors of condominiums, so I could park and not look suspicious.

"You're not telling me we're gonna be running a stake through this guy's heart, are you?" Harry said.

"Listen, we're not chasing down Dracula. We're chasing down a lead." I looked back at him. "Why is it so easy for you to believe that Dantès is hundreds of years old, but not so easy to go with a stake through the heart?"

"So you *are* sayin' he's Dracula?"

"Absolutely not. Besides, I'm not looking to kill Dantès."

"Oh yeah? Then why are we hunting him down?"

I finally told him about the letter. "If I can find Dantès's identity, he'll spare Nate's life."

"Well, *I* wanna kill him," Harry said. "And that way you'll be goddamn sure your son is safe."

It was hard to argue with that, so I didn't. Instead, I moved on to the task at hand. I pulled out my cell phone, located a substation, which turned out to be fairly close, and headed in that direction.

On the way, I thought about *Dracula*, trying to remember

what I could about the book. It'd been a long time since I'd read it—my teenage years—but I'd read it quite a number of times. If I could remember the names of the characters, certainly I could remember more. And Dantès was counting on that, wasn't he?

He was forcing me to travel further into the world of fiction. But I was still fighting it—I was staring hard at the reality around me, looking for it to ground me. Yet the condominiums I passed looked fake, as if they were movie sets, empty of life inside, just mock-ups. The whole neighborhood was nothing but a shadow cast on a blank wall. It wasn't real. Somewhere out there, beyond the stretch of condominiums, the real objects that cast those shadows were visible.

But I couldn't see those objects. Not just yet. Though Dantès had loosened my chains, forced me to consider that reality was a shake and bake of fact and fiction, the fiction part wasn't visible yet.

"So what's in that book?" Harry said.

"I'm going to have to take a look at it," I answered.

"Are you kidding me? You're gonna take time out to read."

"I don't remember the book well enough."

"My bet is you do."

"How do you know?"

"You just finished telling me that books have been helping you all night—even though you don't want them to, right?"

"Yeah."

"But you ain't been *reading* books all night, right? You been moving forward usin' what you remember about them."

That shut me up. When something strikes you as right, you don't have to analyze it. So what else did I remember about *Dracula*? A lot about its plot and a lot about the folklore that Bram Stoker, *Dracula's* author, had created. Folklore that had spawned hundreds of vampire books, comics, TV shows, and films.

And I remembered Jonathan Harker, the novel's main character—the character who bore my name. During his stay in Dracula's castle, he witnessed some bizarre occurrences: Dracula climbing out of a window and crawling down the wall like a lizard, Dracula turning into a bat, Dracula sleeping in a wooden box filled with dirt, and more. Harker dismissed these strange events as hallucinations. Or worse—he thought he was descending into madness.

Was I following in his footsteps?

Harry interrupted my train of thought. "The names made you think about the book, right?"

"That's right."

"What about Dracula? You ain't said nothing about his name."

Names. Wasn't this entire trip through hell about names? Searching for Dantès's true identity. His name. Time to double down on names.

I pulled over.

"What are you doing?" Harry leaned forward in his seat. "We're not at the power plant."

"Checking to see how Bram Stoker came up with the name Dracula." Hopefully the web would dispense that information with ease.

My search quickly yielded that Bram Stoker had gotten the name "Dracula" from a Romanian folk hero who'd lived in the Middle Ages. That was a start, but it didn't help. Luckily it only took a bit more digging to find something that *did* help—something that applied to me directly.

I found an article that had another detail about the origin of the name "Dracula," and if I'd had more faith in my hunches, I wouldn't have had to read the article at all. Our next move was right there in the title. But, as usual, I had doubts about anything that had do with novel therapy, so I read the article.

It explained that Stoker had discovered the name "Dracula" in the Whitby library. Whitby was a small English town, and Stoker had set part of *Dracula* in Whitby as a tribute to its library. Then the article went on to list a dozen other examples of authors who'd also found major elements of their novels during visits to their local libraries.

The point of the article was that libraries had once been holy places for writers, and that this was no longer the case. For centuries, any information writers needed for their stories was waiting for them in that vast reservoir of books known as their local library. But in this day and age, almost any information could be harvested from the web—just as I was doing right then. So writers had lost something when their local library had ceased to be their holy place.

The title of the article was *Libraries: Holy Reservoirs.*

*

Twenty minutes later, we pulled into the employee parking lot of the Cherrydale Public Library—my local library *and* my workplace. Harry hadn't totally bought into this lead, but he wasn't dismissive either. "It was your idea to check out the name Dracula," I'd told him, to help him see it my way.

I got out of the car, pulled Harry's wheelchair from the trunk, and helped him get in.

"Gimme my rifle," he said. "And you take this." He tried to hand me his handgun.

"I don't need it."

"Yeah, you do. It's just that you don't want it, right?"

I stared at the gun. My aversion to the weapon was visceral and powerful.

"Listen," he said. "You saw what he did to Lee. He don't fuck around. If he decides to kill you, you're gonna wanna defend yourself."

I still couldn't do it. "If he decides to kill me, I don't know if that's going to help."

Harry shook his head. "Suit yourself." He shoved the gun back into his waistband. "Then forget the rifle—just get me some extra rounds. Pistol ammo's in the blue box."

I did as I was told, then wheeled Harry to the employee entrance, punched in the access code, and headed inside. To say I was entering my workplace under bizarre circumstances would have been a great understatement. The person who'd walked out of this library less than twelve hours ago wasn't the same person who was walking in now. My life had changed so much as to be completely unrecognizable.

I wheeled Harry through the library's administrative area, past desks piled high with files, and through the double doors into the library's foyer. We rolled past the checkout counter and the bulletin boards advertising local events, then into the main room, where the books were shelved. Tens of thousands of stories, neatly arranged by author, as if organization could bring order to the chaos of fiction.

"Now what?" Harry said.

I had an answer, but it was just a placeholder until I could find out why Dantès wanted us here. "We're checking out the library's copies of *Dracula*."

"So you *are* going to take time out to read?"

"I didn't say that. But checking out those copies might lead to something: a clue scrawled inside a copy of the book, or maybe something down that aisle." *It could be anything*, I thought, based on Dantès's pattern.

And that would turn out to be true. It would be something unexpected—but for once it would be easy to believe it was the right breadcrumb.

On the way to the correct aisle, I scanned everything I passed, looking for the next lead. The displays—one highlighting bestselling mysteries, another graphic novels, another YA books about zombies—didn't call out to me. It was only when my eyes fell on the last display that the trumpets sounded. The call to arms was loud and clear.

I couldn't connect the other breadcrumbs from tonight into a bigger picture yet. A homeless man giving directions to

Dante's *Inferno*; a bartender spouting Plato; a man in a wheelchair waiting in a dingy apartment for a dog to attack him. No, I couldn't see the bigger picture. But on the other hand, I knew that what I saw in front of me fit perfectly:

Barbara's display on Virginia history.

I pushed Harry up to the display. He eyed me suspiciously. "What are you doing?"

"There's something we need in one of these books."

"My eyes ain't that good, but none of 'em say *Dracula*."

"No—think history," I said. That was the recurring motif. That was the part of the big picture I *could* see. "We're talking about the Bellington curse down through the ages. Your genealogy."

"You're barking up the wrong tree. This here's about Virginia history. John Bellington, the Mayflower, Plymouth Colony—that's Massachusetts history."

"Yeah, but remember when you said I'm thinking small?"

He nodded.

"Now you're the one who's thinking small. Think of the country back then. It was all Native American land. Prince William Forest, Cold Falls, the Potomac, and everything up and down the coast. Massachusetts and Virginia were all glorified land if you go back far enough."

Harry shook his head. "What the hell is glorified land?"

I was about to explain that it was a figure of speech, a magical figure of speech that had drawn many kids, including me, to Cold Falls to find that land, when I heard Nate's voice—

"You killed Mom."

I hurried from the display toward the voice. It was coming from the adjoining aisle. Of course, it couldn't be Nate's voice. Unless Jenna had brought him here? *In the dead of night? Why?* Dread bloomed in my chest. Whatever was going on, it had to be horrible.

I peered down the aisle and saw Nate. He was walking toward me from the other end of the aisle. The blue in his eyes was overpowered by large black pupils, cold and hard and fixed on me.

"Nate," I said, racing to him. "Are you okay?"

"Why'd you kill Mom?"

I knelt down to him. "I didn't." I leaned forward to hug him.

He backed away. "Then why didn't you talk about her after she died?" His face was ghostly pale, infused with the agony of doubt—doubt about me. His black eyes bore into mine, searching for an answer.

"I couldn't talk about her—" I began.

"Because you killed her."

"No!"

He cowered away from me, like an animal who'd just been wounded. "You're lying," he said. His lips were quivering.

"I'm so sorry," I said. "I was having a hard time, honey. A hard time letting go of her."

"You're lying. 'Cause you *still* don't want to talk about her."

"No, that's not it. Once you stopped bringing her up, I

just didn't want to remind you about her. I thought it would make you sad."

"I stopped talking about her because *you* wanted me to stop! She doesn't make *me* feel sad. I love her."

"So do I, honey." Tears were forming in my eyes.

"You took me to Aunt Jenna's because the police know you killed her. You're running away from them."

"No… no. I took you to Aunt Jenna's because—" I couldn't tell him why.

"Because you don't want to take me with you," he said.

"That's not it at all. Please, Nate." I reached for him, to bring him closer to me, to hug him and assure him, to let him know I loved him more than anything in the world. But just before I wrapped my arms around him—his head swung down, his jaws opened, and he bit my arm. A vicious, deep bite, like a ravenous pit bull clamping down on a piece of raw meat.

He wasn't letting go.

I screamed out and instinctually tried to push his head off my arm, but his jaws were locked on to my flesh. *This isn't Nate*, I thought, and I pushed his small body as hard as I could.

He tumbled back with a piece of my flesh between his teeth. His eyes were wild, and his black pupils were tinged with a golden glow. He lunged right back at me and savagely chomped down into my shoulder. As a red-hot pain shot through my body, I grabbed at him and tried to shake him off.

Out of nowhere, a gunshot rang out, unnaturally loud, like a wake-up call from another world.

Nate tumbled off of me onto the floor. He was heaving and shuddering.

"Oh my God!" I kneeled down over him.

His neck was ripped open where the bullet had struck, and blood flowed unabated from the wound. I tried to stanch the flow with my hand, but Nate was already in his death throes, wheezing and quivering.

I lifted his small body and held him to me, embracing him. I felt his shuddering and his harsh gasps for air vibrating through my own body as if I were dying with him.

With his head cradled in the crook of my arm, I looked over my shoulder, at Harry. He was at the end of the aisle, gun in hand. His eyes weren't on me. They were on Nate.

"You killed him…" I managed to croak out.

"It ain't him," Harry said flatly.

"You don't know that."

"You still ain't buying it."

"I can't buy it." Nate stopped wheezing and quivering. His body went limp. I held him more tightly. My shirt was warm with his blood.

Harry wheeled forward. "Who do you think you're fighting? We got no chance unless you open your goddamn eyes."

"Who *are* we fighting?"

"Someone who fucks with your head."

I clung to Nate's body. My sweet son, fragile, all hope

extinguished.

Harry waved the gun at Nate. "Look for yourself."

I didn't even have to look—I already felt that the small body in my arms was gone. In its place was cold, clammy air that clung to my arms. It had a weight of its own, pressing down on me. And when I did look, I saw it had a presence, too. Thick, white mist. Foul-smelling.

The mist suddenly dispersed in a rush, revealing a bat. An ugly creature. Scraggly dark gray fur and black, cold eyes— Nate's eyes, at least the ones I'd just seen. It spread its bony, leathery wings and bolted up into the air, then flew over the bookshelves, leaving no sign of mist or Nate or our whole creepy and bloody encounter.

I couldn't have asked for a more direct reference to *Dracula*. Yet it was still hard to accept, and harder still to decipher. The giant shake and bake, where fact and fiction were the same, had been laid bare in front of me. I'd just lived it. This was what Harry wanted me to see.

But I was like Jonathan Harker in *Dracula*. To me, hallucinations and madness were far more acceptable explanations. Like Harker, who'd been trapped in Dracula's castle, witnessing a gala of supernatural events, I, too, was trapped—and my reaction, like his, was to cling to the idea that I was slipping away from reality. I couldn't accept that I'd been dragged into a new world that was just as real as my former world.

But Harker had eventually come around. He'd accepted the giant shake and bake. Was that the lesson here? Courtesy of novel therapy? The therapy I despised? And if I accepted that the threat looming over Nate was supernatural, did that get me any closer to stopping it?

Right then, another critical element of *Dracula* came back to me. Of course, it was my desperation for answers that made this element seem critical. The element had to do with how Bram Stoker had laid out his story. A large chunk of it wasn't about Dracula at all. It was about Van Helsing, an expert on vampires, and his efforts to convince the other characters in the book that such a creature as Dracula existed. *I* needed to be convinced, too.

"Are you gettin' closer to believing what you're seeing?" Harry was eyeing the top of the bookshelves as if he was expecting the bat to return.

I was getting closer, but I didn't say so. "Let's look at that Virginia history display."

Harry wheeled around and headed back toward it. As I followed, I noticed that my shirt was no longer drenched in Nate's blood. It was drenched in the mist's clammy waters, as if I'd been baptized in the waters of a netherworld. A netherworld where doubt turned into belief. Dantès had made his point, and the only thing left for us to do in the Cherrydale Public Library was to find that breadcrumb.

Chapter Thirteen

The Virginia history display featured a dozen books. While Harry clutched his gun and kept a lookout, wary of another attack, I quickly scoped them out. Each book focused on a different period of Virginia's history—from colonial times, through the American Revolution, to just after the Civil War.

When my eyes landed on a slim volume titled *The Forest*, I considered the connection. Cold Falls and Prince William Forest—both forests, as was Windy Run, which ran all the way down to the Potomac, and we'd been only blocks from Windy Run when Dantès had emerged to kill Lee. But this was a stretch—wasn't it?—and not enough to lead to any conclusion. And the author's name, Edna Grayson, didn't strike me as something to get excited about.

But when I got to the editor's name, in small lettering, under the author's name, my breath caught in my throat. *Jonathan Harker*. The character in *Dracula* who had to be convinced he wasn't hallucinating. And my own namesake in this giant shake and bake.

I grabbed the book and flipped it open. From the preface, I learned that Jonathan Harker was a history professor at

Virginia Tech. While he was working on a restoration project in Williamsburg, he'd come across an unfinished short story written by one of the original settlers of Jamestown. He discovered this previously unknown story among the items stored in the attic of a nineteenth-century plantation home, the centerpiece of the restoration project. The story had been hidden in a desktop Bible, slipped in between the Bible's pages, one page of the story inserted every fifty pages or so. The Bible was old, but the parchment pages on which the story was written were far older.

Harker discovered that the parchment and ink were consistent with what had been used at the time of the Jamestown Colony. Also, the parchment had aged at the same rate as other documents from that period. But just to make sure he'd discovered something special, he had a sample from the parchment tested in a lab. The results confirmed his theory. This short story dated back to the Jamestown Colony and, therefore, it was the first story written on American soil.

Jonathan Harker had unearthed the first American short story.

Then he went on to explain that some of the parchment pages that made up *The Forest* were missing—so the story was incomplete, and this greatly disappointed him. At first, he published the incomplete version of *The Forest* in academic journals, but later, he decided he'd try and fill in the missing pieces.

His first task was to find out who'd written the story, and this ended up taking years of extensive research. The author turned out to be Edna Grayson—listed as Mrs. Horace Grayson in Jamestown's official records. She'd arrived in Jamestown with her husband and four children, on the *Susan Constant*, one of the three ships that had transported the original colonists. Harker learned as much as he could about Edna Grayson and about the Jamestown Colony, and using that research as a guide, in addition to the story pages he had, he completed her story. The result was the book I now held in my hands.

"This is why we're here," I said. "A stripped-down version of U.S. history starts with three colonies. The Plymouth Colony—that's where we get the Bellington connection. The Roanoke Colony—that's where we get the connection to Quincy. Dantès killed him on Roanoke Island. And now we have the last of the trifecta—the Jamestown Colony." *And*, I thought to myself, *we have another story*: The Forest.

A rustling sound started to rise in the library, an expansive soft swooshing, seemingly from all around us. Both Harry and I scanned the room, but there was nothing to see. Yet the sound was becoming more distinct, a wing-like batting of the air.

"Let's go," Harry said, spinning his wheelchair around.

I handed him *The Forest* and started pushing him toward the foyer. We looked down each aisle we passed because it was now clear that the swooshing was radiating from the direction of the bookshelves, though the precise source of it still wasn't evident. Harry had his gun ready.

We were just a few aisles away from the foyer when the

books, en masse, began to rock back and forth ever so slightly, almost imperceptibly.

"Do you see that?" I said.

"Yep," Harry said. "You're catchin' on."

The books then began to pitch back and forth with greater force, as if they were reacting to an earthquake.

I picked up my pace, wheeling Harry faster.

The books, their covers various colors—blue, white, yellow, red—were all changing to one color: dark brown. And there was a new sound—a scratching, like claws clicking for purchase on a ledge.

Then the books morphed from their rectangular shapes to oval shapes.

And the ovals grew fur.

We were still about ten yards from the foyer when the books completely morphed into bats—thousands of them.

"Shit!" I took off, pushing Harry—but it was too late.

The bats flew off the shelves in a massive swarm, covering the room in a dark brown, undulating cloud. An instant later, a platoon of them swooped down on me, but not before I was able to give a final push to Harry's wheelchair. Hopefully he'd find safety in the foyer.

Then I desperately swung at the bats, trying to knock them away. But I was outnumbered—they relentlessly charged at me in waves. I lurched my way forward, swatting at the horde, but the attack intensified. They were battering me. Some clung to me with their claws. I swiped at them, but I was met with an unremitting swell of wings and teeth. The blistering pain of dozens of bites and scratches seared through me—I felt like I'd been lit on fire.

For a fraction of a second, through the cloud of brown, I caught a glimpse of the foyer, which looked clear. I forced myself to stagger toward it, stumbling through the sea of rabid monsters. But the room was so thick with bats that I tripped over the ones swarming at my legs and tumbled to the floor.

A fresh horde swooped down on me then, going in for the kill. I swung at them wildly, but it was hopeless. They were clawing and biting me and were now so concentrated that I was having a hard time breathing in without sucking parts of them into my mouth. I spat out wing tips and claws and fur and who knew what else, and choked as I did.

Finally, I whipped my hands up and covered my eyes for fear the creatures would gouge them out. With my eyes shielded, I resorted to willing away the bats as if they were a hallucination. As if *I* were Jonathan Harker in *Dracula*, who'd spent many months after his visit to Count Dracula's castle convincing himself he'd gone temporarily mad and that none of what he'd seen was real.

But the bats were clawing and biting my hands, ripping my skin raw, trying to force me to uncover my eyes and see just how real they were. They were as real as their thousand bites, each cutting me to my core, the agony so overwhelming that my brain was about to shut down.

Fact or fiction. It's all the same.

I believed it—

And before I even opened my eyes, I felt that the bats were gone.

And when I did open my eyes, I saw that, indeed, every one of them had disappeared. The library was silent, and all the books were back on the shelves.

I sat up, bewildered. Not only was the pain gone, but my hands and arms were healed. Not one bite or scratch anywhere on me, and my clothes were completely intact. Not even one tiny rip.

Harry rolled up to me. His eyes were wide with surprise. "You stopped it, didn't ya?"

"Beginner's luck."

"Nah—it ain't luck. Like I said, you're catchin' on."

I wheeled Harry toward the administrative offices, glancing down to make sure he still had the copy of *The Forest*. It was in his lap. He picked it up and waved it at me. "Mission accomplished, huh?" he said.

"You're catching on, too," I responded.

*

We parked in front of one of Arlington's largest electrical substations, one near a shopping center and major roads. We didn't have to worry about nosy neighbors here because there were none. The rising sun was starting to lighten the sky, so the main risk now, other than Dantès, came from the Arlington police. If someone had spotted our car driving away from Lee's body, police cruisers would be on the lookout for us, and with dawn here, our car would be easy to spot.

As soon as I cut the engine, I dove into *The Forest*, picking up where I'd left off in the preface. Every few pages, I filled Harry in.

After making the case that Edna Grayson's story was the first piece of fiction written by an English settler in the Americas, Jonathan Harker—the Virginia Tech history professor, not the fictional character from *Dracula*—launched into a lengthy description of the conditions under which Edna had written the story, explaining that this context would shed light on the story itself.

The original settlers of Jamestown—the Englishmen who'd arrived on the *Susan Constant*, *Discovery*, and *Godspeed*—had built their settlement in Tsenacommacah, a large swath of land which itself was part of a much larger territory known as the Powhatan Confederacy. The confederacy was made up of Native American tribes, all of Algonquin descent.

Unfortunately for the settlers, Tsenacommacah was inhabited by one of these tribes, the Paspahegh. Not that this was a problem at first. Far from it: the Paspahegh welcomed the settlers, and the tribe's hospitality extended well beyond just a cordial embrace. The settlers were poorly prepared for their new environment, and the only reason they survived in this new world was because of the tribe's help.

There were regular meetings, both formal and informal, between the Paspahegh leaders and the colony's leaders. These were men-only affairs, and this is where Edna

Grayson's story really started. She befriended some of the Paspahegh on her own because she was interested in learning as much as she could about her new environment. She wanted her kids to thrive in the new world, and she understood that the Paspahegh could help with that.

But what she didn't know was that the colony leaders, including her husband, Mr. Horace Grayson, were secretly plotting to drive the Paspahegh from their land. Mr. Grayson hid this from his wife.

As it turned out, driving the Paspahegh from Tsenacommacah would have been a far better fate for the tribe than what the settlers actually ended up doing: wiping out the entire Paspahegh population over the course of the next three years.

The confrontations were small at first—mostly skirmishes over right-of-way—so Edna was able to keep up her friendships with the tribe, even though the settlers who knew about these friendships frowned on them. Unlike the majority of her peers, Edna believed that the English and the Native Americans could share this land and live in peace.

After about a year of these skirmishes, Edna discovered that the colony's leaders were purposely provoking the Paspahegh as an excuse to wage an all-out war on the tribe. She tried to convince her husband and some of the colony's leaders that this was a bad strategy. She told them they were only making life harder for themselves. But because she was a woman, and because many of the leaders believed they had a God-given right to this land, her pleas fell on deaf ears.

At this point, the colonists escalated the confrontations with the tribe into larger battles. Those battles always ended with the colonists annihilating entire Paspahegh villages. But still, during this period, Edna secretly maintained her friendships with the Paspahegh.

It was also during this period that she started writing her story. It was based on a Paspahegh legend, one told to her by a couple of her closest Paspahegh friends—friends who were murdered by the colonists when the colonists ambushed their Paspahegh village and slaughtered every last man, woman, and child who lived there. Edna had feared this day would come, prayed to God it wouldn't—and was devastated when it did.

Harker concluded his preface by explaining that in addition to applying what he'd learned about Edna and Jamestown, he'd bridged the missing pages as best he could using Edna's style, language, and voice. He had tried to stay true to what he believed was her intent.

After finishing the preface, I dove right in to Edna's story. It quickly became clear that this slim volume was the bible of what was happening to us. The story it told, four hundred years old, would end up bringing order to the chaos and supernatural phenomena that had engulfed us. But just like the real Bible, this bible was going to require some interpretation.

Chapter Fourteen

The Forest started with an introduction to "Drakho," a powerful warrior who lived on Tsenacommacah land. The Paspahegh were already sharing their land with him when the settlers arrived. An agreement between Drakho and the Paspahegh had been in place for hundreds, possibly even thousands, of years; many of the Paspahegh believed that Drakho was far older than their own race. And because he was so much older, he had learned and perfected special skills. He had powers no Native Americans possessed.

Harry and I both recognized these powers.

Edna wrote that Drakho had the ability to cloud the Paspahegh's minds. He triggered strange and sometimes terrifying visions that were as real as anything the Paspahegh could see or hear or touch when they weren't under his spell. He could cloud their minds even if he was at a great distance from them. At times he also had the ability to read their thoughts. He knew the most intimate details of their personal lives.

And Drakho could transform himself into an animal—a wolf, a dog, or a bat. He'd traverse inhospitable territory in those forms, and he also traveled in the form of mist. Using these forms, he moved with such stealth that he was impossible to track.

Then Edna noted one of Drakho's character traits, a trait that was important to the Paspahegh, because it offered them a way to appease the great warrior. Drakho loved to play games. Complicated games—games based on riddles, quests, and challenges. He'd engage the Paspahegh, as well as other tribes, in elaborate competitions that would last days, weeks, months, years, and even decades. Then he'd award a prize to the winning individual or village. Drakho also liked to stick to the same bloodlines for his games; once he'd chosen a bloodline, he'd forever come back to it, generation after generation.

After introducing Drakho and the Paspahegh, Edna launched into the meat of her story: Drakho's response to the arrival of the settlers.

First, she explained that it wasn't as if Drakho approved of the Paspahegh—her Paspahegh friends had told her it wasn't like that at all. They couldn't read Drakho's mind, but over the centuries, the tribes had come to understand that above all else Drakho loved the land. *His* land, which they said stretched across a great swath of the Atlantic coast—a swath that I knew went from North Carolina to Massachusetts.

The Paspahegh told Edna that Drakho understood that the Native American population would increase, and he understood that with that increase, so would their exploitation of his land. But a crisis point would take

centuries, if not millennia, to arrive, and Drakho was patient.
He was biding his time until that crisis arrived.

Edna wrote that Drakho's reaction to the English
colonization of his land was very different. While he'd
accepted the Native Americans, at least temporarily, he
wasn't so keen on these new settlers. He'd already had some
encounters with the Europeans arriving on his shores, and
they had left a negative impression. That impression was
reinforced when he saw the settlers betraying the Paspahegh.

Still, he didn't get involved until the English began to
massacre the Paspahegh. When they did, he intervened on
the tribe's side. But the settlers were relentless in their war
against the Paspahegh. They were fiercer and more violent
than Drakho had foreseen. So he made a decision. He swore
he'd never allow the settlers to get a foothold on his land. To
that end, he began an offensive against them.

Here, Harker had a rather long footnote about the
historical context of Edna's story. A few years after the settlers
annihilated the Paspahegh, their own population was also
decimated. Eighty percent of the settlers died. Modern
historians called this period "the Starving Time" because
famine caused the vast majority of the deaths.

But Edna's story laid out a different explanation: Drakho
killed the settlers. He was defending his land.

Also in this footnote, Harker explained that up to this
point in her story, Edna had based her tale on an obscure
Native American legend—the legend of Drakho. But now
she was weaving her own life into *The Forest*, including the

calamity. She also brought in the tragedy that struck her own family during these dark days. She lost her husband and three of her children to starvation and disease.

But in Edna's account, Drakho was the culprit. He had destroyed her family, leaving her with only one son, Benjamin. And here, the drama in her story escalated. Edna knew that Drakho was determined to kill all of the settlers. He was going to clear Tsenacommacah—meaning Jamestown—of every last colonist. But she wasn't going to let him kill Benjamin, her only remaining child. And the only way to stop Drakho was to kill him.

But how?

He appeared unstoppable. The revenge he was meting out on behalf of the Paspahegh proved that he was immune to the settlers' every weapon. And his unique abilities made him an even more formidable enemy.

Edna wanted to turn to the Paspahegh for help. Unfortunately, by this time it appeared that the settlers had murdered them all. And if by chance there *were* any left— and she prayed to God that some had survived—she was sure they'd fled.

In the end, she clung to one hope. She'd heard that some of the settlers had tortured a Paspahegh, hoping to extract information from him before executing him. The settlers wanted to know how to stop the vicious warrior who was fighting on the side of the tribe. These settlers didn't have the inside information Edna had about the warrior—that he was an ancient being defending his homeland—but they did have one thing in common with her: they wanted to know how to kill him.

As it turned out, the settlers *had* extracted information from their prisoner. Some of which they understood. You *could* kill the warrior. He had an Achilles' heel—a weak spot. But they couldn't understand the most important part of this information because they didn't understand the Paspahegh language well enough.

Edna did.

And that paid off when she talked to one of the settlers who'd conducted the torture. He told her that the prisoner kept repeating the same words—words she was able to translate.

Amber weapon.

She didn't tell her fellow colonists that she'd been able to translate the words. Instead, she put her own plan together. She'd kill Drakho with an amber weapon and save her only remaining son, Benjamin.

Here, Harker interrupted the narrative, again, with another footnote. He wrote that some of the following pages were missing, so he'd shaped this part of the tale himself.

Based on the word the Paspahegh prisoner had used for "weapon," Edna determined she'd need some kind of knife or dagger. It would form the core of the amber weapon. But she didn't want to steal a dagger from another settler. If she was caught, she'd face severe punishment, and her fellow citizens already distrusted her. Her past friendships with the Paspahegh made her suspect.

So she decided on a morbid course of action. She'd sneak into the cemetery on the edge of Jamestown and dig up the grave of a settler. On his deathbed, this settler had insisted his family bury him with his weapons.

Edna felt sick as she dug up the dirt and peeled the shroud away from the decaying body. She kept her composure during the gruesome task by clinging desperately to one thought: this was the only way to save her son. She retrieved the dagger holstered around the dead man's waist, then quickly re-buried his body.

At this point in the narrative, I took another of the many breaks I'd been taking to fill Harry in. As I was summarizing this section for him, I connected Edna's amber weapon, her dagger, to the knives used to kill Dracula. In the book *Dracula*, Jonathan Harker and Quincey Morris had killed the count using two knives. Harker had slashed Dracula's throat with one, and Quincey Morris had stabbed him in the heart with another.

I dove back into the story, and a few pages later, Edna revealed exactly what the amber weapon was. She was preparing the dagger by coating it with amber. She didn't go into detail about the process, but why would she? How could she have ever foretold that I'd be sitting here in the dawn's early light, four hundred years later, in front of a electric substation, using *The Forest* as a field guide?

After Edna had readied the dagger, she had to figure out a way to get close enough to Drakho to stab him with it. She considered confronting him when he entered Jamestown to wreak his vengeance. He'd been ambushing settlers for months. She'd seen him descend on the colony disguised as a wolf, a dog, a cold, lingering mist, and even as a blanket of darkness from which he unfolded himself in the night. In the end though, Edna decided that Drakho's stealth was so great—he came and went as he pleased—that confronting him in the settlement left too much to chance. Instead her plan was to draw Drakho to her.

Years ago the Paspahegh had told her that Wassamoah Bay, a land of ancient caves and untouched soil, was sacred land for Drakho. Her plan was to ride out to this sacred land and make Drakho an offer. She'd play one of his games for the life of her son. She'd plead for him to give her one chance at saving Benjamin. She'd get on her knees and beg for that chance.

But this would be a ruse. As soon as Drakho was within striking distance, she'd stab him with her amber weapon. She knew this wouldn't be easy. Drakho had the ability to cloud her mind, which meant she'd have to be wary of everything she saw. Her own eyes might deceive her in the moment she needed them most.

When I filled Harry in on this part of the story, he said, "That game she wants to play—for the life of her son—it's the game you're playin'."

"Yeah, but I didn't ask for it," I said.

"She didn't neither, right? She's got no choice."

He was right. The parallel to my story rang true, which made me even more anxious to get to the end of her story to find out if she'd been able to save her son.

Edna waited three nights, for a night with a waxing crescent moon, bright enough to light her way. Her mission had to be carried out at night. The Paspahegh had told her many times that Drakho showed himself in the calm of night or in the darkness of caves, rather than in the frenzy of daylight.

Edna placed her weapon in a sheath that she'd sewn into the inside of her robe, then she saddled up her husband's horse, a noble beast who'd turned despondent after her husband's death. She wished she could explain her mission to the horse, tell him that his former owner would approve of this nighttime trek. If she could explain this to the noble beast, she was sure he'd help her during her confrontation with Drakho.

After riding for two hours, Edna entered the forest that surrounded Wassamoah Bay. Once there, she didn't know where to go—was it all sacred land?—so she rode through the primeval forest toward the bay.

It wasn't long before she heard rustling in the trees. And the rustling got louder the farther she rode into the woods. She thought these were restless nightingales or owls—dozens of them, judging by the denseness of the rustling.

Then suddenly her horse stopped and neighed—and a swarm of bats swept down from the treetops above, bony gray creatures with scaly wings. They sent her horse into a frenzy. The noble beast bucked and whinnied, terrified, as the bats flung themselves at the horse and rider. Edna fought to keep control of the animal while swinging at the mad swarm.

But the horse threw her. She hit the ground hard, and the bats hurled themselves at her like pelting hail. Claws and teeth ripped her robe and gnawed at her skin. The stinging pain was continuous, but each individual blow, each cut, racked her body with new torment.

She tried to swat the bats away, but this only made them fiercer, battering her with more force. She began to reach for the dagger, but then stopped herself. If she pulled it out now, the game was over. Drakho would see the amber weapon. Then she had the frightening thought: Does he already know I have it? *No*, she told herself. Drakho didn't know who she was, so he couldn't know her thoughts.

She didn't pull out her hidden weapon. Instead she cried out, "I've come to play your game! I can play as well as the Paspahegh! Better!" The bats didn't relent. "Please, I beg you! I offer you what you value most: a game!" She felt the onslaught of bats slow. "The Paspahegh told me you are fair, and I believe them."

The swarm of bats thinned out, then flew back up into the trees.

Edna calmed herself and rose to her feet. Her robe was clawed and tattered, and her body was covered in bruises, welts, and hundreds of cuts. But she braced herself and waited for an answer.

She scanned the woods, hoping to see Drakho. But the first thing she saw was that her horse had abandoned her—

the stallion was nowhere to be seen. Did Drakho now expect her to run as the horse had? Or was he considering her offer of the game?

"The game is a good one," she said. "The prize is the life of my son, Benjamin." She scanned the forest once more, glad she'd chosen a night when the moon lit up some of the darkness. But it was an odd light—a pale, unsettling light. The light of an unnatural world.

Then something else appeared in this unnatural world. A mist began to enshroud the forest. She recognized it from the attacks on the settlement. It thickened quickly and took on a foul odor.

She had no doubt that she'd gotten Drakho's attention.

In the distance, through the mist, she saw a shadow darker than the night itself. It was shaped like a man. A very tall man.

"I did not support my people's decision," Edna said, believing she was speaking to Drakho. "Killing the Paspahegh was not a Godly choice. It was evil. Born of the very devil himself." She was telling the truth, for she was a good Christian. She believed in the New Testament God. A God of love and mercy and peace.

"I loved the Paspahegh as my own brothers and sisters. They were Christians even though they hadn't read the words of Jesus. They led their lives as the New Testament asks." The shadow, still quite far away, turned more opaque, more substantial. "My people were wrong to slaughter the Paspahegh. And you are not wrong to seek vengeance on those who harmed them. In the Old Testament, God approved of vengeance on those who had harmed his people. Me—I don't know what to think about vengeance. But I do know what to think about my son Benjamin. He is innocent. He had nothing to do with killing the Paspahegh."

Drakho appeared suddenly in front of her. How he'd moved through the forest so quickly, or changed from shadow to substance so fully, she didn't understand. But he stood before her now—a tall man with dark hair, a narrow face, and deathly pale skin. His black eyes were large and shone with intelligence, cunning, and ancient knowledge. He wore black vestments. He appeared to her like a fallen angel—from the underworld?—in human form.

Edna got on her knees. "Will you consider my proposal?"

"I must take the lives of *all* the Englishmen," he said. His voice was full, stern, and dominating.

"Some of my people are good," she said.

"Letting your people live is like letting disease flourish. In the end, disease kills every living thing it touches."

"That may be true, but I know my son's heart. He is not part of that disease. He doesn't look to war as an answer. He won't grow up to kill the people you choose as yours. He won't destroy your land."

Drakho was silent. Edna looked up from her supplicating pose. From the neutral expression on Drakho's face—no lines on his brow and no curl to his lips—she couldn't tell if he was considering her proposal. The thought crossed her mind: *If he is considering it, should I go through with my plan to kill this ancient being, or should I play the game for Ben's life instead?*

"Please grant me the opportunity to play the game," she said. "If I win, you do not lose. If Ben lives, he will not be your enemy." Edna made her voice small and kneeled even closer to the ground. "You will find that playing this game is more worthwhile than simply taking another life."

"Your people are mindless," Drakho said. "I have tried to play my games with them, but they fail at every one. They don't give a thought to anything. The Paspahegh seek answers to puzzles and look for clues in the words and pictures I leave. Your people cannot see past what is in front of them. They are too easy to trick."

Edna took that as a sign. *She* wasn't so easy to trick. *She* had tricked Drakho. She grabbed the dagger from its sheath, leapt up, and drove it into Drakho's chest, deep into his heart.

He staggered back, his face twisted in shock. His black eyes narrowed and his pale skin took on a pinkish hue. He reached up, clutched at the dagger in his chest, and struggled to pull it out. His body began to weaken and wilt. It shrank inside his black vestments, which began to billow, no longer secured by the weight of his body inside.

Edna watched, slack-jawed and wide-eyed.

Drakho was dwindling to nothingness. She'd driven him from the rank of fallen angel—of eternal being—to that of fallen warrior. He didn't go from dust to dust, but from eternal to nothing.

The vestments fell to the ground in a heap. Drakho was dead. The amber weapon had done its job. *She* had done her job.

Edna returned to the settlement by foot. It took her more than half a day, but she was propelled by triumph, by the joy of knowing she'd saved her son.

No one in the settlement knew about her adventure. But from that day on, the settlers' luck changed. The Starving Time came to an end, and Jamestown began to grow and thrive.

And that was how *The Forest* ended.

Harker then wrote an epilogue. He explained that he hadn't been able to uncover any records that revealed Edna's true fate. He was referring to the author, the real Edna—Mrs. Horace Grayson—and not the fictitious Edna in the story.

He *did* discover evidence that fact and fiction had intersected on one front: the real Edna, like the fictitious Edna, had lost her husband and all her children, save one son, during the Starving Time. But Harker couldn't find any evidence that she and her son had survived the third year of the Starving Time. They could easily have been part of the eighty percent who'd perished. Or it was possible that they had moved to another settlement in the Americas, or even back to England. Harker said there just wasn't enough evidence to come to a definitive conclusion.

He also wrote that what happened to the fictional Edna at the very end of *The Forest* wasn't clear. When the story wound to a close, as was true for other parts of the tale, pages were missing. So Harker had had to shape the very end of the narrative. He was the one who'd chosen a victorious ending, and he went on to explain his decision.

He saw Edna's story as an attempt to make sense of the unbearable hardships in the new colony. The settlers who'd arrived on the *Susan Constant*, *Discovery*, and *Godspeed* were so ill-prepared for the new world that Harker compared it to the trials and tribulations that the first settlers on Mars might have to face. The unexpected adversities far outweighed those few for which they had prepared.

So he believed Edna had intended for her story to be a tale of courage and perseverance against almost insurmountable odds. It was her way of convincing herself that the settlers could, and would, overcome a harsh environment, an environment that showed no mercy. She wanted to believe they would eventually win the battle.

Therefore, Harker's interpretation of the story was that she'd translated that harsh environment into human form by creating the character of Drakho—based on the Paspahegh legend. He was the one destroying the colony, and it was up to the story's heroine to defeat him, save her son, and save the settlement.

So that's what Harker had her do at the end of *The Forest*.

Chapter Fifteen

"There you have it," Harry said.

"There's more," I said.

Harker had also written an afterword to *The Forest*. Reading it made the connections between the story and our present day descent into hell even more clear. In it, Harker postulated a connection between *Dracula* and *The Forest*, laying out the case that Bram Stoker's *Dracula* was based on the Paspahegh's Drakho.

First, he noted his own connection to the material—a strange coincidence that had no practical value as factual evidence, but which had to be addressed nonetheless. How could it be that he, Jonathan Harker, who bore the same name as one of the main characters in *Dracula*, should be the one to discover the origin of the Dracula myth? There was no answer to that question, except that it was a coincidence, one of those strange, grand ones we've all experienced in our own lives. He made it clear that he didn't believe some mystical force had brought him to the parchment pages hidden in the Bible. Then he went on to make his case about the origin of Bram Stoker's *Dracula*.

Harker's research—confirmed by other scholars and academicians—revealed that Stoker had never visited Eastern Europe, the region he'd chosen as Dracula's birthplace and homeland. The accepted wisdom was that Stoker had picked this region because he'd based the character of Count Dracula on Vlad the Impaler.

Vlad the Impaler, whose real name was Vlad Tepes, was a historical figure from the mid-fifteenth century. He was heir to the House of Draculesti, a powerful family whose lineage went back centuries, and he was prince of Wallachia, a region in Romania. He was also known as Count Dracula, derived from his family name, Draculesti. Count Dracula became a folk hero for defending the Romanians against the Ottomans, and he became infamous for his extreme cruelty, which included impaling his enemies.

No historian or professor of literature had challenged this theory. It was accepted dogma: the inspiration for the fictitious character of Dracula was Vlad the Impaler. Of course, there was no reason to challenge this. First of all, *Dracula* was a work of fiction. Digging up new information about this novel wasn't going to change the world. Second, the novel wasn't considered highbrow fiction, so over the decades, scholars hadn't been falling all over themselves actively chasing down new leads about the book's genesis. Such efforts were reserved for the established literary canon, not the likes of *Dracula*.

But Harker couldn't shake the parallels between *Dracula* and *The Forest*—there were so many. Broad ones like

Dracula's and Drakho's lifespans, both apparently spanning centuries, and specific ones like their supernatural abilities, from morphing into animals to traveling in the form of mist. Not to mention the most obvious similarity, their names: Dracula and Drakho.

Here, I couldn't help but think of my own journey—the one which had led me to *The Forest*. Names had been critical every step of the way.

So Harker set out to determine whether Stoker could have heard about the legend of the Native American Drakho. And for that, he needed to uncover the missing link: either Bram Stoker had heard and/or read about *The Forest*, or he'd heard and/or read about the Paspahegh legend of Drakho. Harker would also have to prove that one of these two things had occurred *before* Stoker wrote his masterpiece of horror fiction.

After many dead ends in which he'd tried to prove that Stoker had run across the legend of Drakho in England, Harker moved on to investigating whether Stoker had visited the United States before writing *Dracula*. That turned out to be the better trail.

Stoker wasn't primarily an author. His full-time job was managing the stage tours for one of England's most famous actors: Henry Irving. Henry Irving traveled the world, and as Harker discovered, Stoker was right there with him on almost all of those trips—including many to the United States, where Irving was a favorite.

Irving was so popular in the States that he was invited to the White House and met the president on more than one occasion. This information inspired Harker to do extensive research into those visits to Washington, D.C. He was focused on D.C. because the nation's capital was across the Potomac from Virginia—Tsenacommacah land, Drakho's homeland, and the Paspaheghs' homeland. He eventually found that both Irving and Stoker had taken a trip to Williamsburg, a stone's throw away from the original Jamestown colony.

Harker was getting closer to finding a direct link.

But it turned out the record of Stoker and Irving's visit to Williamsburg was thin. Though both men occasionally wrote personal notes about their trips—letters, diary entries, calendar entries—neither of them had written anything about this particular excursion. So Harker looked for other paper trails: newspaper accounts, hotel records, travel receipts, et cetera.

Through those, he was able to determine that their visit had lasted three days—plenty of time for Stoker to come across the Drakho legend. Of course, except for placing Stoker in the right location, there was no definitive proof that Stoker *had* come across that legend. His visit had come almost three hundred years after the English had slaughtered the Paspahegh and Edna had written her story. And there was also the fact that, as far as Harker could tell, Edna's short story hadn't surfaced during those three hundred years. *And* it wouldn't surface for another hundred years *after* Stoker's visit, when Harker, himself, would discover it in that old Bible.

Still, he thought he'd discovered a strong link, a link far stronger than the accepted wisdom—that Stoker had stumbled across the folk hero, Vlad the Impaler, in the Whitby library, a small library in the English countryside. That explanation didn't account for the entirety of Dracula folklore.

Harker's link *did*. He'd placed Stoker in the heart of Drakho country, in the heart of the Drakho legend. A legend that paralleled Stoker's *Dracula* almost perfectly, including the similar names.

In the first edition of *The Forest*, Harker's afterword ended there, without the evidence of a direct link between Stoker and Drakho. But Harker spent many more years looking for harder evidence.

And he found it.

In the second edition of the book—the one I held in my hands—Harker laid out that harder evidence. He'd discovered Henry Irving's name on a guest list for a lecture given during the actor's visit to Williamsburg. The topic of the lecture was "The Peculiar Myths of the James City Indians." If Stoker had accompanied Irving to that lecture— and from the records of their travels together, it appeared that Stoker was part of Irving's close-knit entourage—then this placed him right where Harker needed him: listening to a lecture on Native American legends that were specific to this region of the country. The county of James City included Williamsburg and Jamestown, home to the Paspahegh—and the clincher was that the James City Indians were what the locals from that time period called the Paspahegh.

So had the lecture that night included the legend of Drakho? Harker couldn't find the agenda for the night, but he did find a mention of the lecture in *The Virginia Gazette*. An article about Henry Irving's visit to Williamsburg— apparently the news media had always been focused on celebrities instead of news—reported on the highlights of his stay and mentioned that he'd sat in on the lecture. It also gave one-line descriptions of two of the James City Indians' myths. One was about "a mystical warrior who once roamed these lands."

Harker was convinced that this warrior was Drakho. How could it not be? Stoker had attended this lecture—there was almost no doubt about that—and then gone on to write *Dracula*, a novel that used every detail about this warrior, including his name. The "mystical warrior who once roamed these lands" *must* have been Drakho.

I, too, was convinced of this. Of course, I was biased. I had experienced Drakho firsthand, so there was no doubt in my mind that the person or creature described in *The Forest* was the same person or creature hunting me down and threatening to kill Nate.

"Drakho," I said. "That's Dantès's real name."

"I guess that means you just tell the fella his real name and you win the game," Harry said.

"I guess so."

"You don't sound so sure."

I wasn't. Regardless of whether Drakho was his true

identity—and couldn't there be another layer still?—hadn't I discovered a treasure trove of information about my enemy? Didn't this story tell me all I needed to know?

It told me that even if I delivered up the name Drakho, and Drakho then gave Nate a reprieve and spared his life, that wouldn't be the end of it. He'd come after Nate again. Edna had reached through the centuries to confirm Harry's hypothesis: Drakho stuck to the same bloodlines for his games. Once he chose a bloodline, he forever came back to it, generation after generation. Which meant Drakho would never let Nate go. Eventually he'd kill Nate, or his kids, or his grandkids. There was only one real McCoy—Drakho—but there were many Hatfields, and that now included my son and me.

"We tell him the name, but that's not all we do," I said. It was time to fight back. To attack. It was time to stop playing checkers and start playing chess. "We're going to kill him."

"It ain't like we got a choice," Harry said.

And that had been Harry's point from the start. We didn't have a choice. For not only were we Hatfields, we were also a deadly disease flourishing on Drakho's homeland.

"We need the amber weapon," I said.

"Yeah, but there's a hitch in that plan," Harry fired back.

I had a good idea what that hitch was. Harry was on the ball—he wasn't going to let it slide. "Harker made up the end of the story," I said.

"Yep. And what if he got it wrong? I mean, Drakho's still around. So we damn well know Edna didn't kill him back then. That part of the story ain't true. Drakho probably killed her. And her son."

"I won't argue with that." I flipped through the pages of the book. "But the part about the amber weapon—that came from the Paspahegh. They're the ones who told Edna about it. The amber weapon wasn't something Harker made up and added to the story."

"I don't know." He was shaking his head, doubt on his face. "What the hell is an amber weapon anyway? When you get right down to it, it's just a goddamn knife."

"That's like saying that when you get right down to it, Drakho is just a goddamn human."

Harry chuckled, and I knew I could close this deal. "When you were firing at him from the car, do you think you hit with one of your shots?" I asked.

"I know I did. Even though I don't see so good, I aim just fine."

"So if bullets can't slow him down, maybe it's going to take a special kind of weapon—and now we know what that weapon is."

Harry glanced down at the book, then looked up at the dawn, now purple and gold. A few beats later, he said, "I know where to get a dagger for the job. You're gonna have to come up with the amber."

I pulled out my cell phone and started googling amber. I skimmed through the mineral's history, then searched for how to acquire some, which turned out to be relatively easy. We could buy an amber gemstone at a local jewelry store. But after a little more digging, I found that coating a knife with amber wasn't going to be so easy. The problem was melting the gemstone. It was nearly impossible to melt without professional equipment.

But there did turn out to be workaround, the same one Edna must've found. Amber had been a precious gemstone since the days of the caveman. Every culture had known about it, *and* they'd also known that it was fossilized tree resin. So I was fairly sure Edna would have known this. She would have concluded that the best way to get amber in the form she needed—liquefied—was to go right to the source: tree resin. She must have coated her knife with tree resin, which was viscous.

"So we're gonna tap a tree?" Harry said after I filled him in.

"Unless you know a professional scientist who's going to lend us his lab to melt a little amber," I said. But I should have taken his question more seriously—for there *was* an alternative, a far better one than tapping a tree.

"We gotta draw Drakho out, too," Harry said. "And that means drivin' to Wassamoah Bay. Sacred land."

"Maybe there's some sacred land up here, too. Edna called it 'untouched' soil."

"From the story, I'm thinkin' untouched land means land that people ain't been on—or hardly been on, right? And up in these parts, *no* land's untouched. Even preserved land ain't really been preserved."

Considering Northern Virginia had become one big

sprawling suburb, à la Southern California or northern New Jersey, that was a good assumption. Still, driving to Wassamoah Bay would eat up the rapidly dwindling hours left to save Nate. Tomorrow was less than seventeen hours away.

So I pulled up a couple of Northern Virginia maps on my cell phone, looking for the least exploited areas. Harry was right—there wasn't much "sacred" land. But I did notice some possibilities much farther out in Northern Virginia. Unfortunately, I would need a more detailed topographical map to determine which of those possibilities were actually in the running. And even *if* one piece of land appeared to be "untouched," how could I be sure it was sacred land?

I also looked up Wassamoah Bay and found that it was now part of the York River State Park. Though it had survived as wilderness, it was probably no longer untouched. Like Cold Falls and Prince William Forest, both also state parks, there were probably trails, picnic areas, and campsites littering the land.

"If Drakho's up here messing with us—and he damn well is," Harry said, "he ain't down there in Wassamoah Bay."

I smiled and shook my head at the clarity of this insight. "That's right."

So we tabled the "sacred land" part of our plan and decided to move on to securing the knife and the amber. Clint "Buck" Gibson, one of Harry's army buddies, was going to provide us with the knife. Buck collected daggers from America's past wars.

We pulled away from the electric substation and headed to Buck's house in Falls Church. The purple dawn had turned into a bright blue morning, and its light invigorated me even though I'd had no sleep. It was refreshing to lose the veil of darkness. Night was gone and the world looked normal, which was reassuring. But I'd already moved out of this normal world and into a world where fact and fiction were interchangeable. In my heart I knew this, but we're always in denial when change first comes a-calling.

Maybe if I hadn't been in denial, I would've expected that Buck was going to play an integral part in this game. But as it stood, I thought he would just provide us with a knife. I had to get more acclimated to playing chess, and the game was getting more complicated. But after Edna's story, which had served as a kind of training ground, my skill at playing Drakho's game was rapidly improving. And that would become more apparent at Buck's.

Chapter Sixteen

Buck Gibson lived in a tiny brick house in one of the only neighborhoods in Falls Church that hadn't been completely gentrified. Judging from his rickety front porch and the ancient, beat-up Ford Taurus in his driveway, Buck, like Harry, wasn't in the best financial shape.

The interior of his house backed that up: worn carpets and tattered furniture. But Buck, an older man who appeared to be in great shape, had a disposition that was diametrically opposed to the state of his house. He was cheerful and extremely happy to see Harry. They hadn't seen each other in years.

Harry had called ahead, so Buck was ready for our visit. He led us into his dining room, which was really nothing more than an alcove off of his living room. Here, on a small dining table, he had laid out his dagger collection. There were a dozen knives, each with its own history, which Buck proceeded to fill us in on.

I didn't interrupt Buck's lecture, though if Harry and I were going to move on to the task of collecting amber, I'd soon have to. The mini-history lessons about each dagger included the type—trench knife, knuckle knife, push dagger, and more—and how each type was used in warfare. It all brought home the nature of what we were attempting to do: murder Drakho.

As Buck spoke, I studied the daggers, looking for a sign that one was better than another. Even though I was in denial, I was almost expecting one knife to radiate some kind of supernatural quality. And considering what I was planning to use it for, that didn't seem so unreasonable. In addition to studying the daggers, I listened carefully to Buck in case the history of one of the daggers revealed that it was *the one*. I was looking for any sign whatsoever, based on fact *or* fiction.

The knives on the table were from the Civil War, World War I, World War II, and the Korean War. Buck had told us he had no interest in the wars that followed, but it wasn't clear if this was because he didn't care for the knives used in those wars or because of political objections to the wars themselves. After about fifteen minutes or so, during which Buck had covered the history of six of the daggers, I was getting anxious about the time we were wasting. We had to make a decision and move on to getting the amber. So before Buck started telling us about the seventh dagger, I interrupted.

"What do you think, Harry? Is there one you like?" I asked.

"They all seem mighty fine to me," Harry answered.

That wasn't what I wanted to hear. I looked them over again, hoping a mystical quality would leap out at me from one of them. It didn't. Maybe that was because Drakho wasn't messing with us right now. In Buck's house, maybe there was no other world beyond the ordinary world. Maybe fact and fiction weren't a giant shake and bake.

Buck began telling us about the next dagger, a World War I dagger, and painted a vivid picture of the young soldier who'd once owned it. He described the brutal trench warfare—the signature horror of that conflict—so well that I couldn't help but see it: the young soldier in a muddy channel, fighting hand to hand with another soldier, both of them confused and scared, both fearing they'd never go home, both fearing they'd end up rotting in this open grave—and neither of them ever having imagined that war would mean fighting face to face with someone who looked exactly like you.

"No drones back then," Buck said, "and no launching missiles from a naval ship parked in the middle of the ocean hundreds of miles from the battlefield. You couldn't whitewash war back then. For the most part, you had to look your enemy in the eye if you wanted to kill him. If you ask me, not that anybody does, we wouldn't be so quick to get into all these damn wars if we went back to that."

"I hear ya," Harry said, and I heard him, too, but his political leanings didn't really register, as I was still focused on the job at hand: staring at the knives, willing myself to see if any of them was the shadow of another knife, a knife on the other side of reality—the knife that would aid us in our battle with Drakho.

But still none of the knives called out to me. So I figured it was time to pick a dagger at random and hope that any dagger, as long as it was coated in amber, would do the job. The only other option was to come right out and ask Buck the most ridiculous question he'd ever hear: *If you were going to kill Dracula, which knife would you use?*

I didn't ask him that, but the thought of asking him led me to another question: *What if there* was *a specific kind of knife that would kill Dracula?*

Edna hadn't mentioned the type of knife she'd used in *The Forest*, but maybe Bram Stoker had mentioned the types of knives Harker and Quincey had used to kill the count in *Dracula*. I couldn't remember.

"I've got to make a phone call," I said. "I'll be right back."

Buck eyed me suspiciously, like he wasn't buying my excuse to walk away from his lecture. His good cheer dropped a notch or two.

I hurried from the alcove, through the living room, and stepped out onto the front porch. I pulled out my cell, and it didn't take me more than a minute to find an online copy of *Dracula*. Using the word-search function, I immediately went to the passages where Stoker mentioned knives. Sure enough, he'd stated exactly what kinds of daggers Harker and Quincey had used. Harker had used a Kukri knife, and Quincey had used a Bowie knife.

I hurried back through the living room and heard Buck and Harry speaking in hushed tones in the alcove. They stopped as soon as they heard me approaching, as if they were hiding something from me. At the time, I dismissed that impression, chalking it up to my own growing paranoia, not to mention my lack of sleep; that burst of energy from the morning's bright light was fading fast. But I'd soon find out that my impression had been right on the money. Everyone who was sucked into this nightmare had secrets.

"Buck," I said, getting on with it, "is one those daggers a Kukri knife or a Bowie knife?"

"Yep," he said, and pointed to a large knife. "That one there is an original D-Guard Bowie knife from the War Between the States."

I knew that some southerners used that term for the Civil War—and that those who did usually had an unnatural obsession with that war. I had no problem with that, but some of them were also virulent racists, and that sickened me. My bet was that Buck fit right into that category, and it was just a matter of time before he showed his stripes.

"I bought that D-Guard knife from a fellow in Manassas about thirty years ago," he said. "It was passed down to him by his great-granddaddy, who defended Virginia in a battle not more than twenty miles from here." He picked up the knife and turned it over in his hand. "It's a beaut. The fellow had to sell it 'cause he needed the dough. Sometimes money's more valuable than memorabilia. But I gave him a fair price 'cause I didn't want bad luck coming along with the knife."

Even after giving that disclaimer, Buck averted his eyes and lost a little of his cheer, again, as if he did feel a little guilty for taking advantage of someone else's misfortune.

After a couple of seconds, he looked back at us. "So you wanna borrow this one?" he said, his cheeriness restored. "It's a fine choice."

I got the impression that putting the D-Guard knife to good use would assuage his guilt. And it appeared, from the clue in *Dracula*, that the game called for this knife.

"That's the one," I said.

Buck smiled. "I don't got an original sheath for it, but I got a reproduction off eBay."

"Then wrap 'er up and we'll be on our way," Harry said, rolling himself out of the alcove. Buck and I followed.

In the living room, Buck motioned toward the hallway. "Why don't you stick around a bit longer and check out the war room?"

"Since when do you got a war room?" Harry said.

"Since I got nothing but time on my hands."

"We really have to go," I said.

But Harry glanced at me and mouthed, *He's lonely*, then began to wheel himself toward the hallway. "We can spare another couple of minutes, Buck," he said.

I reluctantly fell in line, perturbed by this waste of time, and that's when I realized there'd been something weird about Buck and Harry's interaction over the knife: Buck hadn't asked Harry what we were planning to do with it. You'd think that would've been a wake-up call for me—that things weren't exactly as they seemed. But it wasn't even close to a wake-up call. Instead, I rationalized it this way: Buck trusted Harry's judgment completely.

But I was way off the mark.

The war room was decorated with Civil War memorabilia, which validated my hunch: Buck was obsessed with the War Between the States. I was now fully expecting his next lecture to include his ugly beliefs about race relations. The room was like a mini-museum, curated with attention to detail. On the wall hung framed Confederate uniforms under glass, battlefield photographs, detailed maps of battles, Confederate money, sabers, guns, and the front pages of yellowed newspapers.

"Ain't this something?" Harry said.

"Everything you see has got to do with battles that took place right here in these parts." Buck walked over to one of the uniforms. "All the uniforms are from soldiers who defended this part of Northern Virginia." He motioned over to one of the framed newspapers. "See that? It's the original reporting on the Battle of Arlington Mills, one of the first battles in the war. That stand kept the Union army from getting too deep into Northern Virginia."

Then Buck stepped over to one of the maps. "This here's a map of a more famous battle that took place on that very same day. The Battle of Fairfax Courthouse."

That map caught my attention. In addition to methodically illustrated troop movements, it also boasted meticulously drawn topographical details. Hillsides, cliffs, valleys, streams, and even copses of trees.

"Do you have any other maps of Northern Virginia like this one?" I asked. "I mean ones where the geography is so detailed."

"You bet." Buck moved over to a cabinet and opened it, revealing more than a dozen long cardboard tubes. "Any particular area you're interested in?"

"Yeah—land that's still undeveloped today."

"Not much of that left. But you're still going to have to narrow it down for me. I got lots of maps."

I looked at Harry, not sure where to start. He shrugged.

"What is it exactly you're looking for?" Buck said.

I couldn't say sacred land or untouched land, so I went with, "A place that hasn't changed... at all."

Buck rifled through the tubes, grabbed one, opened it, and pulled out the map inside. He knelt down on the floor and unrolled the map. "This land here runs along the Potomac in Loudon County. Goose Creek cuts through it."

I knelt down and checked out the map, searching for some hint that this land was sacred land. The map was as meticulously drawn as the other one, but there were no troop movements or battle lines.

"Why doesn't this map have troop movements on it? " I said.

"General Ewell—a Lieutenant General in the Army of Northern Virginia—wanted to gain an advantage over the Union Army. He thought he could do that by learning the lay of the land down to every anthill. So he had maps drawn for the entire area. This is a copy of one of those original maps."

Buck opened another tube and pulled out another map.

"This one shows land near Mount Vernon. Some of it is still parkland." He unrolled the map. "Ewell was a mighty fine man. You know what he wanted to do with the slaves?"

Okay, here it comes, I thought. Buck was about to unleash his racism.

"He told Jefferson Davis to free them," Buck said, "and let them fight for the Confederacy. I know it don't sound like much to modern ears, but he also put his money where his mouth was. He said he'd lead a brigade of freed slaves. Jefferson and the rest of 'em thought the man was crazy. *And* they thought it was a terrible strategy."

He stopped there, but as I looked over the Mount Vernon map, I kept expecting him to say what was really on his mind. He didn't.

As for the map, nothing jumped out at me, so I switched my line of thought from Edna's untouched land to *Dracula*. The book had yielded up which knife to choose, so maybe it would yield up the sacred land's location. But my only lead along those lines, without actually searching through the book, was that the count had brought soil from Transylvania with him when he'd moved to London. The casket in which he slept was packed with dirt from the old country. That was *his* sacred land.

I stared at the map, trying to make a connection between soil from the old country and what I was seeing in front of me: beautifully rendered line drawings of hillsides, valleys, and caves. And it was when I saw the caves that I made the connection. Not to Stoker's novel, but to our own bible, *The*

Forest. Edna had mentioned a specific characteristic about Drakho's sacred land. Of course, it could've been Harker who'd embellished that part of the story, but it was all I had.

I brought it up with Buck. "Are any of the lands you're thinking of known for their caves?" For Edna had said that Wassamoah Bay was a land of ancient caves.

"Yep," Buck said. "And sometimes Confederate soldiers hid in those caves to ambush Union soldiers."

Bingo, I thought, and then made another connection, one I should have made earlier. Drakho had led me to caves once already: through Dan T.'s account of Plato's famous cave. Why hadn't I always been on the lookout for caves—fact or fiction?

Buck pulled out a third map and unrolled it on the floor. "This is where the Battle of Front Royal took place. The land is tricky here. Lots of peaks and valleys and streams and caves. Jackson drew the Union Army into the area, and the army got divided up, confused, and lost. They were forced to retreat. Anyway, there are lots of caves there. Old limestone caves going way back. Soldiers hid in them, and some even signed their names on the walls."

I took pictures of the map with my cell phone. There was no way to know if this was sacred land, but it met the only requirement I had at the moment: caves. And Buck said *going way back*, which to my ears sounded like another way of saying *ancient* caves.

"Front Royal is part of the Shenandoah Valley," Buck continued. "You know Skyline Drive and the Blue Ridge

Mountains?"

I nodded. Skyline Drive was a big Northern Virginia tourist attraction. But wasn't that problematic? "I don't know if you could consider that land unchanged," I said. "There must be trails all over it."

Buck countered easily. "Parts of the Shenandoah Valley have hardly been touched at all."

I wasn't convinced that this was sacred land, but I took more pictures of the map, hoping I was on the right track. Then Harry and I thanked Buck for the D-Guard Bowie knife and the tour of the war room, and we all made our way out to his rickety front porch.

That's where the final verdict on Buck's racism was rendered. I shook hands with him, then wheeled Harry carefully down the three steps, and as I started toward the car, Harry said, "Hang on a minute. Swing me back around."

I did, and Harry looked up at Buck, who was standing on the top step. "Listen, I'm sorry I didn't say anything," Harry said.

Buck's cheery demeanor fell away; it was replaced with a somberness that made him look every bit his age. "That's okay," he said. His voice was soft.

"I meant to," Harry said, "but I just kept putting it off. Then…" Harry took a breath and gathered his thoughts.

Buck's eyes watered, and he rubbed them.

"I was gonna say something today," Harry said, "but I didn't see any pictures of her in there. So I thought, well, maybe you guys went your separate ways or something before…"

Buck shook his head. "Never." He looked back at his house. "I took her pictures down because I couldn't look at them all the time. They reminded me of how sick she was at the end."

"Jenny was my favorite of all the wives," Harry said. "Smart as a whip, the best sense of humor, and gorgeous, too. I'm sorry."

"Don't be sorry. I was a hell of a lucky man to have roped her in." Buck walked down the steps and pulled out his wallet. "When I feel up to it, this is the picture I look at. And I've been looking at it a lot lately. You know, it's like the good times are coming back, and I'm forgetting how she was when she was dying. I might even put some of her pictures back up."

Buck opened his wallet and showed Harry the photo. I looked over Harry's shoulder and took a peek. The picture was one of pure happiness: Buck, smiling wide, in a red and yellow Hawaiian shirt, with his arm around a pretty African-American woman, caught in the middle of a joyous laugh. She was wearing a white dress that highlighted the pink and green lei around her neck. Sunlight sparkled gloriously on the blue Pacific Ocean in the background.

"That was the last vacation we had," Buck said, a hint of melancholy in his voice. "I'm glad we splurged."

"She was a keeper," Harry said.

Buck looked at the photo for a long beat—lost in the past—then quickly closed his wallet and stuffed it back in his pocket. "I'm glad you said something, Harry. I appreciate it."

As I helped Harry into the car and loaded his wheelchair into the trunk, Plato's cave came back to me in a new light. This time it told me how badly I'd misjudged Buck. My assumption that he was a racist was another example of focusing on the shadows on the cave wall, rather than looking at the reality behind them. I hadn't wanted to consider that there was more to the man than met the eye. And what made it worse was that he'd basically told me so right up front.

If I'd paid attention to exactly what Buck had been saying during his history lecture—*You couldn't whitewash war back then. For the most part, you had to look your enemy in the eye... We wouldn't be so quick to get into all these damn wars if we went back to that*—I wouldn't have seen him as a pro-war collector of weapon memorabilia. His stance against the perpetual war our country was waging would have been obvious.

All this was another sharp reminder that my life was changing. I had to let go of my old beliefs.

*

As we pulled away from Buck's house, Harry immediately asked me how I knew which knife to choose, so I filled him in on Bram Stoker's account of Dracula's death. Then I moved on to the next task at hand: tracking down amber.

"We're headed to Home Depot," I said.

"They talk about Home Depot in *Dracula*?" Harry laughed at his own joke.

I let him enjoy himself for a few seconds, then told him what I was thinking. "Melting amber would've been impossible for Edna."

"I got that part," he said. "I figured, just like us, she didn't have access to high-tech lab equipment."

"And it doesn't really make sense that she'd have tree resin just lying around."

"She probably got it from a tree, just like we're fixing to do."

"Well, I can't rule that out," I said. "But there's a better alternative. Something that would've been easy for her to get. And considering Jamestown was a colony, with building going on all the time, I'd say she had easy access to this."

"Okay—cut to the chase." Harry frowned at me impatiently.

"Varnish."

He cocked his head, then grinned. "Made from tree resin."

"Exactly. And that's what we're going to pick up at Home Depot."

Harry leaned back in his seat, seeming to accept my conclusion. But only for a second. "I don't know," he said.

"How else could she have coated her dagger in amber?"

"Tree resin—from a tree."

"So you're telling me you prefer tapping a tree over picking up a can of varnish?"

"I'm not tellin' you nothin'. It's just that we're getting farther and farther from the story. And if stories tell ya all you need to know… well…"

Harry had a point, but I didn't know how good a point it was at the time. Just as it was true that you had to interpret the Bible to understand its lessons, you had to interpret *The Forest*. And that was proving to be a major challenge. Centuries had passed since *The Forest* had been written, so the real context would always elude me. Plus, I had to be content with the missing pages as well as Harker's edits and embellishments.

When we got to Home Depot, I parked, googled which types of varnish were made purely from tree resin, and headed into the store. Harry waited in the car because I expected a quick trip—I knew exactly what I needed to pick up.

But that expectation died as soon as I stepped inside.

There was not one other person in the store. There had been plenty of cars in the parking lot, so this didn't make any sense. I told myself to ignore what I was seeing and just head to the aisle with varnishes. Drakho was clouding my mind—and doing a damn good job of it.

Though there weren't any people around, the store itself looked normal. I passed aisles for light fixtures, paints, tools. The lack of customers exaggerated the store's cavernous size—all these goods and no one to purchase them.

I picked up my pace, and then suddenly the overhead lights started turning off—from the back of the store to the front. That prompted me to hurry even more, but the darkness was sweeping through the store quickly, like a tsunami of gloom. Unless the varnish was in the next aisle or two, I'd be searching in the dark. It wasn't—and then the last set of lights went out.

There were a few seconds of total darkness—during which I stood there, indecisive, debating whether to leave or continue—before I saw her.

She was standing halfway down an aisle, holding a lit torch that bathed her in fiery light. Her lush blond hair and luminous ivory skin shone in a radiant aura, as if she were a goddess. As if I'd entered her world and left mine.

Otranto's emerald green eyes stabbed at me. "There's another way to end the game," she said. "You don't have to tell Dantès his real name."

Was she making me this offer because she knew that I'd found his real name? Or did she know I'd discovered Drakho's Achilles' heel?

"I can show you the way out," she continued, "so you don't have to play this game at all." Her torch flared up and the flames momentarily lit the aisle behind her—but it was no longer an aisle. It was a stone passageway, like the entrance to a tomb, stretching out into the distance. Strange hieroglyphs were carved into its walls.

She turned and started walking into the tomb. "Let's go."

I didn't move.

"I'll give you what you want most," she said.

"I want to save Nate's life."

"That's not what you want most."

"It is."

She turned back, her green eyes wider now, beautifully malicious. "That's a lie."

Of course she'd know there was something I wanted more. Something I could never have. It was what we all wanted after losing someone we loved.

"You *can* have what you want," she said, then walked farther into the tomb.

I followed, tempted to see if she could deliver. Could she bring forth a miracle? One straight from the Bible? The *real* Bible.

I told myself I should be thinking more rationally, but I couldn't convince myself to actually do so. There was no difference between fact and fiction—reality was a giant shake and bake of both—and here was the living proof: I was walking through a tomb in the middle of a Home Depot.

The deeper I moved into the tomb, the more the temperature dropped. But my attention quickly turned from the cold to the hieroglyphs on the wall. I was close enough to Otranto now that they were visible in her torch's light— pictograms of men, women, and children trekking through a lush forest toward the banks of a wide river. Then, after a few yards, the hieroglyphs changed. The men, women, and children had now reached the banks of the river. They seemed to be waiting at the water's edge for something or someone to appear.

The temperature dropped even more, and the tomb walls started to close in on us as if the passageway was narrowing. The pictograms were larger here, and the story they told had progressed. Boats appeared at the river's edge, and the people were boarding them, children first. Farther down the wall, the boats were crossing the river, and that was when I made the connection.

The hieroglyphs fit in perfectly with what I wanted most. These men, women, and children were crossing the river Acheron, the river that separated the living from the dead. Drakho was once again using Dante's *Inferno*, for in that work of fiction, Dante crossed the river Acheron into the world of the dead.

Up ahead, past Otranto, I saw that our narrow passageway opened up. I assumed we were headed into a large mausoleum and was shocked when instead I found myself stepping outside, as in outdoors—

I was on the banks of a rippling, dark body of water that stretched out to the horizon. Up above me was a black sky without stars. The water rhythmically lapped at the shore, maintaining a steady, eerie cadence—it was the only sign of life in this dead place.

Otranto approached the river, her torch held high. Across the water, about thirty yards away, a boat appeared from the darkness—and in its bow stood the woman around whom my every thought revolved. The woman I loved. The woman with whom I wanted to spend the rest of my life.

My sweet Lucy.

I strained to see her face, wanting to read her expression. Was she joyful or sad? She was too far away to tell. I hurried up to the river's edge.

"If you take your own life," Otranto said, "you can join her. She'll come to shore and take you with her—to the other side."

Otranto's proposal sounded reasonable. She had delivered it in a voice buoyed with hope.

I strained to see Lucy more clearly, and for a second her face came into focus. It looked soft and fragile. Her eyes glistened with tears, and her mouth was slightly upturned in the saddest of smiles. She whispered something to me, words that went with her sad smile. But I couldn't make out those words. Not yet. It would take a minute or two for them to reach my ears.

Was she waiting for me?

"There's a place where the dead are alive," Otranto said.

"She's not real," I said, my rational side attempting to fight back.

"She is. You just can't imagine it from this side of the river. You have to cross over."

I understood what Otranto was telling me. She was asking me to take my own life in the hope that Lucy was still alive, waiting for me, just out of reach. That would be the biggest leap of faith yet. Far bigger than believing in and following the trail that had led me to *The Forest*. By comparison, my plan to rely on an amber weapon to end this nightmare was the most logical plan ever conceived.

Then Otranto upped her offer. "If you sail away with Lucy, Dantès will accept that as the end of the game. He won't take Nate's life tomorrow." She looked up at her torch and let out a soft breath. The flame flickered and fluttered and died, plunging us into absolute darkness. "Your son lives, and you join Lucy," she said, her voice the only living thing.

Then light slowly returned as if it were coming from an unseen sunrise. It was a dark, rich, orange-yellow light—an *amber* light.

And in this light, I saw I was no longer standing at the river's edge.

I was now standing in front of a large tree. Its trunk was charred black and its branches were barren of leaves. And where the river had once been, there was now a landscape of dead trees, surrounded by bronzed, dry dirt, untouched by even a hint of vegetation. It was the bleakest landscape I had ever seen.

I looked behind me, checking for the tomb's passageway—my way into this place of death—hoping it would be my way out. But it was gone, replaced by more of the somber, lifeless vista. *Endless.* And the dark amber light bathed it all in gloom.

Was *this* the amber weapon from the story? This oppressive light from which there was no escape?

I turned back to the large tree. A noose hung down from one of its branches, and a series of boards were nailed to its black trunk: rungs of a ladder leading to the noose. The orange-yellow light, which hung heavy over the rest of the landscape, played a different role here. It highlighted the noose, foregrounding it in blazing amber.

The noose beckoned me.

This was the amber weapon that would save Nate.

Right then, I understood that Harker had been completely mistaken about the ending for *The Forest*. His analysis had led him to write the wrong ending. But I knew the right ending: Edna had sacrificed herself for her son. She had taken her own life; Drakho had accepted it and let her son live. That was the ending she'd written. The true ending. The ending lost to history.

Didn't it make sense that a mother would sacrifice her own life to save the life of her child?

I'd do the same. I *was going* to do the same. I would give up my life, and Nate would be spared. That had to be way this game ended. That was why Lucy had appeared on the river Acheron. Sure, I'd be reunited with her, but that wasn't why she'd come. She'd told me her purpose, for those were the words she had whispered to me across the dark water:

Give up your life for Nate.

Those words were the reason for her sad, fragile smile. She knew I had no choice.

I climbed up the rungs of the tree and crawled out along the branch. I grabbed the rope and pulled the noose up from below.

Nate would live.

I put the noose around my neck and was submerged in amber light. It chilled my skin and bones. I would join the barren landscape—the dead trees and the dead earth. They were waiting for me. They were waiting to receive the only living man in this world—

Or was I already dead?

Was life and death a giant shake and bake, too?

The noose felt tight around my neck.

No—it was fact and fiction that were a giant shake and bake.

Life was where the line was drawn.

There was a clear line between life and death. That was why Drakho played games of life and death. Those were the real stakes, the only stakes. Life was where the line was drawn.

I grabbed the noose from around my neck, slipped it off, and let it fall. It snapped to a stop ten feet from the ground. The sharp sound echoed through the dead world. I crawled along the branch and climbed back down the rungs.

My thoughts were thick and hard to process, and I was glad for it. I didn't want to think right then. I just wanted to leave. To get as far away as possible from this dead world.

Though I couldn't see the tomb's passageway, I moved in that direction as if it was still there. It had to be the way out, just as it had been the way in.

At first, I trudged along the dry soil, passing barren trees. But after a while—I couldn't be sure how long—the amber light began to darken, and then it disappeared. I found myself walking through the tomb once more. The hieroglyphs hadn't changed. The men, women, and children were still crossing the river Acheron. I walked on, and the tomb widened and warmed until I stepped back into the Home Depot.

Chapter Seventeen

The store was no longer empty. A few yards from where I stood, a couple was checking out floor tiles, and farther down the aisle, other customers did the same. Bewildered, I didn't move. I stood there like a statue lit by the fluorescent lights above—lights whose glare I normally disliked, but which I now welcomed.

Finally, I looked over my shoulder. The tomb was gone. I tried to reorient myself to what was now a normal Home Depot. The river Acheron no longer flowed through it and the dead world was gone. I turned back. The nearby couple was now staring at me as if my confused state might pose a threat to them. I quickly walked down the aisle, leaving them to get on with their shopping.

Then, amid the other customers, I got on with my own shopping. The thickness which had slowed my thoughts had worn off, so I forced myself not to think about what had just happened in order to concentrate instead on getting what I needed: fast-drying varnish and a brush with which to apply it. I also picked up a couple of flashlights in case we ended up meeting Drakho in one of the Shenandoah Valley caves.

In line, at the cashier, I found myself glancing around the store, still bewildered by the normalcy of the place. Laborers, housewives, couples, and contractors walked the aisles and examined items. There was no sign of Otranto or the bleak landscape.

Or Lucy.

*

In the car, Harry and I ran through our "sacred land" options one more time and concluded that the Shenandoah Valley was the best option in Northern Virginia. And there was another benefit to heading toward those limestone caves. The Shenandoah Valley was more or less heading south, so we'd be one hour closer to Wassamoah Bay.

So I pulled out and started toward Front Royal, the town that was the gateway to the Blue Ridge Mountains, Skyline Drive, and the Shenandoah Valley. Once we were on Route 66, I convinced Harry to start coating the D-Guard knife with the varnish, so it'd be dry by the time we got there.

As he applied the first coat, I told him what had happened in the store. He listened without saying much. Maybe that was because he was doing an excellent job of coating the knife. Even though he wasn't convinced that varnish was the equivalent of Edna's amber weapon, he was applying it with the confident, even brushstrokes of a craftsman.

When I finished my tale, I tried to explain how taking my own life had seemed like a perfectly reasonable way to save Nate.

Harry said he understood, but I didn't believe him, and he must have been able to tell, because he then told me a story that explained *why* he understood. A story he'd never told anyone else. There'd been no reason to—until now.

"It happened after the attack in Prince William Forest," he said. "I was still in the hospital. My legs had been amputated and I'd been all drugged up for a while. A long while. But they were finally startin' to take me off the drugs. I was feelin' pretty bad. You know, it ain't easy to get used to not walkin' no more. You gotta learn to take care of yourself all over again. Hell, I didn't like it. Not one damn bit.

"Anyway, they started teachin' me how to help myself. How to get in and outta the wheelchair—hard as hell when you start—and all sorts of other things. And every night I'd lie there in the hospital room, scared, like a little baby who'd lost his mommy. I didn't think I could make it on my own. And the more they took me off the drugs, the more I really believed that. My life was shit."

I glanced over at him. He was applying a second coat of varnish, using the same even brushstrokes he'd used for the first.

"So one night, this nurse comes in," he said. "A new nurse, blond and pretty, with the greenest eyes I've ever seen."

Otranto, I thought.

"I was awake," Harry said, "feeling bad for myself. Not wanting to go back to Quantico. And in the back of my mind, I thought I wasn't ever gonna go back to Quantico—

that they were gonna warehouse me somewhere. I knew life
was gonna be shit no matter what. But the nurse says to me,
like she knew what I'd been thinking, 'I'm taking you to see a
place where things are good.' And she don't even make me
get in the wheelchair by myself. I should've known
something was wrong right there. They'd all been forcing me
to do things on my own. But not her. She helps me slide
right into the wheelchair.

"Then she wheels me to the elevator, and we head down
to a floor lower than the basement. I didn't remember a floor
down there, but it was right there on the panel of buttons—
as plain as the nose on your face. The elevator door opens,
and she pushes me into an alleyway. I'm thinking, *Where the
hell are we?* and I look back at her to ask—but she's still in
the elevator and the door is closing.

"So I try to wheel my chair around, but I wasn't so good
at steering the damn thing yet, and by the time I got it right,
the door was closed and there wasn't no button to call the
elevator back. So I wheel back around and check out the
alleyway. I see nothin' but dumpsters and trash.

"I'm thinking to myself: *I just been dumped from the
hospital.* I'd heard about that kinda thing on the news. Maybe
the VA stopped paying my bills or something. The buildings
in the alley, well, their walls were black, like they'd been
through a pretty bad fire, and their windows were all busted
out. I start to wheel myself forward to get outta there, and
from what I can see through the windows, the buildings are
all burned up on the inside, too."

He continued to apply the varnish, meticulously, without missing a beat in his story.

"I kept goin' until I made it out of the alley. It turns out I was in a city. I hate cities, and this one was bad. It was all rundown. The buildings were cracked and falling apart, like they'd all been abandoned. And some of 'em were burned out."

"But in front of me, across the street, there was a river—a wide one—and on the *other* side of it, I saw my favorite place, my favorite town: Culpeper—where I grew up. It's not like the streets in Culpeper are paved with gold or nothin', but it's nice. Small and friendly. I could see the town square, and people were goin' about their business, headin' to their offices, or lunch, or eatin' ice cream cones, shootin' the breeze."

Harry finished the coat of varnish, picked up the knife, and examined his handiwork.

"I'm thinking I got to get over to the other side. I'm askin' myself, *Can I swim?* I got no legs, but I got arms. And I'm trying to decide if my arms are strong enough. Staying in the hospital made them weak. I look down at the river, and it's moving pretty fast. I don't know if I can make it across.

"When I look back up from the river, I see Art Craig on the other side. My best buddy is lookin' at me from the shore, standing there, smiling, like Drakho never killed him. I'm thinking, *Art wants me to swim over there*. Why else would he be here? And I *wanted* to go over there, you know? I wanted to see my buddy and go back to my hometown.

Who wouldn't?

"So I decide that's exactly what I'm gonna do. And I knew how to do it. There was only one way to swim over there. And as soon as I decided I was gonna do it—boom, I'm back in my hospital bed.

"It's the middle of the night now. I knew, 'cause they dimmed the room lights when it got real late, and there was less hustle and bustle—no doctors, no visitors, and hardly any nurses around.

"This was the perfect time to do it. The perfect time to swim across that river. So I pull out my IVs and I do what they been teaching me to do. I get into my wheelchair by myself. But this time I *want* to do it. I use my arms and shimmy to the side of the bed. I push myself up, holding on to the bed, and get myself into my chair."

Harry was turning the knife over in his hand. The fresh coat of varnish flared in the sunlight.

"Then I roll myself into the bathroom and up to the sink. I use the sink for leverage and pull myself up so I can reach the cabinet. I pull out my shaving razor and fall back into my chair, snug as a bug in a rug. And then I get right to it. No use wastin' time. I open the razor, pull out the blade, and slide it across my wrist. The bleedin' starts right up.

"I know that this is the way to swim across the river and get to Culpeper and see Art, so I push the blade down harder to make it go faster. And it's workin'. I'm bleeding pretty good, and I'm swimming across. I feel the river water on my skin. It's thick like blood.

"Then I hear someone calling me: 'Harry!' And I look back and see Macon. He snatches the blade out of my hand. Then he grabs a towel and wraps it around my wrist, and all the while, he's yelling at me, 'What the fuck are you doing, man?' over and over again. Then he tells me to hold on to the towel, and he wheels me out of the bathroom and down to the nurses' station. He's got tears rolling down his face. He tells the nurse what I was doing, and she tells the other nurse to grab some supplies. Then she wheels me back to my room, telling me I got plenty to live for, it's just a bad time now.

"Macon isn't saying anything, just following us. We get back to my room, and the nurses put me back in bed. Then they hook me up to the IVs and start to patch up my wrist. They're tellin' me they'll get someone to talk to me— someone who knows what I'm going through—and it'll all work out.

"The whole time, Macon's just standing back, staring out the window, or staring at the bathroom, or staring at some 'get well soon' cards I got. The only place he isn't looking is at me.

"The nurses finally leave, and he stays quiet. Me too. I'm ashamed of what I done. It takes him another couple of minutes, but he finally looks me, and he says, 'Why?'

"'I'm sorry...' I said, and I was. He said, 'I looked up to you. You're the good one...'

"I told him I'd been having a hard time. I told him it had been really bad. But he didn't answer me. He's got tears in his eyes and he just leaves. He took off." Harry took a breath and looked over at me. "You know that saying: 'hero to zero'?"

"Yeah."

"Well, that's what happened. I wasn't no hero no more to him. I was a lowlife cripple. Just a sad sack of shit."

Harry started applying a third coat of varnish to the knife, and he didn't say anything more for a few seconds. Then he said, "This last coat should do it."

His story hung with a physical weight, pressing down on me, the same awful sensation I'd felt right after Lucy died. The same weight Harry must've felt in the hospital—a star football player, a strong and smart soldier, cut down, adjusting to a life where he could no longer walk.

I drove for a while in the warm, clear light of the Virginia afternoon. A light with no hint of heavy amber. A light colored by a powder blue sky and a radiant yellow sun. A light that melted away that heavy weight so I could ask the question I had to ask.

"… Did you think it was Drakho trying to get you to do it?" I said.

"You mean trying to get me to kill myself?" Harry shot back.

I nodded.

"Not till today. Not until you told me your story. I thought it was withdrawal from the drugs. But who the hell really knows, right? Ain't that the whole point of this not knowin' what's real and what ain't? I was feeling pretty down back then. Hell, the only reason I didn't try again was because of Macon."

"Macon? Why?" From what Lee had said about his dad and from what I'd seen in Dan T.'s Firegrill, there was nothing about the guy that would inspire anyone to do anything good.

"I know it don't make sense," Harry said. "Back then, he was no different than he is now—a lazy drunk, just scraping by. But I got to thinking, if I offed myself, he'd sink even lower. Just getting my shit together again would help him keep *his* together. If I stuck around—hero or no hero—he'd be all right. Don't fool yourself—a man can go pretty bad even if he's bad already, and I didn't want that for my brother. And it worked. I mean, he didn't sink no lower, and you know why that was good?"

I shook my head.

Harry turned toward the window. "Because of Lee," he said. "Macon wasn't a great dad. He wasn't even a good one. But somehow he was good enough for Lee to turn out okay. Lee got it together in the end, and that's the truth."

The queasy helplessness of loss welled up in my stomach, but I pushed it away before it turned into melancholy. I thought instead of *The Forest*, reviewing passages I'd read, as a pastor might review verses in the Bible looking for a lesson. Neither of us spoke for while.

*

As we got closer to Front Royal, the suburbs thinned out, and when we entered the edge of the Shenandoah Valley proper, there were far fewer housing developments and far more forested patches of land. Thirty minutes later, we were driving through rolling hills and farmland, bearing down on Front Royal. It was time to talk business again.

"I don't think Drakho is just going to show up like he did in *The Forest*," I said. Actually, I couldn't be sure if he'd ever showed up for Edna either, since that part of the story had been Harker's addition.

"If you tell him that you got his real name," Harry said, "then he's got to show up to collect it, right?"

"Maybe."

Harry touched the D-Guard's blade. "The varnish is dry," he said, then sheathed the knife. "So there you go: he shows up, you stab him, and everything's hunky-dory."

"Too easy?"

"Not that it's got to be hard, but it still seems like we're getting too far away from *The Forest*."

I didn't have a response for that, because I hadn't been able to latch on to anything else in the story. To take the pastor analogy one step further, my Bible verses weren't offering up any new lessons.

As soon as I drove past the Front Royal city limits sign, housing developments once again reared their ugly heads. But at least they were small, and few in number. We entered the town, where many blocks had been redeveloped, another indication of just how far south the D.C. suburbs had sprawled into Virginia. We were seventy miles from the nation's capital, but based on some of the boutiques we passed, we could just as easily have been driving through Georgetown or Old Town Alexandria. There were still a few country stores with rundown wooden facades and hand-painted logos, but they were overwhelmed by the far more numerous faux-quaint shops and retail chains.

On the other side of Front Royal, we hit Skyline Drive, the gateway to the Blue Ridge Mountains. After a dozen more miles or so, I pulled in at a state visitors center, where I hoped to get more information on the ancient limestone caves—the landmarks that connected Edna's story to whatever sacred land might be in these parts.

Harry stayed in the car and skimmed *The Forest* while I headed inside. The center was empty of tourists except for an elderly couple checking out a giant map of hiking trails that covered an entire wall.

A gray-haired docent sat behind an information counter. She flashed a grandmotherly smile at me, which I returned before walking over to a rack of pamphlets. The pamphlets advertised the various attractions along Skyline Drive, and it was clear at a glance that Skyline Caverns was the main attraction.

I plucked a few pamphlets from the rack and started to peruse them, looking for a clue. A clue about the caves. Maybe a Native American name, or a reference to colonial times, or a description of a supernatural monster—a local legend—that haunted the Shenandoah Valley, or something that hinted at *Dracula* or *The Forest* or Dante's *Inferno*.

But nothing jumped out at me except the ancient caves

themselves. The pamphlets went into the history of the limestone caves—the caverns—and the highlight was the discovery of a rare geological formation there, a six-sided crystal called an anthodite. But since the pamphlets weren't giving up any clues, I walked over to the giant map and located Skyline Caverns. I wanted to see if the map revealed anything about the caverns that indicated they were sacred land. Although if tourists were going in and out of the caverns all day long, I doubted Drakho considered them untouched.

As I looked over other parts of the map, checking more remote areas in the Blue Ridge Mountains, out of the corner of my eye I saw the docent get up from her chair and walk out from behind the counter. She made her way over to me and said, "Is there anything I can help you with?"

"Sure," I said.

Her face lit up with enthusiasm. "Fantastic. Nowadays we don't get much traffic in here because of the Internet. Everybody just goes online."

"I know what you mean—I'm a librarian." But my life had changed so much in the last twenty-four hours that claiming I was a librarian seemed like a lie. It was fiction, and my quest to kill Drakho was fact.

She motioned to the map. "What are you looking to do today?"

"I was thinking of exploring the caverns."

"A great choice! I've been working here for forty years and it's still my favorite part of the Shenandoah."

"Which cavern is the oldest?" I hoped that would make it sacred land.

"Even though it's called Skyline Caverns, it's really just one big cavern with multiple sections." She motioned to it on the map. "The entire site is fifty to sixty million years old. And that's even more amazing when you consider it was untouched until 1937."

"Untouched?" She'd used the right word.

"Yes—it wasn't discovered until then. When the state of Virginia was building Skyline Drive, they hired a retired geologist to look for caves along the route. They wanted to find tourist attractions to get people out this way. Well, boy did that work out. The geologist came across a sinkhole and decided to dig it out. Next thing he knew, he'd made one of the greatest geological discoveries of all time."

My thought right then was that it *had* been sacred land. It hadn't been polluted by humans until 1937. Until then, Drakho would've loved it. A Dracula-type lair, underground, and pristine. But when this geologist discovered it, when it became a tourist attraction, had it become spoiled? Contaminated by humans?

"Are there other sections?" I said. "Sections that weren't opened up to the public?"

"No, but believe me, there's plenty for you to enjoy there. You'll love Mirror Lake and Rainbow Falls." She pointed to one of the pamphlets in my hand. "You can find all the tour times listed in there, but you can explore on your own, too."

This was a dead end. Though the caves had been

untouched decades ago, I couldn't buy the idea that Drakho was going to show up in the heart of a tourist attraction.

"Are there any other caves?" I said, knowing that there must be. Buck had said that soldiers had hidden in caves in these parts during the Civil War, and that was well before the discovery of the caverns. "I mean, caves that aren't part of Skyline Caverns?"

"There are a few others. But they're hard to get to."

"That's okay. I'm ready for an adventure. And to be honest, I'm looking for something less touristy."

"I understand," she said, and smiled sympathetically. "Some people come out here for a little peace and quiet. I don't blame you."

She stepped over to another part of the map. "Here we have Briggs Cave. But you have to hike in quite a ways to get to it. And it's not nearly as beautiful as Skyline Caverns."

Now we were getting somewhere. "Anything else?"

She pointed to another part of the map. "Allegheny Roughs. Three caves. But not many tourists get out that far. They're mostly visited by campers."

Then she looked over the map as if she was making sure she hadn't forgotten any other caves. I noticed her eyes stop on one spot, and her smile disappeared a second later. Then she quickly turned away from the map.

"That's really about it," she said. Her smile was back. "But I can tell you about some of our other terrific attractions." She headed toward the information counter.

"No other caves, huh?" I knew she was withholding

information.

She glanced at me and shook her head no, but her smile was waning.

"I'm pretty sure I heard or read about another cave." I wasn't letting her off the hook. "I guess I can just check online."

She circled around to her side of the information counter and nestled back into her seat. I stepped up to the counter.

"But I'm sure you know more than some random website."

That got her. She glanced at the elderly couple, leaned forward, and lowered her voice. "Well, if you're talking about Hadley Cave, I don't recommend it. It's too dangerous."

"Dangerous?"

"It's under Paspahegh Falls."

My heart almost leapt out of my chest. I could've jumped across the counter and kissed her. She'd made an unmistakable connection. She'd resurrected the slaughtered Paspahegh so they could guide me, just as they had guided Edna.

"Paspahegh," I said. "Sounds like a Native American name."

"Yes—it is." She quickly looked down at the counter, at a visitors' registry, which had only a few names in it. She straightened the pen next to the registry as if she was anxious. "Would you like to sign the registry?" she said.

"Sure." I grabbed the pen and started to sign my name. I had no doubt she was withholding more information about

Hadley Cave. "So climbing under Paspahegh Falls is dangerous? That's why you don't recommend Hadley Cave."

She looked back up at me. Her smile was gone and her lips were pursed as if she was trying to keep her mouth shut.

"But it sounds like it's far from the beaten path," I said. "No tourists. It may be worth a trip."

"It's not," she said, and lowered her voice again. "The entrance to the cave is sealed."

"Really? Why is that?"

"It's just too dangerous climbing down under the falls."

I weighed whether to press her with another question, but I opted instead to just meet her eyes and wait. My bet was that she'd fill the awkward silence with more details. My bet was right.

"... Two boys died there in the fifties," she said in a quiet, conspiratorial voice, "so the entrance was sealed. But a few years ago some troublemakers went down there and opened it up again without permission." She leaned forward a little closer. "You know, when I first started working here, my boss called it 'Hades' Cave, and you know what 'Hades' means."

I nodded. It meant "hell." As in Dante's *Inferno*. As in Dan T.'s Firegrill. It meant that this was the next clue and the place to go. But did it mean it was sacred land? It wasn't completely untouched—at least not if the docent's story was true—but at least it was relatively untouched.

The docent let out a breath, smiled again, and dropped the conspiratorial tone. "I recommend sticking with Skyline Caverns. They really are amazing—'awesome,' as the kids say.

Then if you really want to try something less crowded, and don't mind a long hike, check out Briggs."

I thanked her for the suggestions, checked the pamphlets I'd picked up to see if one of them showed the way to Paspahegh Falls—it did—and then headed back out to the car.

I filled Harry in on what I'd learned, then got on my cell to see what else I could dig up about the two boys who'd been killed in the fifties. I wanted to see if there was a connection to Drakho. I tried combining different kinds of deaths—accidents, homicides, suicides, et cetera—with different locations—Hadley's Cave, Shenandoah Valley, Skyline Drive, Front Royal. I finally came up with an article that had appeared in the *Richmond Times-Dispatch*. It didn't contain many details, but one stuck out.

The boys had been playing hide-and-seek, the same game we'd been playing as kids in Cold Falls when we'd first come across Drakho. Games were Drakho's domain, and hide-and-seek was apparently one of his favorites. And though there was already no doubt in my mind that Paspahegh Falls was the new breadcrumb and Hadley's Cave—Hades—was our new destination, this detail was extra confirmation.

The pamphlet showed that Deer Hill Trail was the fastest way to get to the falls, so thirty minutes later I was turning off Skyline Drive and onto a dirt service road headed toward Deer Hill Trail. What followed was a bumpy ten-mile stretch where the underbrush had crept over the road. The park rangers, or whoever had once maintained this road, had apparently long ago abandoned it. At last it dead-ended without fanfare at the head of the trail. The dirt parking spaces and turnaround lane were completely covered with vegetation.

I cut the engine and Harry said, "Guess this is where you go it alone, huh?"

I hadn't even thought about that. Of course hiking was out of the question for Harry. Nevertheless, I said, "Let me check it out."

"Why? You ain't gonna be pushing a wheelchair for—how long is it?"

"Three and half miles—"

"Uphill," he continued, "on a trail that probably ain't been cleared in thirty years." Harry grinned. "But this is just the way Drakho wants it."

"How?"

"You, alone. You're the one who got the letter. You're the one he's playing the game with."

I'm the one who's "it," I thought.

Harry grabbed the sheath and thrust it toward me, but I knew he wanted to be part of this. He'd been waiting decades to confront the monster who'd crushed his legs.

"Just hang on to it for a sec," I said, then got out of the car.

I starting hiking up the trail to get a better look at it. For about thirty yards, the trail was fairly wide and the dirt was packed down and smooth, as if inviting hikers in. But then the trail narrowed and the dirt turned pockmarked and wildly uneven. Even farther ahead, vegetation encroached from the forest.

Pushing a wheelchair up Deer Hill Trail would be impossible.

I hiked back down to the head of the trail, and Harry swung open the passenger door. "Not gonna happen," he said. "Right?"

"Not with the wheelchair," I said.

"You want me to fly?"

"How about a piggyback ride?"

"You think you can swing that?" He looked doubtful.

"I'm up for trying. But we're going to have to take breaks along the way."

Harry checked his watch. "Can't take too many or we'll be hiking in the dark."

"Then let's go."

I took the sheathed knife, dropped it into the Home Depot bag, which had the flashlights in it, and gave the bag to Harry. Then I maneuvered him onto my back—and immediately slumped under the weight.

"You sure you can make it?" he said.

"Yeah." But I wasn't sure at all. Harry could only wrap himself around me with his arms, so his body weight wasn't evenly distributed. That made the heavy load hanging from my shoulders even harder to bear.

We started up the trail, and it wasn't long before the path became even more ragged than what I'd scouted out earlier. There were pitfalls every step of the way—dips, cavities, vines, roots. I took it one step at a time, breathing evenly, trying to fall into some kind of rhythm, hoping that that would keep me going. But the footing was so uneven that every step felt like I'd gone a mile. My legs were sore, and my lower back was aching under the strain.

Harry must have felt my body weakening because he asked, "Why are you doing this? You don't gotta have me around to pull this off."

Why *was* I doing this? Was he actually going to be of any help? He'd brought his gun, but I didn't believe for a second it was an effective weapon in our battle. I turned the question over in my mind, and just as the burden of carrying him turned almost unbearable, a sudden epiphany hit me and lightened my load.

"If it wasn't for you, I wouldn't be here," I said. His stories had led me through Drakho's maze of clues just as much as *Dracula*, *The Forest*, and the Allegory of the Cave had. And that led to another reason I needed him. "Besides," I said, "I might need another story, and you've got thousands of them."

"More," he said.

The hike became more treacherous, and at one point, after fighting through a long stretch of vegetation, I lost the trail completely. Or more precisely, the forest took the trail into its clutches and hid it from me.

I put Harry down and scouted up ahead until I found it again. After another mile and a half and four stops for rest, I heard water and knew we were on course. According to the pamphlet, the Shenandoah River was just ahead of us.

The trail started to parallel the river, but the forest was so thick here we couldn't actually see the water. The hike became steeper, so I had to take more breaks. I was drenched in sweat, the muscles in my legs were burning, and my lower back felt like it was about to give out. But I forced myself forward and into a routine: travel roughly twenty-five yards, stop and slide Harry to the ground, reboot myself, then start up again.

The river grew louder, its waters thrashing downstream, fast and wild, propelled by the Paspahegh Falls above.

"You're getting the workout of a lifetime, ain't ya?" Harry said.

"I might be dead before we get there."

"Then leave me here. 'Cause if you're dead, you ain't gonna stand a chance against Drakho."

That made me laugh. "Nah, I can't give up now."

And I didn't. The final stretch, though a short distance, took a hell of a long time. I stopped five more times before I got to the top of the trail. There I was greeted with a familiar sight—so familiar it gave me the confidence that we'd come to the right place. Giant gray boulders, just like those that bordered the Potomac at Cold Falls, also surrounded Paspahegh Falls.

However, that's where the similarity ended. Despite its name, there were no falls at Cold Falls; here, the water plunged down a hundred and fifty feet in a vertical drop.

I slid Harry off onto one of the larger boulders. Then I

scanned the falls, letting the spray of its waters cool me down. I was trying to spot the entrance to Hadley's Cave, but it quickly became obvious that there wasn't a clear view from our perch up here.

"I'll be right back," I said, and I started climbing down the rocks, angling for a better look. It took a while to spot something, but finally I did. About forty feet or so above the foot of the falls, I saw a narrow ledge, wet and uneven, running behind the cascading water.

If there was any way to get to the cave, that had to be it. But just to make sure, I climbed all the way down to the foot, where the waters raged and churned in a mad maelstrom. From what I could see, there was no other way to get behind the falls.

On the way back up, I resigned myself to the fact that Harry wasn't going to be accompanying me on the final leg of this journey. If getting to Hadley Cave meant navigating that narrow ledge, there'd be no piggyback ride. It looked like Harry had been right: I'd be facing Drakho alone.

When I made it back to him, he must've seen the disappointment on my face because he said, "Let me guess: it ain't handicapped accessible."

"Good guess."

"But you found it?"

"I think so."

"Then you'd better get to it. And don't worry—I ain't going nowhere." He laughed.

It crossed my mind that if I didn't return, he'd never be

going anywhere again. There was no way he could drag himself back to civilization, not with the trail and the abandoned road in front of him. He'd die somewhere along the way.

Harry handed me the sheathed knife and one of the flashlights. I tucked the sheath under my belt and stuck the flashlight in my back pocket. Then I reached out to shake his hand.

He grabbed it and said, "You'll be fine," but his voice wavered with uncertainty.

I could have turned this into a long goodbye, but that would've been an admission of my own doubts, so instead I took off. I climbed back down the falls until I was even with the narrow ledge, then I moved closer to the torrent of cascading water. The spray became heavier with every step. It was soon striking at me like a heavy rainfall, stinging my face. I forged ahead, climbing over the boulders, and stopped just short of the ledge.

Here, the sound of water plummeting down and hammering the Shenandoah River below was both deafening and disorienting. I took a beat to gather myself and to scope out the path ahead. The ledge stretched under the falls, receding and protruding unevenly from the sheer cliff wall. It was a jagged and treacherous path—and calling it a path was an exaggeration. I had to wonder if the boys from the fifties had even made it *into* the cave—they could have easily fallen from the ledge into the raging waters below.

Before moving forward, I tried to get a better view of the

cliff wall itself to see if the entrance to the cave was visible. But I couldn't see far enough under the falls. There was just no way to know if Hadley's Cave was actually there without going under and taking a look.

I took a deep breath, let it out, and stepped onto the ledge. It was no more than twelve inches wide here, so I immediately leaned up against the wall to brace myself. Then I started to inch my way along, moving under the falls. My eyes were fixed on the path ahead, and I willed myself not to look down, tempting as it was, but also understanding that this might cause just enough vertigo for me to lose my balance.

Progress was slow, and the farther along I went, the more the temptation to look down grew. After fifteen minutes or so, with no sign of the cave, I finally gave in and took a peek below. What I saw was far more frightening than vertigo. The falls hit the Shenandoah River with such a fierce and violent force that the frenzied vortex looked like a living, vicious creature, carved from water, angry, and warning me to keep away from its deadly clutches.

I hugged the wall more tightly, took another deep breath, and continued on. I wasn't tempted to look down again.

As it turned out, I didn't have to. Five minutes later, the wall began to curve inward and the ledge started to widen. After a few more yards, the wall gave way to the mouth of a cave. I stood there for a few beats, catching my breath, thankful that I'd avoided tumbling into the ferocious mouth of the creature below.

Then I entered the cave.

Inside was nothing but darkness. I pulled out my flashlight and flicked it on. The cave got progressively bigger until, about thirty yards in, it opened up rather suddenly into a large and magnificent cavern. Beautiful stalactites—white crystal spikes—hung down from the ceiling, and stalagmites—small pillars of all shapes, sizes, and colors—sprang up from the floor. Tiny rivulets of water ran down the walls.

The spectacle before me, elegant geological art, made by nature and not man, led me to one thought: this was untouched, sacred land. But that was how *I* saw the cave. What mattered was how *Drakho* saw it. Was it sacred land to him? Had he killed those boys because they'd trespassed on this magnificent, unpolluted territory?

I moved deeper into the cavern, shining the flashlight across the walls and floors, in awe of the majesty before me. But this sense of grandeur quickly gave way to something else—a physical sensation of malevolence. Something was pressing on me from all sides, a dampness in the air—thick, like an invisible fog. And it became thicker the farther in I went. I rubbed my arms, trying to brush it off as if I were trying to remove some gelatinous cobwebs. It didn't work. I was wrapped in what felt like a sentient mesh.

Then the cave suddenly pulsed—like a heartbeat.

Th-thump.

The stalactites quivered—I swept the flashlight beam across the cavern.

Th-thump.

The stalactites quivered again. What was going on? Was this the incipient rumbling of an earthquake?

Th-thump.

This time the heartbeat was stronger. The stalactites trembled violently, and I had the craziest thought yet: Was the cave alive? Did sacred land mean *living* land?

Th-thump—

I had an even more bizarre thought: Was the cave Drakho?

With each heartbeat, the walls, ceiling, and ground shook more savagely, and the dankness clung more aggressively to my skin. The wet air turned clammier, stickier, and more viscous—and it now had a distinct odor. Metallic, like iron or copper.

Was this how Edna had killed Drakho? Had she literally entered Drakho's very own body at Wassamoah Bay? Entered his heart?

Th-thump.

In the flashlight beam, I saw that the invisible dampness now had a crimson hue. It was turning into a dark red haze. I could taste it in my mouth, too—the tang of copper and salt and pungent honey.

The taste of blood.

Th-thump.

Frightened, I turned around and aimed my flashlight at the cave's entrance—but it was no longer visible. The mist of blood obscured everything.

Th-thump.

Panicked, I hurried toward where I had last seen the entrance, but the blood had become so thick I started choking on it. I was breathing blood in, and also trying to spit it out. Gagging, I picked up my pace. It felt like I was running through a reservoir filled with blood.

My coughing turned spasmodic, and I doubled over. My breathing was now so labored I didn't think I could make it out alive.

In desperation, I suddenly pulled the D-Guard knife from its sheath, ready to attack Drakho, but without a plan as to how. I swiped at the air, whipping the knife wildly through the crimson mist, hoping I was slicing through some sort of living tissue—slicing through it and killing it.

Th-thump.

My wild stabs at the mist were futile. I needed to cut through *real* tissue—Drakho's heart. Did that mean going for the walls? Were the walls his flesh?

I couldn't even see the walls through the crimson miasma. If I ran at them, I'd be charging blindly, an aimless attempt to lash out at an invisible enemy. An enemy who had somehow been able to engulf me completely.

Choking, fearful, and defeated, I knelt down, ready to give up—but when my knees hit the ground, I realized: there *was* flesh to stab.

Th-thump.

I raised the knife and drove it down into the ground with all my might.

The bloody mist instantly began to swirl all around me. Huge eddies cascaded over each other, surging forward, then retreating in fierce waves. Over and over again the waves swelled and rolled and churned around me. It was as if by stabbing the ground, I'd created a raging sea of blood.

Then Drakho stepped out from this raging sea. He appeared exactly as Edna had described him: thin and unusually tall, with a narrow face and deathly pale skin. His large, black eyes radiated cunning and intelligence.

I was too shocked at his sudden appearance to move. Now it was my own heart that was thumping violently. So violently I could hear it. I was still kneeling down, so it looked like I'd come to Drakho as a supplicant. Except my hand was clutching the knife, its tip buried in the ground.

I had no time to weigh my next move. I could either tell him his name and hope that he'd keep his word and give Nate a reprieve, or I could follow through with what I'd come here to do: kill him and end this forever.

Th-thump.

I made my decision in a split second. I wrenched the knife from the ground, lunged to my feet, and sprang at him.

He partially blocked the knife with his hand; it sliced his palm, and blood seeped from the wound.

I continued to drive forward and plunged the knife into his chest.

He stumbled back, so very human in that moment. I was ready to press my advantage—to drive the knife into his flesh again—when I saw something so unfathomable it stopped me.

Blood wasn't oozing out of the deep cut in his chest. Instead, the thick mist of blood that hung in the air, surrounding his wound, was oozing *into* the open laceration.

I looked up at Drakho's face. His pale skin glowed with a healthy, rosy hue, as if he was more alive than before I'd stabbed him, not less—and his black eyes shone brightly. His face wasn't contorted in pain, but was instead serene.

Then the miasma of blood that filled the cave, still churning and ebbing, *all* of it began to flow toward him, slowly at first, then gaining speed.

Th-thump.

The blood was streaming into the laceration in his chest, past the torn flesh.

Th-thump.

With each beat of the cave's heart—or was it Drakho's heart?—the blood in the cavern drained into Drakho, until the crimson mist, along with its cold and clammy weight, was completely gone.

The cave was majestic again, just as it had been when I'd entered. The ancient stalactites and stalagmites were undisturbed, watching over the sacred land.

My eyes went to the cut in Drakho's chest. It had healed.

Drakho swept toward me then—and I ran. I felt a cold wind at my back, as if the monster was on my heels. I picked up my pace and considered swinging around and stabbing him again. But that would have been an act of desperation. The amber weapon had failed. It was nothing but a symbol of my futile attempt to save Nate.

Still, what choice did I have? I could either die as a coward on the run or die trying to save Nate. I slowed down, clutching the knife, ready to swing around—when I saw daylight up ahead. The mouth of the cave. A way out.

I sped up and felt the web of dankness engulf me again, returning as if commanded by Drakho. I was still "it." He wanted to play more of his game, but daylight was just a few yards away—and I was sure that my momentum was strong enough to carry me forward out of his dank web and into the oblivion of the falls.

And that was the new choice. Hurtle off the ledge and risk death in the furious, violent waters below, or face Drakho and *surely* die.

I sped up and leapt off the ledge.

The sensation of plummeting down while embedded in the waterfall wasn't thrilling, like I'd seen it depicted in countless movies; I didn't feel like a triumphant hero who'd braved a great escape and found it exhilarating. It was agonizing and terrifying to know for certain that I was going to be fed to the frenzied vortex below.

Which was precisely what happened next. The falls threw me violently into the raging maelstrom, burying me deep in the waters of the Shenandoah River. There was no way to fight back. The falls were pushing me down with brutal force, so I just held my breath, hoping that force would relent. And all along I feared that my death was yards away—that the falls were about to drive me into the river bottom and break me into a thousand pieces.

But the force abated, and as soon as it did, I began to kick and swim, not up against it, but laterally, away from it, parallel to the river bottom. At least I hoped that was the direction I was moving in; I was too disoriented to know for sure.

After thirty seconds or so, I couldn't hold my breath any longer, and I reflexively inhaled—and water flooded my lungs. I gagged and lost my bearings. A wave of dizziness coursed through me and I realized I was about to lose consciousness.

I had to make a move if I was going to live through this.

I inhaled again, lightheaded, taking more water into my lungs, then kept my mouth shut and frantically glanced around. A few feet to my right, the water appeared lighter in color, so I kicked in that direction, hoping it would lead to the surface.

My lungs felt like they were going to explode. I forced myself to keep swimming, but my body was leaden and my kicks weak.

My thoughts turned hazy as my lightheadedness bloomed. My vision left me, and I saw only white. Giving up was the best way out. Breathe in, let the water flood my lungs, pass out, and let the Shenandoah River carry my body to the dead world.

I broke through the surface and immediately spit out water, gasping and coughing, while fighting to suck down air. My arms and legs felt like dead weight, but I forced them to move so I wouldn't sink. My vision returned—I saw blurs of color, then the river came into focus.

I treaded water as I caught my breath and got my bearings. As soon as I stabilized, the pain from my collision with the river came roaring back. I felt as if I'd been used as a punching bag. Still, though bruised and battered, and aching from head to toe, I was thankful to be alive.

I swam slowly toward the Deer Hill Trail side of the river, then climbed out, sat down on a boulder, and stared back at the falls. My thoughts were on the D-Guard Bowie knife. Not because it was lost somewhere in the river, but because it hadn't done any damage at all. Instead, it had been part of some supernatural extravaganza, some ritual in which Drakho and the ancient cave had become one living thing.

The amber weapon had no power.

I'd misinterpreted Edna's story.

As I hiked up the trail, toward Harry, I turned *The Forest* over in my mind. Had Harker gotten it wrong? Had he misinterpreted Edna's story and filled in the missing pieces with useless knowledge? Or had the amber weapon failed Edna, too? Or maybe Edna's story *had* once told you all you needed to know, but all you needed to know was now forever lost in those missing pages.

Chapter Eighteen

The hike back up was hard. With every step I took, weariness and soreness coursed through my body. With every breath, my throat and chest burned—the residual effect of choking on the mist of blood and on river water.

As I approached the cluster of rocks where I'd left Harry, I had a sudden fear: he wouldn't be there. And as soon as I stepped off the trail, that fear was realized. My eyes fell on the gray rocks that bordered the falls—Harry was gone from his perch.

I scanned up and down the falls. Surely he hadn't tried to drag himself back to civilization. I hadn't been gone that long. Or was my impression of time warped? The events in the cave had unfolded in that other world, the one beyond the shadows, and maybe time in that world had its own scale. Maybe my supernatural meeting with Drakho had unfolded over hours and not minutes.

A quick look to the sky, and the position of the sun, confirmed that everything had passed in "real" time—it was still late afternoon. I hadn't been gone very long. So I climbed up onto the rocks to get a better look around, and immediately spotted Harry. He'd scaled some of the boulders and was now perched closer to the edge of the falls. His vision was fixed on something below.

"Hey," I yelled, over the sound of the falls.

Harry swung himself around, took in my waterlogged, beaten-down appearance, then shouted, "What happened?"

I climbed over to him and told him about my encounter, which I could have summed up in four words: It was a bust.

"Well, you get a partial victory," he said.

"How do you figure that?"

"It sounds like you got the sacred land part right."

"We can't be sure."

"If he shows up in person, then you're at the man's house. Or at least, one of them."

His logic was sound.

"And come to think of it," he added, "you got another victory. The bastard let you go."

"I told you, he didn't let me go. I ran."

"You think you got away 'cause you *outran* him?" Harry scoffed. "He let you go so he could play his game, just like he did with me. But he's got a soft spot for you—he let you keep your legs."

I'd been too panicked to realize that this was exactly what had happened. Of course I hadn't escaped.

"He's sticking to the rules of the game," Harry said. "The game is for your son's life, not yours." He looked back down at the falls. "But give him time—and he's got plenty of it—and he'll get around to yours, too."

"Meanwhile, we get another chance," I said.

Harry smiled. "Yep—but we gotta get it right this time."

*

The clock was ticking, so even though I would have preferred to have spent a few minutes recuperating, we began our trek back. Carrying Harry down should have been easier than hauling him up, but the punishment my body had taken from the falls made it harder. Every one of my muscles ached, and every time my foot hit the ground, it felt like the falls were punching me again. These new body blows made the going very slow.

During one of our frequent stops, I told Harry what I'd concluded earlier: that Harker had misinterpreted what Edna had meant by an amber weapon, or I had. "Or the weapon just don't work no matter what," he said. "And the story is just that—a goddamn story with nothing to it."

"No—that's throwing the baby out with the bathwater," I shot back, defensive, as much out of exhaustion as stubbornness. "The story laid out his powers perfectly. It told us everything about him."

"Okay then, here's something I got from the story. Something you ain't said nothin' about. He's been here for a hell of a long time. Way before those settlers came over, and way before the Indians made Virginia their home. Nothing's beat him yet. The proof is in the puddin'."

"So you think this is a lost cause? I thought you were all for this."

"I'm sayin' we need more than stories to kill him. If stories were all it took, I could kill him myself. I got a thousand stories."

*

The ride back from Front Royal was somber. I weighed whether to give up. What if novel therapy was failing me again? It had guided me into a world that was a giant shake and bake of fact and fiction, one where supernatural events were a part of life, but also one where death wasn't hidden—where it couldn't be shunned or ignored but had to be accepted.

I'd seen Lucy, so fragile and sad, beckoning me to cross the river Acheron.

In that way, this world was the opposite of the world I'd left just a day and half ago: the world of American culture, mores, and tradition, which dictated that we should avoid dealing with death and should bury our grief as if it were unnatural.

So was novel therapy working or not?

The only way to come up with the answer to that question was to answer another question: Was it helping with my battle to save Nate's life?

The answer to that was "no," which meant that as soon as I got back to Arlington, I'd go and see Nate. I'd spend this evening with him and as much of tomorrow as possible; I'd give him some sort of birthday celebration after all. I'd spend every hour I could with him before Drakho took him from me.

He'd have a blast, unaware of his fate; but for me, it'd be hell on earth. A voyage deeper into Dante's *Inferno*. The hell of knowing that my precious son was going to die. And when he did die—

"What am I not seeing about *The Forest*—about Drakho—about *Dracula*?" I blurted out, hoping to stem the feeling of dread welling up from my soul, the bitter agony of losing my child. A grief so great as to be unfathomable.

"Maybe he ain't Dracula," Harry said.

"Maybe," I said, though I didn't believe that for second. Drakho *was* Dracula, the original Dracula. That's where the trail had led. Bram Stoker's *Dracula* had led us to *The Forest*. It wasn't possible that this had been just a coincidence. The connections were too great to ignore. And the more I'd dug, the stronger the connections had become.

And that took me deeper into novel therapy, where another connection started to crystallize. It required a bigger leap of faith than the ones I'd already taken—but what choice did I have? I either had to double down or give up.

This new connection meant believing and accepting a bigger picture, a canvas of fact and fiction that spanned centuries. A canvas that had been painted by three people: Edna Grayson, Bram Stoker, and Jonathan Harker. If I could accept this bigger picture, I'd be able to devise another strategy for playing Drakho's game of chess.

When we got back to the sprawling suburbs of Northern Virginia, I told Harry that I might have a way forward, or at least a way to find out what our next move should be.

"So what are you waiting for?" he said. "Lay it on me."

I did, but I was expecting resistance. "Edna wrote her story at the very start of the seventeenth century," I began. "Then, almost three hundred years later, just before the turn of the twentieth century, Bram Stoker wrote *Dracula*. And then, a hundred and ten years after *Dracula*, Harker found Edna's original story—"

"Thanks for the history lesson, but so what?"

"You wanted me to lay it on you, so hear me out. Harker finds this four-hundred-year-old story and fills in the missing pieces. But he's basically from our generation, and he knows the same stories we know. So he's filling in the missing pieces with what he knows."

"So?"

"So he sees the resemblance between Drakho in *The Forest* and *Dracula*. I mean, anyone reading *The Forest* would see the connection. Even a twelve-year-old."

"Okay, I'll give you that—but I don't see where you're going with this."

That worried me. Harry was smart, and I was hoping I'd get him to see where I was going before I got there. It would've validated that I was headed in the right direction, that the big picture I was seeing had merit.

But this wasn't to be, so I made the connection for him. "What if Harker used *Dracula*, a book published hundreds of years after *The Forest*, to fill in the missing pieces of *The Forest*? Just think about it for a minute. *Dracula* didn't exist when Edna wrote *The Forest*, so her story was based solely on whatever she knew back then. It was based on what the Paspahegh told her about Drakho. Her story wasn't based on ideas that came three hundred years later."

"I'm still not seeing what you're getting at."

That added more doubts to the ones I already had; I'd thought he'd definitely start connecting the dots by now. Still, I forged on. "What if Harker filled in the missing pieces of Edna's story with things she couldn't have possibly known? I mean, what if he used elements that came hundreds of years later to complete her story? After all, we're talking about fiction; he was embellishing a *story*, make-believe. So it's not like anyone would really care about these made-up details."

"You do," Harry said.

I had to laugh. "Ridiculous, huh?" He grinned and I went on. "Here's the long and the short of it: What if Harker shaped Edna's story so that it fit in neatly with the Dracula story he *already* knew. The Dracula story we *all* know. The detailed mythology we can't help but absorb even if we have no interest in Dracula. You know, all that stuff we grew up on: biting necks, blood, capes, coffins, the whole bit. The Dracula legend that Edna would've had no idea about. Harker was writing about Dracula; *Edna* was writing about Drakho."

Harry didn't respond for a few seconds. Either he was trying to wrap his head around this or he was disgusted. "Okay... I get your point," he finally volunteered. "But I still don't see how that gets us our next move."

"It might get us a different weapon," I said. "The right weapon. If we're lucky."

"At least you're talkin' weapons." He grinned again. "That I can buy."

"Okay, good. So how about this? What if Harker based the amber weapon on *Dracula*—the rules laid down by Bram Stoker, and not by Edna? We need to see exactly what Edna wrote about the amber weapon and what Harker added."

"No one's stoppin' ya."

That was my cue. I pulled over, reached into the back seat, and scooped up *The Forest*. I dove back into it, determined to isolate exactly which sections of the story Edna had written and which sections Harker had written or embellished.

I already knew that Harker had written the very end of Edna's tale, the section where Edna defeated Drakho, the section I'd used as my field guide, the section that had ended in triumph for Edna and failure for me. But now I focused on exactly what Edna had actually written about the amber weapon. What did the *original* text say—her words?

Harker's detailed footnotes were meticulous on this front. And as it turned out, the only time Edna had written about the weapon herself was in the section where she described how she'd learned of it.

I reviewed that section once more. She'd learned about the weapon from the settler who'd tortured one of the Paspahegh, and not directly from the Paspahegh prisoner. I made a mental note of that, as well as noting that at this point in the story there was no doubt that Edna was looking for the same thing the rest of the settlers wanted: a way to stop the vicious warrior from slaughtering the residents of Jamestown.

The settler had relayed to Edna the words he'd heard from the Paspahegh, and Edna had translated those words as "amber weapon." She hadn't been ambiguous about those words. But she didn't give any other details about the weapon. It was Harker who had written the rest of the information about the dagger—from Edna coating it in amber to her stabbing Drakho with it.

It took me less than five seconds to realize what this meant, and I couldn't believe I hadn't noticed it the first time around. But I understood why I hadn't. The first time around, I hadn't yet seen the bigger picture. But now I did, and this is what it told me:

Edna had never once called the weapon a dagger or a knife. That was all Harker.

Why would Harker have assumed the amber weapon was a knife? The answer seemed obvious. How would you go about killing a creature Harker believed was the basis for the myth of Dracula? Well, you'd kill him in the traditional way: by stabbing him in the heart. With a knife.

It was only natural that Harker would have come to that conclusion. I supposed he could've opted for a stake through the heart, which was also part of the myth of Dracula, but it wasn't part of Bram Stoker's *Dracula*. In Stoker's book, knives had killed Dracula: one to the count's throat and one through his heart.

But the point was that Edna wouldn't have known about either stakes or knives. Stoker's novel wouldn't come along until three hundred years after her death.

So what *did* she actually know?

The answer to this question was lost in *The Forest's* missing pages—which were now lost to history. The only clue Edna had left behind was the term *amber weapon*.

I needed to drop my assumptions—and Harker's—about what those words could mean; I needed to start fresh. First, I couldn't assume the weapon was a knife or dagger of some sort. And second, I couldn't assume that Edna had used amber to coat her weapon. This "coating" idea had also come from Harker.

I had to start at the beginning again and research "amber." But this time, I didn't want to use my cell phone. I wanted to do a more thorough search. But I had no home in which to do it, and I couldn't go to the Cherrydale Library.

"Does Buck have a computer and Internet access?" I asked.

"Why wouldn't he? Just 'cause he's into the Civil War don't mean he's living like a caveman."

I explained that I wanted to go back to the drawing board with amber. So Harry called Buck.

On the call, once again, the knife didn't come up. You'd think Buck would have wanted to know how we'd used it. And, once again, I didn't ask Harry *why* Buck wasn't curious. Maybe I just didn't want to know that there was yet another layer to this nightmare.

On the way to Buck's, Harry laid out *his* plan. "Buck's got some explosives—dynamite. I say we load up, go back to Hadley's Cave, and when Drakho shows up, we blow the shit out of him."

"And why do you think that'd work?"

"Hell, I didn't come up with the idea. The army did. And not just the U.S. Army: all armies, all military powers, no matter when or where—they all know that the bigger the bomb, the more you wipe out your enemy. It's kinda like if you can't kill your enemy with bullets, drop a goddamn megaton bomb on 'em and that'll do the job. Hell, that's why we kept building bigger and bigger bombs until we got the king of all bombs: an atomic bomb. You just blast an entire city." Harry glanced at me. "I know what you're thinking, so don't get me wrong. I'm not sayin' that blowing up entire cities is the right thing to do. I'm just talking about a tried-and-true tactic. Somethin' we can use."

"So we destroy the entire cave, huh?" He had a point.

"Yeah. And if he's in it, or if he's somehow part of the cave, like you were describin', then he ain't gonna survive."

"We'd have to surprise him—ambush him."

"Then that's what we'll do," Harry said, folding his arms.

This was a plan all right, but it didn't fit into the complicated game of chess we'd been playing. On the other hand, it wasn't like we were winning the game. The best you could say was that we hadn't been checkmated yet.

I guess we'd have to see if I could uncover what Edna's

amber weapon actually was before ruling out Harry's crazy idea. And that thought led to a question.

"Why does Buck have dynamite?" It had dawned on me that explosives didn't seem like collectable memorabilia.

"Well, he might not, anymore," Harry said, "but I remember him telling me he and his wife were gonna plant a garden in the back yard. He got dynamite to blast out two tree stumps. Then his wife got sick and they never did get to plantin' that garden."

*

It was evening when we got to Buck's place. The afterglow from the setting sun was red, the kind of brilliant red that makes you stop and stare at the sky in wonder. But this evening, on this last night of Drakho's game, the night before Nate's life would either be won or lost, I saw this spectral red glow as a sign that Drakho's land—his sacred land, from North Carolina to Massachusetts—had been colonized by settlers. For this spectacular sunset was the result of pollutants from the millions and millions of those settlers on his land.

Buck had made spaghetti and meatballs for dinner and had set the table for three—the same table on which he'd earlier displayed his knife collection. We didn't have time for a meal break, but we were starving, so I scarfed down my food and then quickly excused myself; rude behavior, but I had more pressing concerns than whether or not Buck found me lacking in the social graces.

Harry was left at the table, entrusted with the task of

coming up with an explanation—a lie—as to why I was in such a rush. Buck had already set up his laptop for me in the war room, and I got right down to it. I searched "amber," and this time I took a closer look at the gem's history. Amber had been widely admired as jewelry for thousands of years— archeologists had even found examples of prehistoric man using the gem as ornaments. So it stood to reason that Edna would have known of amber primarily in the context of jewelry. But what could she have meant by "amber weapon"?

Or more to the point: What had the Paspahegh prisoner meant when he'd used the term "amber weapon"? After all, the phrase had originated with the prisoner; he'd said it over and over to the settler who'd interrogated him. Edna had merely translated it.

Of course, it was possible that the interrogator had misremembered the phrase, or that Edna had mistranslated the Paspahegh language. Which meant perhaps the prisoner had never actually meant to refer to amber at all. But I wasn't ready to concede that possibility yet, because if that was true, then there was nothing left to go on.

I moved on from the history of amber and instead turned to information about the qualities of the mineral itself. This led to the discovery that amber exhibited a special property. Thales, a Greek philosopher, who lived in the sixth century B.C., discovered it. When you rubbed a piece of "elektron," which was the Greek name for amber, the mineral acquired a special property—what Thales called a unique force. This force was able to attract pieces of straw. People thought this force was some kind of trick, or even magic. It would take another two thousand years to discover that this force was what we now call static electricity. And it would take even longer to discover that static electricity was part of a greater force—electricity itself.

When I read this, I felt immediately vindicated: my latest foray into novel therapy seemed to have paid off big time. I'd just discovered the missing link, the missing connection—the one that tied the amber weapon to Drakho's weakness. The same weakness that Harry had discovered many years ago.

Drakho feared electricity.

And that explained why Drakho stuck as much as he could to the wilderness in Northern Virginia. The wilderness was the land least contaminated by electricity. So with the connection between amber and electricity now clear—and it couldn't get any clearer; even the word "electricity" was derived from the Greek word "elektron" meaning "amber"— it was time to go back to my bible. *The Forest.*

Edna hadn't coated a knife in amber—or in tree resin. Her weapon had been *amber itself.* Harker had made the wrong choices when embellishing and completing her story. Of course, he'd had no reason to think his choices would ever affect anyone or anything; he'd simply been restoring a piece of fiction, and factual accuracy wasn't how fiction was judged. He couldn't have known that for me, fiction would be a matter of life and death.

Buck wheeled Harry into the war room, and Harry asked, "How's it going?"

"Good," I said, wanting to blurt out everything but stopping myself. I couldn't fill Harry in with Buck in the room.

"What'd ya find?" Harry asked.

I glanced at Buck, who smiled curiously. The silence grew until it became awkward.

Finally I said, "I think we've got what we need. If you're ready, we can hit the road."

"First tell me what you got." Harry wheeled himself closer to me.

Why was he putting me on the spot?

"Buck knows," Harry added.

"What?" In one fell swoop, this explained why Buck hadn't asked us any questions.

"They didn't call him Drakho," Buck said. "The Confederate soldiers called him the Nightman. It's in some of their diaries. The Union soldiers also talked about him in their diaries, but they saw him differently. They thought he was the devil himself. The way they saw it, since God wasn't going to help the South, the devil was doing it. But no matter what side you were fighting on, the soldiers agreed on one thing: Virginia was his homeland. That's why it's just the soldiers in these parts who saw him."

"So you believe this Nightman is real?" I said.

"Hell if I know, but I'll tell you this: when I visited Harry in the hospital all those years ago and he told me what went down in Prince William Forest—I believed *him*. And it reminded me of something I'd read in my great-grandfather's diary when I was kid. My great-grandfather was a Confederate soldier, and he was one of the ones who wrote about this Nightman. I believed *him*, too."

"Let's hear what you dug up, John," Harry said.

I wanted to hear more about the Nightman, but I knew it'd have to wait, so I told Harry what I'd found out about amber and then laid out my conclusion.

"We know Harker made up the ending of Edna's story because those pages were missing. My bet is that Edna used amber against Drakho. Not a knife coated in amber or tree resin, but amber itself—the raw material, or maybe a piece of jewelry. She understood that the 'weapon' part of amber was this strange force—the static electricity—created when you rubbed it. The Paspahegh had figured it out. Just like you figured out that Drakho stays away from electric power stations, they figured out that he stays away from that strange force created with amber."

"So Edna used amber to protect her son—to ward off Drakho," Harry said.

"Yeah, and that part fits because we know for sure that Edna didn't end up killing Drakho—he's most definitely still around."

"So it looks like Harker latched on to the wrong part of *Dracula*," Harry said.

"What do you mean?"

"From what you're sayin', amber was jewelry, so don't it stand to reason—if reason got anything to do with this—that Edna had her boy wear a necklace around his neck—"

I got where he was going and filled in the rest. "Like a garlic necklace wards off Dracula."

"Yeah. But I still got a problem."

"What?"

"Are you tellin' me we're gonna kill Drakho with static electricity?"

"No—not *static* electricity. The key thing here is that he's susceptible to electricity, period." I looked at the battle maps on the war room's walls. "Let's say that hundreds of years ago, it took only a small amount of electricity to ward him off, so static electricity did the job. But as we became more industrialized, Drakho gained more tolerance. He *had* to. Electricity is now everywhere, and to survive, to interact with his environment, to interact with us, he had to be able to tolerate stronger electrical fields."

"We all adapt or die," Buck said.

"I'm living proof of that," Harry grunted.

"The bottom line is you're right, Harry," I said. "We're going to need more than static electricity."

"You're gonna need a bigger boat," Buck said, and chuckled.

"Especially if we're gonna kill him," Harry added. "And if I remember right, in *Jaws*, they never did get a bigger boat—they killed the shark with an explosion."

"Yeah," Buck said. "They stuck an oxygen tank in its mouth, shot the tank, and blew that fish to smithereens."

Was warding Drakho off a better strategy? Harker hadn't been able to uncover whether Edna and her son had survived the Starvation Time or not. If she *had* survived—if she had withstood Drakho's onslaught of Jamestown—then she had probably succeeded by using her amber weapon to keep Drakho at bay.

But could Nate and I spend the rest of our lives next to a strong electrical field? I supposed it was possible. We could move to a house or an apartment that abutted a substation. And then what? Would Nate only attend schools that were near substations? Would he only visit friends who lived near power plants? How would he travel from place to place? It was clear that no matter what, Nate would eventually find himself vulnerable to attack. It just wasn't possible to make sure he'd spend every minute of the rest of his life in close proximity to a strong electric field.

"We're going to have to use electricity to kill him," I said.

Harry shook his head. "How are we gonna do that? We can't just cut down a power line, hand it to the fella, and say hold on to this."

"No, but there has to be a way to do this."

Harry's brow furrowed, and he leaned back in his chair. Buck nodded like he was thinking this through.

I got back online.

"What are you lookin' up now?" Harry said.

"How strong the electrical fields are around those substations." That information was easy to find. People didn't want to live near substations, and the power companies wanted to show it was safe to do so, so there were plenty of studies that measured these electrical fields.

"Harry, when you lived off Columbia Pike, you said Drakho stopped following you when you were about a hundred yards from the power plant," I said.

"Yeah."

That turned out to be good news. The electrical field from a substation was relatively weak at that distance, which meant a portable generator might be powerful enough to inflict damage on Drakho—*if* we could get him close enough to it. I looked up generators and found a few models that could do the job.

I filled Harry and Buck in, and Harry said, "Just how are we going to draw him to a generator?"

"We meet him in his favorite place—a cave," I said. "And this is the part you're going to like: we trap him inside by dynamiting the cave shut."

"You're right," he said. "I do like it."

"Good—then maybe you can come up with a way to get a generator into a cave that Drakho considers sacred, then rig the cave with dynamite without him catching on."

"Maybe I can," Harry said.

"I'd like to come along and help," Buck said. "Since I'm donating the dynamite."

Harry glanced at me, and I could tell he didn't like that idea. He took a beat, then turned to his friend. "We could use an extra pair of hands, Buck, but if you get into this, and we can't kill the bastard, I guarantee you'll become part of this. I know you don't worry about yourself none, but your family becomes part of this guy's game, too. The Nightman takes a liking to bloodlines. I know you got your daughter, Beth, and her family, and your son, Henry, and his family. If you come with us, you're riskin' their lives, too. And their kids' lives. I mean, you're lucky your great-grandpa only wrote about the fella and didn't tangle with him."

Buck took this in and then looked over the memorabilia in the war room.

Everything Harry had said applied to me, too. It reinforced that I was doing the right thing. Warding off Drakho wasn't enough. The only way to save Nate, and the family Nate would someday have, was to kill Drakho.

"It ain't worth the risk," Harry said, adding a coda to his speech. "If you want to help, go ahead and add the Nightman to the war room. So when others come looking for what's after them, they got someplace to go to find some answers. They'll know they're not crazy."

Buck nodded, though he didn't look happy with his decision.

I went back online for one last bit of information. Something we'd need to know if we wanted to trap Drakho: the area in Northern Virginia that was the least touched by man-made electromagnetic fields. Sacred land may once have meant land untouched by humans, but I was sure it now meant land untouched by these fields.

I tracked down an environmental watchdog site with a special set of maps. Each of the fifty states had an overlay of man-made electromagnetic fields. I magnified the Virginia map until Northern Virginia filled the computer screen. The areas with the most powerful electrical fields were covered in a red hue, a brilliant red like tonight's sunset. These parcels of land featured power plants, factories, manufacturing parks, TV stations, arrays of satellite dishes, and medical complexes.

Next came areas covered with orange hues, where the electrical fields were strong but not overwhelming. These were the densely populated parts of suburban Virginia which included townhouses, apartment complexes, and all the business districts.

Then came areas covered with yellow hues. These were the wealthiest parts of the suburbs, where the homes were on huge lots and where there were plenty of parks, including a few lakes.

White hues indicated the weakest levels of electrical fields, and that was what interested me. These were the rural areas with few homes. It included the wilderness areas along the Potomac, Northern Virginia's state and national parks, and a good chunk of the Shenandoah Valley. These were the places where Drakho felt the safest. They included Cold Falls, Prince William Forest, and Hadley Cave.

But I was hoping to narrow it down much more. I wanted to find Drakho's sweet spot. An electromagnetic-free zone. *If* it existed. Drakho hadn't been able to keep mankind from touching every inch of his homeland, but was it possible that mankind hadn't yet infected every inch with an electrical field?

I magnified the map as much as the website would allow, then scrolled through the regions overlaid with white—

through national and state parks, through wilderness preserves, and through the Shenandoah Valley. I was ready to give up, to settle for another trip to Front Royal and Hadley's Cave, when it appeared—a small patch of land untouched by an electrical field. An area in the middle of the Bull Run Mountains, not far from Paspahegh Falls. It wasn't covered in red, orange, yellow, or even white hues. This was the last untouched part of Drakho's homeland.

I was reminded of *Dracula*. At the end of Bram Stoker's tale, Dracula retreated to his homeland in the Carpathian Mountains. But in Drakho's story, Drakho wasn't retreating—it was his homeland that was retreating.

I googled maps of the Bull Run Mountains, trying to scope out more topographical features about this specific patch of land. It turned out to be a valley between two shallow peaks, but it still wasn't clear exactly what was there—caves, woods, marshes? From one map, it appeared there was a col—a small pass—between the peaks, so I plotted out the best way to access this col: Route 66 to Fauquier County, then a series of small rural roads.

The last of these roads led to a trail that would take us close to this spot. But to get to the col, it looked like we'd have to go off-trail. I downloaded a GPS app to my phone, since getting lost in that remote area was a real possibility.

While I called Home Depot and placed an order to rent a generator, Buck retrieved the dynamite from his garage. Then we loaded the sticks of dynamite, along with blasting caps, into the trunk of my car. Buck gave me a crash course in explosives, from how to prepare the blasting caps using a mechanical match, to where to place the dynamite so the explosion would dislodge enough stone to seal the cave.

As we all said our goodbyes, I again considered my other option: warding Drakho off for the rest of my life, then passing that burden on to Nate. And again I couldn't see that as a viable option. Maybe it had worked for Edna and her son.

And maybe not.

Chapter Nineteen

At Home Depot, I picked up the generator, a couple of empty gas cans, and a cart for hauling the generator through the wilderness. It was a quick trip this time. The river Acheron wasn't flowing through the store.

After filling up the cans at a gas station, Harry and I headed to Fauquier County.

"Why doesn't Drakho just leave this area—get the hell out of Dodge?" I said. "Why doesn't he go to a place that's totally free of electrical fields? There must be a few of those spots left somewhere on Earth."

"The same reason any man wouldn't leave," Harry said. "This is his homeland."

Of course, I thought. *Some things aren't that complicated.*

Harry glanced at me and said, "I never got to ask you something."

"Better go ahead then—this might be your last chance."

"How did you and Lee get to be friends? I know you were just kids, but it still don't seem like you two would be hangin' out on the same side of the tracks."

That was an easy question to answer. "He made me cool. I

was a nerd and got picked on a lot. Lee, on the other hand, was a mean kid—but not the kind of mean kid who was a bully. He didn't need to pick on kids, because all of us were already scared of him. We saw that if you crossed him, he'd get angry."

"Yeah, that boy had a temper."

"I guess it came in handy sometimes, because that's how we became friends. I was waiting my turn to play four square, and Lee was in line, too, ahead of me. His turn came up and he went in. And when the next kid fouled out, I went in, too.

"But no one liked to play with me, the nerd, and I didn't really want to play, either, but Mrs. Baxter, our teacher, forced us to do group activities during recess. She said it built character. So for me it worked like this: to get rid of me, the kids made sure I fouled out as soon as I got in. You know, for carrying the ball or double bouncing or whatever, even if I didn't actually do it. And I never argued.

"And that's how it went down this time, too. At least that's the way it started to go down. I hit the ball, and one of the kids called it out and told me to take a hike. Of course, it wasn't out. It hit inside the line, but like I said, I never argued. Well, Lee argued. He said it wasn't out. And for some reason the other kid insisted that it *was* out. Maybe the kids were all used to getting rid of me, so it was a habit, or maybe he hated me so much he thought it was worth the risk of crossing Lee.

"Anyway, it was a big mistake. Lee got in his face and yelled, *Are you saying I'm blind? Or a dumbass? Is that what you're saying?* And he punched the kid. Just like that. The kid started crying and Lee told him to shut up. If Mrs. Baxter came over, he'd punch him a hundred times. So I stayed in the game and we all kept playing. Lee didn't say anything to me. And I didn't foul out until I really did hit the ball out.

"Later, after school, I went up to him, to thank him, but before I said anything, he asked me to explain a math problem to him. He didn't say anything about defending me and neither did I. But that was it. We were friends from that day on."

"You know what?" Harry said, "You're pretty good at telling stories yourself."

I laughed.

*

After that we didn't talk much. There wasn't much left to say. We both believed Drakho would show up. He'd damn well know humans were in his pristine lair.

I saw this trip to the Shenandoah Valley with different eyes this time. It wasn't just a journey from the densely populated suburbs—beleaguered by housing developments, shopping malls, and office parks—to the rural areas of Northern Virginia. It was a journey through electrical fields. Angry red fields, then buzzing orange fields, then mellow yellow, and finally calm white.

When I reached the Bull Run Mountains—a lush expanse of peaks and valleys, thick forests, and rocky cliffs—I pulled off Route 66 and headed down the rural roads that would carry us to the most sacred of lands.

The first few roads were paved. We passed picnic areas, trailheads, and turnouts with scenic views. Then we hit a series of dirt roads, each narrower and more desolate than the last.

A metal cross bar blocked the last road. The cross bar was locked in place with a padlock and chain; both were covered in a thick coat of rust, as if they hadn't been touched in many decades.

We were way too far from our destination to start hiking, so I grabbed a rock and started pounding on the padlock. On about the twentieth blow it broke open. I unraveled the chain and began pushing the cross bar. It creaked and groaned, trying to resist, but eventually it gave way.

After driving a couple more miles, it became obvious that not only had the padlock not been touched in many decades, neither had the road. The forest was encroaching on it from both sides, threatening to take it over; saplings were even growing from the road itself. I had to stop the car several times to get out and yank the saplings from the dirt in order to clear a path farther into the wilderness.

Then we reached a point where the forest had almost completely taken over. Vestiges of the dirt road were still there, but instead of saplings springing from it, larger trees had taken root, and the underbrush here was as thick as in the bordering woods.

The only way forward was on foot, and that meant roughly a four-mile hike to the col.

"You ain't gonna be able to haul the generator and carry me on your back," Harry said.

"What about trying to use the wheelchair?" There was still the hint of the dirt road.

"You gotta be kidding me."

"I'll alternate between the generator and pushing you."

"And when you get to the trail?"

"The hike to the col is short." But what I didn't say was that we'd have to go off trail to get to the col.

"Listen, I wanna help, but I don't see how I can," Harry said. "Last time I'm guessing I was good for moral support—kinda." He grinned, then turned serious again. "You had doubts then. But you ain't got doubts now, right?"

I did have doubts. I didn't doubt Drakho would be at the end of the trail, but I doubted we'd be able to trap him. He might even have been tracking us already, and was busy preparing for our next move.

"You go alone and you go faster," Harry said. "*And* you're in better shape when you get there."

It was in that moment that I realized why Harry had to come with me. Or maybe I'd known it all along, but it wasn't until now that it finally crystallized into the right words.

"Someone has to tell the story," I said.

"What?"

"You're Edna Grayson. You're Bram Stoker. You're Jonathan Harker."

"And you're off your rocker."

"Stories tell you all you need to know, and *you* have to tell *this* story, Harry. Without stories, the Hatfields never have a chance. The McCoys—the real McCoy always wins. It was your story that gave me a chance."

Harry leaned back and stared at the peaks in the distance. His face looked resolute. This was about as serious as I'd seen him, as if he was weighing my words carefully and considering the journey ahead.

"Your story will fill in those missing pages," I said.

Harry looked from the peaks to me. "If you don't make it and I do," he said, "I'd have to crawl back on my own. Now *that* would be a story worth tellin'."

"One you'd want to tell?"

"Hell yes." He smiled. "But I'll settle for the one where we both make it back."

*

After filling the generator with gas, then strapping it to the cart along with the dynamite, blasting caps, and flashlights, I pulled the cart about a quarter mile down the road, navigating through the underbrush. Then I went back for Harry and the wheelchair. The path wasn't smooth, but pushing him was better than carrying him.

Still, after a mile or so, the forest had done such a good job of reclaiming the land that it became tougher to drag the cart, and pushing the wheelchair forward was altogether impossible. So from that point on, I alternated between carrying Harry on my back and dragging the cart—two trips every fifty yards or so.

The closer we got to the trail, the lusher and more wild the terrain became. It was possible that hikers had trekked out this way, but this land was so isolated—nestled and lost between the shallow mountains—that it was more likely that Harry and I were the first to come this way in a long, long time.

It took about four hours to make it to the trail, which was so overgrown it was barely visible. Here, I tried to use my GPS app, but it wouldn't work—no reception. I knew that our final destination, the col, was about a half mile away, so I left Harry and the generator behind as I went on to scout.

I followed the traces of the trail, or what I thought to be the traces, and I must have done a good job of it, because when I continued past the trail, into the woods, I soon hit the col—the electromagnetic-free zone I'd pinpointed at Buck's. There was no doubt this was the place—a low pass between two peaks.

I scanned the hillsides up to those peaks, searching for a cave entrance or some geological formation Drakho might favor, paying particular attention to the ridges and rock outcroppings. Nothing stood out except one particularly large ridge on the east side. The land here was so thick with trees that it was hard to know for sure if I'd missed something, but as far as I could tell, there were no caves. Which meant no place to trap Drakho.

After studying the terrain for another fifteen minutes, I was seriously regretting the decision to come here. Maybe we should have gone to Hadley Falls again—or to another area with a weak electric field. An area that we were sure had caves.

But we didn't, I thought. *And there's no turning back now.* If I was going to have any chance of saving Nate by tomorrow, I had to work with the cards I'd been dealt—even if I'd dealt those cards to myself. And right now, it looked like I had dealt myself a bad hand.

But as I hiked back, I didn't focus on my awful cards. Instead I racked my brain, trying to come up with a new battle plan. Unfortunately, when I got back to Harry, I still hadn't come up with anything.

I filled him in on what I'd seen, and he summed up what should have been obvious from the start.

"He don't need a cave here because there ain't no electrical fields," he said. "He feels pretty safe in these parts."

"So how are we going to trap him?"

"We should've brought a bear trap instead of dynamite," Harry said.

"He'd probably just gnaw his leg off and regrow it," I countered.

"Nah. Dracula didn't regrow limbs."

I could go along with that—I'd built my entire theory on the legends of Dracula and Drakho, and there was nothing in those myths about regenerating limbs. A bear trap might actually have worked out just fine. We could have snared him and then dragged the generator over to him. Didn't that parallel trapping Dracula in sunlight? For Drakho, electricity *was* sunlight.

"Can we build our own bear trap out here?" I said.

"Even if we could, how we gonna draw him in?" Harry cocked his head. "With animals, you draw them in with food. But Dracula?"

"With Dracula—I guess you'd do it with blood. With Drakho... who knows? Edna didn't give us any help there."

My eyes fell on the weapons we'd brought: the dynamite and the generator. Regardless of what we did or didn't know, we had to make do with these. Edna had used her amber weapon to ward Drakho off, to keep him at bay. I wondered: could we use the generator to do the opposite? We had brought it here to kill Drakho—but could we first use it to draw him in?

And then it suddenly hit me: "If you can't *draw* an animal into your trap, you *herd* it into your trap," I said.

Harry glanced at me. "I like it so far."

"There's a massive ridge on the east side of the pass," I said. "What if we rig it with dynamite, then drive Drakho up under it?"

"Not bad. But how we gonna drive him up there?"

"The generator. We draw him to us, flip it on, and he hightails it up to the ridge."

Harry nodded. "You're gonna have to detonate the dynamite at just the right time," he said.

"Yeah..."

He grinned and leaned back, and I could tell that he'd caught on to the part of the plan he might not like. "And I'm the decoy," he said.

"Hopefully just a decoy, and not a sacrifice." I wasn't grinning.

"Either way is fine with me. I been waitin' a hell of a long time to kill this bastard."

So the plan was set. I would carry Harry and the generator to the col, to a spot that ran under that ridge. Then I'd come back here, grab the dynamite, blasting caps, and mechanical match, hike through to the woods to the ridge, from the backside, and plant the dynamite.

"So when Drakho comes after me in the col," Harry said, "I'll fire up the generator and we pray to sweet Jesus that it drives him up to the ridge."

"That's right." But then I brought up the flaw hanging over this entire operation. "Of course, if he knows we're here, none of this is going to fly."

"Kinda late to be worryin' about that now. Besides, the guy's got other Hatfields he's playing games with. And even if he does know what we're up to, he's sticking to the rules he put down."

"You mean I have until tomorrow."

"Yeah. But he's still gonna mess with ya."

I believed part of this. The part about Drakho playing by the rules. I knew my enemy well enough by now to understand that these games were his life—the Paspahegh had told Edna that hundreds of years ago. And without the rules, there was no game.

But that didn't mean he wasn't watching me, mocking my plan, preparing to counter it at any time. Harry's theory that

Drakho was out messing with other victims, playing a myriad of games, was plausible—it explained why Drakho hadn't been messing with me every second of every hour since I'd received the letter. But I couldn't be certain. The only thing I could be certain of—or at least *felt* I could be certain of—was Drakho's respect for the rules of the game.

Now that we had a battle plan, I moved on to the next order of business. I gassed up the generator—our amber weapon—and hauled it to the col, where I positioned it directly below the ridge. Then I hiked back, picked up Harry, and carried him back to the col.

"Turn on the generator at eight fifteen," I said.

Harry's eyes swept up the hillside, past the ridge, to the sky above. "You think you got nightfall goin' for ya, don't ya?"

"I think so." While I'd been hauling Harry to the col, a small revelation had come to me—or maybe it was just a desperate attempt to boost my faith. I had realized that Drakho had never shown himself in daylight. Not with us, not with Edna, not in Bram Stoker's tale. Never. And nightfall would hit the col at around eight fifteen.

Before I left Harry alone—which under any other circumstances would look like a horrible and cruel prank: leaving a man who couldn't walk stranded in the middle of the wilderness—I felt obligated to let him know how big my doubts were.

"This whole plan, and everything leading up to it—it could all be wrong," I said. "All the connections and threads and links might only exist in my head." I motioned to the wilderness around us. "And not out here."

"That don't make it any less real, does it?"

I smiled. He'd nailed it. Fact and fiction were a giant shake and bake.

Chapter Twenty

By the time I was closing in on the ridge, dusk had fallen, bringing with it a chill in the air and long shadows cutting through the woods. The darkening sky was a haunting violet blue, disturbingly luminous, as if heralding Drakho's imminent arrival.

During my hike up, I'd been on the lookout for signs of Drakho, but twilight brought on another fear. I was now wary of a change in scenery—a literal one. A vision, a hallucination, a warping of reality.

And the closer I got to the ridge, the more I wondered if I was already hallucinating. Was I seeing what Drakho wanted me to see and not what I needed to see to fight this battle?

I scanned the terrain below, trying to spot Harry and the generator. But the forest was too thick to offer a clear line of sight, and I didn't have time to look for a better view. I had miscalculated how long it would take me to hike out of the col and circle up to the ridge. I should've told Harry eight thirty. As it stood now, Harry would be turning on the generator in less than ten minutes, which meant I needed to hurry.

I ran to the underside of the ridge, where the air was cooler, the trees thinner, and the shadows darker. Then I scouted for a spot to plant the dynamite, a crevice in the ridge that fit Buck's parameters. Of course, I was adapting his instructions; he'd told me where and how to plant dynamite so it'd have maximum impact when it came to sealing a cave, not bringing down a ridge.

I went with a fissure that ran lengthwise in the stone, near the center of the ridge. I securely planted the dynamite, rigged up the blasting caps and the fuse, then attached the mechanical match. To ignite the fuse, I'd have to come back and pull the ring from the match.

Then I hiked out from under the ridge, scouting for a location that would protect me from the explosion. The dusk had turned darker now, and with it the tenor of the pass had changed. The haunting purple light had gone from luminous to dull and heavy, and the sounds emanating from the hillsides—cawing, croaking, rustling, buzzing, and crunching—reverberated with an unnerving dissonance. I wondered if the other world had suddenly enshrouded the pass, but I also knew it didn't matter.

I moved forward until I spotted a cluster of boulders that were a safe distance from the ridge. Then I looked down toward the col—and my heart immediately started pounding.

There was a clear sightline to Harry, and what I saw was impossible to process. Harry was *walking*—on his own two legs—toward the generator. It was as if Drakho had never crippled him. My perch was far from the col, and my view was obscured by the approach of night, but there was no doubt that Harry was walking.

He stepped up to the generator, hovered over it, and then a few seconds later a low hum filled the pass. *Harry couldn't have walked up to the generator. So was the generator off or on?* There was no way to know.

But one thing I did know: Drakho was here, and he was clouding my vision.

I scanned the hillside, looking for a sign that Drakho had arrived with the night. I saw nothing. I looked back at the ridge—and my throat went dry—

There was a castle where the ridge had been. Its moldering gray walls stood stark and silent; its menacing battlements, turrets, and towers loomed over me. *And why not?* I thought. The final confrontation in *Dracula* had taken place in Dracula's castle in the Carpathian Mountains. And although I didn't know where Edna's final confrontation had taken place—or even if there'd been one—my bet right then was that she had confronted Drakho in a castle.

Drakho was playing chess. He was tying everything together, bringing the game full circle. For not only had the final confrontation in *Dracula* taken place in the count's castle, but the first supernatural novel was *The Castle of Otranto*, and that tied the game together in a nice, neat, novel therapy bow.

I stared at the castle, trying to see through it and past it, willing myself to see what was *also* there—the ridge—so I could locate where I'd planted the dynamite. But all I saw was the medieval monolith, a gloomy fortress dominating the pass.

And the fortress was inviting me inside for the final battle. Its gates—heavy oak, and iron eaten with rust—were open.

There was no seeing past the castle to the ridge and to the fissure where the dynamite lurked. Fact and fiction were a giant shake and bake, but I needed to see both—and right now. If I couldn't see the dynamite, I couldn't detonate it.

It was time to up my game or lose the game. I'd cast my lot—I hadn't come here to tell Drakho his name. The only thing that mattered now was whether novel therapy was going to be enough to beat him at his own game. He clearly thought it wouldn't, which was why he'd chosen it. He'd challenged me on my own turf to make it a worthwhile competition, but he'd never believed he'd lose.

I suddenly started running downhill—away from the castle and toward the pass below. I had a plan in mind and was going for broke, betting that Harry *had* turned on the generator. If I was right, then I was rapidly approaching a strong electrical field.

As I ran, I intermittently glanced back at the castle. After fifty yards or so, the first part of my plan paid off—there was no castle. The ridge was back.

And so was Drakho.

He was on the ridge, silhouetted by the darkening sky, keeping his distance from the electrical field. My bet had paid off. Drakho couldn't cloud my mind and change my world if I was far enough inside the electrical field.

Now it was time to execute the second part of my plan. I started back up toward the ridge, toward Drakho, until I made it to the point where the ridge was once again transformed into the castle. Drakho was gone—but I knew he hadn't disappeared. He was inside the castle.

I retreated again until the castle disappeared and the ridge returned—but this time Drakho wasn't on the ridge. I didn't have time to worry about where he'd gone; I had to focus on the location of the dynamite. Staring at the fissure where I knew I'd planted it, I climbed toward the ridge again, slowly, until the castle reappeared. I made a mental note of exactly where the dynamite was located *inside* the castle. Once I was certain of that spot, I turned and raced down through the thick woods toward the generator. A pale light from the rising moon lit the way.

I found Harry just as I'd left him—not ambulatory.

"I saw him," he said as soon as I stepped into the col.

"Me too."

"Then what happened to blowing him up?"

"I'm not done yet. I'm going back up there. Give me three minutes, then shut the generator down. When you do, he's going to head down here. If you see him or even if you just sense he's nearby—turn the generator back on."

There wasn't time to explain any more. I took off, hurrying uphill, until I made it back to the edge of Drakho's power—the edge of the electrical field—where the fact of the ridge met the fiction of the castle, both as real as anything I'd ever know.

And then the hum of the generator died out. And without the resistance of the electrical field, the castle immediately grew larger, sturdier, more ominous. It sprawled out farther, sweeping past the length of the ridge, taking up a wide expanse of the hillside.

In awe, I waited quietly and still, hidden in the forest. I was sure that as a result of Harry shutting down the electrical field, Drakho would now take care of business. I pictured him traveling downhill as a lone gray wolf—the same husky, powerful wolf from that night in Cold Falls so long ago— hunting his prey. With the generator off, this col was once again the wolf's sacred, untouched land—land that Harry and I had just polluted. Drakho would clean it up as fast as he could.

I waited for the hum of the generator to fill the air, the sign that Harry had sensed Drakho's approach. But I didn't hear the generator's gentle hum—and never would again. Instead, Harry's shrieking cry took over the col, followed by horrifying, wet, ripping sounds—a mauling, a fast and vicious one—

And then silence.

The wolf had struck. Harry had become the sacrifice, and I had to make it worth it.

I raced through the woods, toward the castle's oak and iron gate, knowing the wolf was already on the hunt for me. I tried to keep my mind off of Harry's death, telling myself he had believed that sacrificing himself was worth it *if* it helped me complete my mission.

I ran through the castle's gate and into a courtyard. Massive wooden doors—the entrance to the stronghold— greeted me from the other side. But rather than continue toward them, I ran to the east side of the castle, toward the dynamite, until I came to another entrance: an arched entryway with no door.

I darted through it and found myself in an empty room with doorways on either side. I took the one that led east. This led to another room, a much larger one. It looked like an abandoned banquet hall. A long wooden table, covered with a thick layer of dust, sat in its center, surrounded by scarred, high-backed chairs.

I took a second to figure out where the dynamite was in relation to this banquet hall, not by searching for the explosives, but by weighing whether I was far enough east along the ridge; I was scrolling through the giant shake and bake of fact and fiction in my mind. This *wasn't* far enough east, I decided—so I continued through the room and out into a narrow hallway that dead-ended at a set of stone stairs. The stairs led up into a tower.

Somewhere in this tower, somewhere above me, was the fissure where I'd planted the dynamite.

I was so sure of this that I suddenly had an epiphany: *I have some control over fact and fiction.* I had exerted that control back in the library, when I'd stopped the bats from mauling me; and now I had carved out my own trail within Drakho's world—within this other world. Novel therapy was working.

I hurried up the circular stairs. They wound up at a steep angle, along a narrow passage no more than three feet wide. After a minute or so, I passed a small arched doorway on the inside wall—but there was no time to explore. If I was on course, the dynamite was farther up the tower.

I kept climbing, expecting to come across another doorway, the one that would lead to the dynamite. But when no door appeared, just more and more steps, panic crept up on me. Had I made a mistake and misjudged where the dynamite was? Had I misjudged my ability to wrangle with fact and fiction?

I slowed down and glanced back. *Did I need to* will *a doorway into existence? A door to the fissure in the ridge?*

The clicking of paws slapping down on stone steps filled the narrow passage. Drakho was steadily making his way up the tower. This was the final move in our chess game. If I couldn't ignite the dynamite, the game would end. And Nate would die.

The clatter of paws intensified, growing louder and faster.

Was telling Drakho his name still an option? It wasn't. That was the sobering truth. I didn't know his real name— his true identity. Sure, I knew the origin of the Dracula legend. And sure, I knew that Drakho was an ancient and supernatural being. And I knew that he was the Nightman. He was the creature behind every scary story ever told and behind every dark tale ever written. He was the vampire, the werewolf, the witch, the shape shifter, the ghost, and the devil. He was the supernatural reality behind them all.

And I knew that every civilization in every age told stories about this creature, because every one of us needs to be reminded that he exists. That he preys on us when he chooses. And that there are ways to fight him.

Stories tell you all you need to know.

It was time to write my own story.

And as soon as this truth crystallized in my mind, the inside wall of the tower flickered and softened. The stone was melting away, morphing.

Then the clicking of the paws stopped for a beat—as if Drakho was suddenly aware that *I* was writing the story.

This is where the dynamite is, I thought, and I reached toward the morphing wall. My hand moved through the stone—and the tower disappeared.

I was standing under the ridge, in front of the dynamite, which was embedded in the fissure—just as I'd left it.

The paws started up again, clattering against the stone steps—which also still existed—more furiously and aggressively.

I pulled the ring from the mechanical match, lighting the fuse. I now had sixty seconds to get away from the detonation. I raced along the underside of the ridge, hoping to write a triumphant end to my story. I cleared the ridge, sprinted through the woods, and dove behind the cluster of boulders just as—

A deafening *KABOOM* filled the pass.

The explosion roared through the air like a sudden crack of thunder. The violent clap reverberated between the peaks, rumbling up and down the hillside. Then, as the echoing began to subside, the night was filled with sharp cracking and popping sounds.

The ridge was fracturing.

I peered over the cluster of boulders, my ears still ringing from the explosion, and saw the ridge disintegrating. As I watched, the sturdy monolith turned into a torrent of crumbling rocks, cascading into the pass below. A cloud of dust and debris rose up into the night, painting the entire vista gray.

Had Drakho been trapped under the collapsing ridge? There was no way to know for sure.

After the last big chunk of rock had dropped into the pass, I scanned the hillside looking for the ancient and supernatural being who had become my nemesis. The pale moonlight wasn't strong enough to cut through the cloud of dust, so my view was obscured. But my view *wasn't* obscured by some strange vision—and that was a good sign.

I moved around the boulders and stared at the ashen night vista, almost daring Drakho to attack me if he was still alive.

After a few minutes, during which the dust cloud cleared enough for me to see more of the forest, I spotted Otranto.

She was above me, where the ridge had stood. She was looking down, and in the moonlight I saw that her eyes were green pools of sorrow—a sorrow I recognized. I'd seen it in my own eyes whenever I'd looked in a mirror after Lucy's death. It was a sorrow reserved for grief.

Drakho was dead.

I took off, running toward the trail.

Chapter Twenty-One

As I drove back to the suburbs, my heart was heavy. Heavy with grief. For Harry, for Lee, and always for Lucy. But this wasn't the grief of overwhelming hopelessness—the grief I'd carried since Lucy's death. This was the grief of acceptance. A grief that lived in my heart—but didn't take over. There was room for Nate and for whatever else came my way. I'd had to be driven out of my cave to understand this, to feel this. And I'd had to be forced to see that novel therapy was the way out of that cave.

It had saved Nate, and it had saved me.

But there was no way of getting around the tragedy of *how* everything had played out. There was no sugarcoating the randomness of it. That a lone camping trip I'd taken as a child—a trip I could just as easily not have taken—had hung over my life for decades, and had then pounced. A random game of hide-and-seek. A game that had taken Lucy from me and left a sadness in my heart that would stay forever.

Still, there was comfort in accepting the randomness. The randomness that came from the shake and bake that was *life*.

*

I arrived in Arlington a couple of hours before dawn, too early to head to Jenna's to see Nate. So I pulled into the parking structure at the Ballston Common Mall, parked my car, reclined my seat, and fell sleep almost instantly.

The light of dawn that crept into the structure didn't wake me. And the beehive of activity that overtook the mall—the human swarm that Drakho had feared would take over his homeland—didn't descend until ten o'clock on Sundays. So I finally opened my eyes a little after nine, awakened by the arrival of the mall's employees.

I drove over to Jenna's.

She was making breakfast for Nate, and as soon as she let me into the townhouse, Nate raced up to me and hugged me. I held him tightly, and when he was ready to move on, I didn't let go. I kept him wrapped in my embrace. Then, against my will, tears welled up in my eyes.

I tried to turn away from Jenna, but she saw the tears and looked me over carefully. I hadn't thought about my appearance until right then—unshaven, unkempt, and disheveled. Hopefully—even though she'd seen me almost break down when she'd brought up Lucy on Friday—she knew me well enough to dismiss the thought that I'd gone off on an alcoholic or drug-fueled binge in an attempt to bury my sorrow.

I let go of Nate before the tears fell from my eyes.

"Dad—did you pick up the birthday cake?" he said, eager for the day to get started.

"Ah—no, not yet." I wiped my eyes.

"Can I come with you to pick it up?"

"… Let's see how the day goes first."

"Okay, but I can go, right?"

Before I handed out another vague answer, Jenna interrupted in an attempt to help me out. "Go on back into the kitchen and finish your breakfast, sweetheart, and then we'll figure out what's next."

Nate glanced at her, then back at me, looking for guidance.

"I'll be right there, honey," I said. "Let me talk to Jenna for a minute."

"Okay." Nate raced back into the kitchen.

Jenna stared at me, and neither of us said a word for what seemed like an eternity. She had a soft expression on her face, curiosity mixed with compassion. *If you want to talk, I can listen*, she was saying. *But if you don't want to talk, that's okay, too*. This was the empathy that made her a great nurse.

I felt warmth in my eyes. It was the tears returning, and I fought them back.

"There isn't going to be a birthday party," I said.

"What?"

"My house is gone."

"Gone? What do you mean, 'gone'?"

"There was a fire. It… it destroyed everything."

Her brow furrowed as if she was having a hard time registering what I'd just said, and then her eyes widened. "Oh my God, John—what happened?"

"I don't know. But the entire place went up in flames."

She instinctually hugged me. "I'm so sorry."

I accepted her hug, but I didn't hold on long for fear of giving in to the urge to tell her everything. "I don't know how I'm going to tell Nate," I said. "I should probably just stick to telling him the party's not going to happen. That's enough bad news for one day."

"It's all he's been talking about," she said. "He's going to be crushed."

She and I stared at each other, and again I had the urge to tell her everything. But I knew that I'd never be able to tell her any of it, much less all of it. Not her, not anyone else. That's the way this worked. Even if Jenna listened, and I was sure she'd be a sympathetic listener, she wouldn't believe it. No one would. They'd think my grief had gotten the best of me.

I had written my own story, but there was no one to whom I could tell it. At least, that's what I was thinking then. I hadn't yet understood how my story fit in with the other stories.

"Let's have the party here," Jenna said. She was focused on solutions.

"You're kidding."

"Why not? Just tell everyone to come here instead of your place."

"I canceled it already."

"So? Call everyone. Tell them it's back on, but it's here. I'm sure a good number of them can still make it."

That sent a wave of joy through me. It felt as warm as the tears had felt, but without the sting.

Jenna and I joined Nate in the kitchen, and I told him we'd pick up the cake together after he finished breakfast. He was excited and started talking about the magician. Remembering that I'd canceled him, I excused myself and called him. He was still available and gladly agreed to come.

After breakfast, while Nate got dressed, I called the parents of the kids who'd been invited to the party and told them it was back on, then gave them Jenna's address. Everyone said they could make it.

Then I told Nate the party would be at Jenna's place because we'd had a gas leak. I wasn't ready to tell him he'd lost his home. At first, he wasn't okay with the sudden change of venue, but within two hours, he was so swept up in the whirlwind of preparation—from gathering the party supplies to getting the townhouse decorated—that he was more than on board. In fact, he was excited that Jenna was going to be part of the fun.

The party was a success. Full of laughter, games, and oohing and aahing over the magic show. Nate had a blast. But the best part came after all the kids had gone home and Jenna and I had finished cleaning up.

I walked into Nate's room and found him lying on the floor, exhausted. He was using the little energy he had left to examine one of his birthday presents: a three-dimensional maze game called the Perplexus. "The most challenging game on Earth," it had said on the box, and I couldn't help but think of Drakho.

I sat down on the floor next to Nate, ready to tell him he'd be spending the night at Jenna's again. She'd offered to let us both stay until I found another place. My insurance company had arranged for a hotel until we found temporary housing, but I thought it'd be better for Nate to spend a few more nights at Jenna's before that transition. Plus, I still hadn't told him what had happened to our house.

"That was a great party, Dad." Nate's eyes were focused on the Perplexus.

"I'm glad you liked it."

"I'm glad we had the party over here."

"Me too."

"Mom would've liked it."

"She sure would've."

Nate took his eyes off the Perplexus and looked at me. "Things are getting better," he said. His eyes shone with truth.

I was taken aback by his raw honesty. And I almost hid my reaction—but then I stopped myself and opened up instead. "They are. And they have been. And I'm sorry I didn't see it sooner." I kissed him on the forehead. "I love you."

"I love you too, Dad." He handed me the Perplexus. "You try it."

I tried it, and he gave me some pointers. We handed it back and forth until he was so exhausted, he actually volunteered to go to bed. I followed suit and slept on Jenna's couch that night. My sleep was deep and overwhelming, like I'd been knocked out. No tossing, no turning, no dreams—but no fears, either.

The next morning, I drove Nate to school, then headed to work. On the way, I began to wonder if I'd really made it out of the woods. But soon enough, the normalcy of the drive to the Cherrydale Public Library convinced me that I had. I'd played Drakho's game and had saved Nate's life. Sunday had come and gone, and my son was still alive.

It wasn't until I was in the library that this sense of normalcy took a hit. When I passed the display on Virginia history and saw the empty space where *The Forest* had once been, uneasiness crept over me. That small void—where the book should have been—was a reminder that the other world was right here, waiting to reveal itself.

The next day, I brought the copy of *The Forest* back and surreptitiously placed it back in its spot. But there were still some loose ends.

The local media had reported Lee's death, and both the local and national media had run stories on the explosion deep in the Shenandoah Valley, where a mutilated body had been found. But so far no report had connected Harry and Lee, though undoubtedly the police had already identified them as uncle and nephew. I had no idea what theory the police would come up with to tie the murders together, but one thing was certain: it wouldn't involve Drakho. He was the stuff of fiction.

The loose end I was most worried about was the

generator. It tied me to Harry's death. I had rented it and never returned it. I'd been smart enough to pay in cash and use a fake name for the rental, but there was still a chance the police could trace it back to me. Maybe the surveillance cameras at Home Depot had taped the transaction or caught a glimpse of my car. Maybe the cashier or the clerk who'd shown me how to work the generator remembered me well enough to give the police a good description.

The rest of that first week back, I pored over news items related to Lee's and Harry's deaths, trying to determine what the police knew. And in case an officer showed up on my doorstep asking about the generator, I tried to work out a decent explanation for how it had ended up in the Shenandoah Valley at the scene of a crime.

I settled on a relatively simple explanation: I'd rented it for Nate's birthday party and it'd been stolen. Of course, this explanation still had a hole in it. Why did I need the generator for the party? I was leaning toward saying I'd rented it to go along with one of those bouncers. Of course, there was no record that I'd rented a bouncer, and why would I rent a bouncer without an operator who'd bring his or her own generator?

There was also another loose end that loomed on the horizon should the police connect me to Lee—a troubling one. My house had burned down on the night Drakho had murdered Lee. If the police placed us together that night, they might think the fire and the murder were connected, especially because the fire appeared to be arson. So would they think I was involved in the murder? Maybe I'd killed Lee for burning down my house. Who knew? Again, the only thing I *did* know was that the police wouldn't have the fictional element they needed to pull it all together. They wouldn't have Drakho.

After another week passed, I began to worry less about the police showing up. There were no more news items about the murders or the strange demolition of the ridge, but I did come across notices about both Lee's and Harry's funerals. I wanted to attend, but I knew I couldn't. That would've been handing the police a direct connection between them and me.

A few days into the third week, Nate and I moved into a rented duplex paid for by the insurance company. This was the move I hadn't been willing to make six months ago when I'd first realized I could no longer afford the life I'd lived with Lucy. Instead I had clung to my old life, both financially and emotionally.

It was a move that was long overdue.

I was now fully engaged in Nate's life, focused on the present and no longer pining for the past. When Nate talked about losing the only home he'd ever known, I listened and talked about it, too. This didn't make up for the many months when I'd avoided talking with him about losing his mom, but it did lay a strong foundation for our fresh start.

And that start was going well, until one evening, six weeks after I'd first received the letter.

The doorbell rang just before I was getting ready to cook

dinner. Even before the chime fully died out, I was uneasy. The only visitor we'd had at the duplex was Jenna, and as far as I knew she hadn't been planning on dropping in. So I wasn't too surprised when I opened the door and found a man sporting a crew cut, a neutral smile, and a gray suit standing on my doorstep. Before he said a word, I knew why he'd come.

He flashed his badge and introduced himself as Detective Miner from the Arlington Police Department. Though I wasn't prepared to answer his questions—I'd long since stopped planning for a visit from the police—I invited him in.

As I led him into the living room, I tried to keep my composure. At the same time, I didn't want to act as if I'd been expecting cops to show up on my doorstep, which would have looked just as suspicious as if I freaked out.

"I hope you're not bringing more bad news," I said, hoping the distress in my voice hit the right level of anxiety.

"What do you mean, more bad news?" he said.

I didn't believe that he hadn't checked me out before heading over, but I played along. "The last time a police detective came to my door, it was to tell me my wife had died."

"I'm sorry," he said. He used an even tone, which gave nothing away. "My condolences."

"Thank you."

We sat down.

"I'm working on a homicide case from a couple of months

ago, and your name came up."

I nodded and didn't say anything, hoping to avoid implicating myself by stupidly blurting out information. I waited for him to fill me in.

He did, but it only amounted to telling me that he was investigating Lee Bellington's murder. Then he jumped right in to the reason for his visit—a loose end that I had only considered for a millisecond.

"Macon Bellington—Lee's father—told us you were with Lee on the night of his murder," he said. "Mr. Bellington said you were with Lee at Dan T.'s Firegrill in Alexandria."

"That's right," I said, not wanting to act like I had something to hide. But how had Mason known who I was? Neither Lee nor I had even hinted at my identity during the brief exchange, and he certainly didn't remember me from my childhood. We'd seen each other just a few times back in those days, and every time he'd been drunk. I had dismissed this loose end within the first few days of my return from the Shenandoah Valley.

Miner must have read that question in my expression because he answered it. "Dan T., the bar owner, said he had a conversation that night with two belligerent men, so we got to thinking, maybe it was the same two men who argued with Mr. Bellington. We took a look at the surveillance tapes in the bar, and bingo—there you were with Lee. It took a while to ID you... but here we are."

I didn't say anything, running through what I *should* say.

That gave Detective Miner the opportunity to press me

with questions, which was exactly what he did. "How do you know Lee?"

"He was a childhood friend."

"Childhood? As in you weren't friends anymore?"

"Yeah—pretty much… I mean we were still friends, but I hadn't seen him in twenty years." I knew what he would ask next, and I was frantically trying to come with an answer.

"So did you get back in touch with him, or did he get back in touch with you?"

Off the top of my head, I could only come up with one reason we'd reconnected—a reason that made some sort of sense, especially because I'd already laid the groundwork with the first thing I'd said to the detective. "I reached out to him when I found out he'd lost his wife. As I said, I'd lost my wife, too, and I thought he might want someone to talk to. You know, someone who went through the same thing."

Miner nodded and was appropriately solemn, but in that neutral way. I supposed he was either doing his job, which meant not getting emotionally involved, or he didn't believe a word I was saying.

"And how long before that night at the Firegrill had you been in touch with him?" he asked.

This was going to sound bad. "It was that night—that was the first time."

I expected him to flash an *I got you* look, but he didn't. He just went on to the next question as if the coincidence of my barging into Lee's life on the night of his murder meant nothing.

"And did you notice anything about his state of mind?"

"It was bad," I said. And that was the truth. But I didn't add that Lee's state of mind had improved greatly when the opportunity to mete out revenge on his wife's killer had come up.

"That was clear from the way he'd let his place go to pot," Miner said.

"That's why I thought we'd go out—he needed to get out of there." For once my answer *did* make sense.

"After that, did you go back to his place or try another bar?"

"The flare-up with his dad put a damper on the night. Not that the night was going well anyway. But after that, he was ready to call it quits."

"Around what time did you drop him off?"

"I don't remember exactly. Probably somewhere around eleven."

Miner leaned back, nodded, then completely changed his line of questioning. It was as if he knew I was getting too comfortable. "I understand that you lost your home in a fire that same night," he said.

"Yeah. That's right." I had to be careful about what I said next. Maybe one of my neighbors had placed me there with Lee.

He stared at me, calmly, waiting me for to say more.

"It was awful…" I said. Then I added, "I mean first my wife, then my home. Like I was cursed." *By Drakho.*

"I'm sorry," he said, then again waited for me to say more.

When I didn't, he did. "Do you think it had anything to do with Lee's homicide?"

"No—are you thinking it did?"

"The fire's being investigated, but nothing's turned up yet." Miner glanced around the duplex, then back at me. "You'd heard about Lee's murder before I showed up, right?"

"Yes."

"Then why didn't you come forward and tell us you'd been with him on that night?"

My guilt was about to betray itself on my face if I didn't push it back down right then. I was about to become a suspect, and it wouldn't have surprised me if Drakho had planned this all along. That he'd left breadcrumbs for the police—breadcrumbs that had led them straight to me.

"I don't know," I said. "I mean, I remember thinking about it. I didn't actually read about Lee right away—it was the week after, when I was at work. I was shocked, since I'd just seen him after all those years." I realized I was rambling, but I had no choice but to forge ahead, to keep the guilt off my face. And wasn't this why the detective was here? To get under my skin? To get me to ramble.

"I made the connection that it was the same night, but it just seemed like a weird coincidence," I said. "I do remember thinking that I was one of the last people to see him—but honestly, I didn't think of going to the police. I was dealing with the loss of my house and trying to find a new place to live and dealing with everything else that I'd lost in the fire. And I was worried about my son."

Detective Miner nodded again and didn't say anything. Again, it seemed like he was waiting to see if I had more to say.

I didn't. I'd said way more than enough. I looked him in the eye.

"So why *exactly* didn't you come to us?" he said.

"I don't know," I answered. "I guess that's what I'm trying to say. I just don't know." And before he could press me with another question, I followed that up with something that at first I regretted—but weeks later, I thought that maybe this remark was precisely what had taken me out of the running as a suspect. "Or maybe the truth is, I'm still upset at you guys because you don't have any leads on who murdered my wife."

"I'm sorry about that," Miner said. "And I understand your frustration." He stood up. "I'm sure we put a good man on the case, but I can take a look at it again if you'd like."

"Sure," I said. "Thank you." I felt awful. Though I'd used Lucy's unsolved murder to end the questioning, I hadn't meant to send him on a wild goose chase. He was already wasting time trying to solve Lee's case, and now he'd be wasting more time. Time he could use on other cases—cases that didn't involve Drakho.

We both headed to the door, exchanging pleasantries, and just before he walked out, he let me know that we'd probably talk again, which was worrisome. I'd been connected to Lee's death, and I was worried that Miner would eventually also connect me to Harry, my comrade in arms. Connecting me to both victims would undoubtedly make me far more of a suspect.

But as it turned out, Detective Miner visited me only one more time. He went through the same set of questions, and had a few more when it came to the argument between Lee and Macon. My impression was that Macon had become a suspect. I supposed it was because he was the link to both Lee and Harry, though Miner never brought up Harry.

In the third month after Drakho's death, I started to think about Otranto again, mostly while at work. She was another loose end, one from the world of fiction, so I dove into fiction to see if I could uncover her true identity. I read *Dracula* again and *The Forest* again, then moved on to *The Castle of Otranto*. When those stories refused to yield up any clues, I dove into a slew of classic supernatural stories: stories by Edgar Allan Poe and M.R. James, by Ambrose Bierce and Algernon Blackwood. Then I started in on supernatural novels, from *The Picture of Dorian Gray* and *The Monk* to more modern fare like *Ghost Story* and *Carrie*, both of which featured women antagonists.

But if there was a clue to be found in one of those stories, it must have been buried deeply. So deeply that I wasn't able to find it. It took me months of reading to finally accept that Otranto was going to remain a loose end.

And as soon as I did, it dawned on me: maybe the reason none of those stories contained a clue about Otranto's identity was because Otranto's story hadn't been written yet.

And I realized what this meant.

It meant that there *was* someone I could tell my story to. I could tell it to everyone—in the form of fiction. And I could start with Otranto. For *she* would be the way into my story. My story would begin with the mysterious and beautiful Otranto, and then it would lead to Drakho, or Dracula, or the Nightman, or whatever I chose to call this creature—this cunning creature who randomly preys on some of us. My story would be fiction, just as Edna's and Stoker's had been, but it would be just as real, too. And if I was wrong about Drakho—if he had survived, or if there were other creatures like him out there—then my story, too, would tell you all you need to know.

THE END